ANNA SPARROWS

Spencer's Satisfaction

Littles & Lace Book 4

Cover Design by: Ky at Blue Brolli Graphics

First edition

This book was professionally typeset on Reedsy.
Find out more at reedsy.com

For the wonderful members of the kink reading community.
Thank you for including and supporting me in your world.
I promise* to keep supplying you with sweet Boys, hot Daddies,
and plenty of delicious, delicious steamy goodness.
(*Just keep on indulging my praise kink.)

Contents

Preface

While this is a low-angst, sweet & cute romance, this book contains discussion of undiagnosed/non-ascertained neurodivergence* and self doubt, mentions of homophobia, anxiety, and panic attacks.

Also, please bear in mind that this book is an MM Age Play/Age Regression romance between consenting adults and **does** include ABDL and wetting (more than previous books in the series).

I am a firm believer in not yucking someone else's yum, so if this kink squicks you, don't read it. As I always say: life is too short to read something you don't enjoy.

*I am absolutely not an expert in neurodivergence, but between my own ND brain and my kid's, I drew on our personal experiences and behaviors when I wrote Tony. Upon a re-read, I discovered a *lot* of myself in him, which was…*interesting*, to say the least. Nevertheless, I am aware that everyone's experiences are different, so please know that this story is by no means intended as a generalization or an 'all encompassing' representation of, in Tony's case, potential or non-ascertained neurodivergence. It's just very similar to my own.

Acknowledgments

Where to begin? Once again, I have to acknowledge and profusely thank my beta readers for their guidance and feedback. I can honestly say that without Amur and Cindy, who kindly volunteered their beta reading services a second time around, this book would not be the book you currently hold in your hands/kindle. I am forever thankful for these wonderful people - for their friendship, support, and advice. Cindy and Amur, I am so lucky to have found on this journey of mine. (PS - Amur, I wrote that bedtime story scene after all. Enjoy!)

I'd also like to give a quick shout out to my fellow Age Play author, Myf Wren, for listening to me whine my way through bouts of imposter syndrome and self doubt. Myf, your cheerleading and unwavering support really helped me to regain my confidence and kept me going when I needed it the most. You are another friend I am so glad to have met on this crazy path I've taken.

I am also eternally grateful to you, dear reader, for giving an unknown author a chance. *Especially* indie authors like myself. With every KU page turn, every ebook and paperback sold, I'm encouraged to keep writing, to keep learning, and to keep growing as a writer and as a person in general, and it's people like you -and my brilliant beta readers, and my fellow authors- who help me to do so.

Chapter One – Spencer

"**A**nd that's a wrap," Becky, the studio engineer and producer I've been recording with for the last couple of days declares cheerfully from behind plexiglass. "I think that was a record, Spence."

I pull off my headphones and give my wild hair a shake out, stretching my neck and grinning back at her. We've worked together on a few projects now, and it's starting to show. We're like a well-oiled machine at this rate.

"Not many bloopers this time around," I acknowledge, chuckling. "Should we stage a few for J.C.? I hear some authors are sharing our fuckups as bonus content these days."

I leave the booth and meet her outside the door.

"Whatever sells the books, babe," Becky shrugs, before her plump lips pull into a smirk, "and you still gave me plenty to work with on that front, don't worry. I mean, yesterday you completely forgot to switch your voice into Melody's for the sex scene, remember?"

I cringe. "Ugh. Rookie error for sure. I still blame you

for making me record that one first up before I had enough caffeine in my system."

She cackles like a 1960s *Batman* villain, throwing her head back, making her long dark hair sway with the movement. "It. Was. Gold." She proceeds to deepen her voice into a mockery of mine as she re-enacts some of the scene in question.

"Shut up," I huff, then frown and point my index finger at her for good measure, "that shit could be taken as transphobic. Maybe in my creative interpretation of Melody's character, she's MTF. Who are you to judge?"

"She got pregnant in the first scene you recorded, dumbass. Your logic is flawed."

I can't help snorting at that. With my hands held in surrender, I shrug. "All I'm saying is that there are women out there with deep voices, too."

Hell, most of my female characters are spoken in a softened version of my own voice. I don't buy in to the practice of pitching my voice comically higher. As a listener, I think it can come off condescending and cringe-worthy (not unlike a woman making her voice sound ridiculously deep to voice a male character, like Becky just did playfully).

She arches one of her eyebrows at me. "You're serious."

"I am." We haven't really ever shared any deep and meaningful discussions in our past interactions, so my reticence to come off even at all offensive or exclusionary might come as a surprise to her. Nevertheless, 'live and let live' is an adage I genuinely try to practice.

"Shit, Spence, I'm sorry. I just thought it was funny."

"No, no," I realize that I might have come on a little too strong with my ideologies, too, "it was. I mean, in context it was hilarious." We'd had tears rolling down our faces at the time. The re-take had also taken an hour longer than either of us had planned because one of us would inevitably start laughing again once the other had calmed down, setting the whole thing off again. On a sigh, I add, "I'm just sensitive about these things. Y'know…inclusion. LGBTQ rights. The whole shebang."

And don't get me started on my 'Bi/Pan Erasure' rant. Bisexuality and pansexuality exist, damn it. But if I'm dating a woman, people assume I'm straight, and if I'm dating a man, they assume I'm gay, and God forbid I publicly flirt with both men and women at the one event!

"Of course, babe. I'm sorry. I wasn't…I didn't mean…"

Crap. Now I feel bad. I honestly don't mean to talk *at* people like that. Or to lecture like that. Or to make people feel bad for just having a little fun. I don't. But, at the same time, I struggle to just let potentially offensive stuff go. I mean, in the right context there was nothing malicious about it, but what if someone had walked into the studio and misunderstood where it was coming from?

"No, I know; I'm sorry." I scrub a hand down my face and curse myself for having derailed the conversation so spectacularly.

Well done, Highland. Can't even carry on a conversation with a colleague...

Grimacing at the turn my thoughts have taken, I add, "I guess it's been a long day and I'm more tired than I thought."

Becky waves me off with a smile laced with understanding. "You're a good guy. It's nice that you think of other people's feelings."

"It's all that romance I read," I jest, trying to lighten the mood. "It puts me in touch with my softer side or whatever."

"Uh huh." Becky doesn't sound convinced, but the smile toying at the edge of her lips is playful. She bumps my shoulder with hers. "I'm sure that's it."

I scoop up my satchel from the floor outside the booth and fiddle with the strap as I loop it over my shoulder. I'm always a little awkward with goodbyes, even professional ones.

"So," I say, aiming for casual despite the clusterfuck of the conversation we've just shared, "it was awesome working with you again. You'll call if anything needs to be re-recorded?"

Becky nods. "It was," she agrees, "and I will." She cocks her head to the side. "Rumor has it you've got yourself a home studio now. Do you do your own post-production?"

"Yeah. It's…*ugh*. Honestly, I hate doing it. But it keeps my overheads low and maximizes my profits, so…"

"I get it. If I could perform, I'd be set. But, trust me, *nobody* wants me reading their books." She sighs dramatically. "Turns out acting isn't in my wheelhouse."

"You could take lessons," I offer helpfully. "Performing for narration purposes isn't the same as acting – it's all vocal work, and you don't have to memorize anything." The face she makes has me chuckling and holding my hands up in the universal gesture of surrender. "Or not. It was just a suggestion."

"To be fair, my job keeps me busy enough. But the idea of starting my own company with the ability to work from home has its appeal."

As someone who took the plunge and invested in building a small studio in their basement, I wholeheartedly agree with her. I still take on jobs for publishing houses and established production companies but having my own space and being able to offer my services as a narrator or voice over artist under my own company name (and rates) has been incredibly liberating.

Becky and I walk together and continue our conversation as we leave the building which houses the recording studio and their offices and meander towards the parking lot. She asks me about how much it cost me to set my home studio up, and I happily give her all the information I have. She's not my direct competition, after all, and it's always nice to talk to someone else who understands the intricacies of my job.

The guys I'm closest to try their best, but I'm pretty sure they all think it's a walk in the park. After all, how hard can it be to be paid to read a script out loud with no physical audience? Harder than they think, I assure you.

After we say our goodbyes, I head home, smiling when I'm greeted at the door by my cat. He's a rescue from the local shelter, sleek and black and vocal as fuck.

"Hey, Frank," I greet him, earning myself a loud, drawn-out *'mrrrrow'* in return. He winds around my ankles, butting his head into my shin. "I missed you, too, bud."

After dropping my satchel on the side table in the entryway, I reach down to stroke my hand over his back, smiling as I always do when he arches up off the floor for more, purring deep and loudly.

"At least I can get *someone's* engine running," I mutter to myself as the rumbling sound starts up.

Frank twists around with that effortless grace gifted to all felines and nudges my hand for more pets. "Alright, alright, you attention whore," I grumble lightheartedly, picking him up and cradling him against my chest. His purr vibrates against me, soothing away the remaining stresses of my day.

My friend Chance (probably my closest friend, considering I hang out with him more than any of the other guys in our social circle, especially since they've all started finding partners to settle down with) gave me no end of grief when I first adopted Frank.

"Cats are assholes," he'd said, trying to convince me to get a dog instead. "They're selfish and aloof and not at all affectionate. And they break shit. Like, on purpose. They look you dead in the eye and do it. I've seen it on YouTube."

I'd argued that cats are generally cleaner, more willing to entertain themselves when I'm out at work, and I've never had to strap a leash to a cat and walk it for hours on end. Cats also don't cause noise disturbance for the neighbors or during my recording sessions. As much as I also love dogs, a cat was a better fit for my lifestyle at the time (and still is). Plus, Frank had totally proven Chance wrong when it came to how affectionate he was when I first saw him.

And, yeah, the fact that Emma, my ex, had also loved cats had been a draw card, too.

I'm just glad she didn't fight me for custody. I wouldn't have gotten through the last couple of years without my furry little companion.

Frank meows again as I walk towards the kitchen. He's got our routine memorized at this point, and he knows that his dinner is about to be served. I talk to him about my day as I pull out a can of gourmet cat food (shut up, he's fussy) and then set him down on the tiled kitchen floor in front of his food and water bowls.

He eats his meal while I reheat myself some leftover Chinese food from last night and then perches himself on the armrest of the couch as I settle in to eat and watch TV, occasionally reaching out a soft black paw (complete with the cutest pink toe-beans) in an attempt to steal from my fork as it moves towards my mouth. And if I give in and hand feed him little bits of braised chicken, nobody else is any the wiser.

'You're spending another Friday night alone with your pussy again, aren't you?' Chance's text message comes through midway through my attempt to catch up on the last season of *The Great British Bake Off.*

I roll my eyes and text back, *'For a gay man, you're kind of obsessed with what I do with pussy.'*

'I take that as 'Yes, Chance, I am channeling my inner old lady again'. You're not fooling anyone by deflecting.'

I snort. He knows me too well. *'You got me. All I need is a pair of knitting needles and I could be someone's grandma.'*

'Come out to The Grove tonight.' He replies, cutting to the chase. I groan. Before I can respond, he adds, *'Please?'*

I'm pretty sure he knows I'm going to give in even before I send my response. *'Fine. But you're buying the drinks.'*

Chapter Two — Tony

"Get your nose out of that book and help me, would ya?"

I roll my eyes at my sister's demand, but I still swing my legs off the armrest of the armchair I've been sprawled across and down onto the floor, tossing my book onto the coffee table in front of me. I give the cover (adorned with glistening abs and a jawline that could make a nun swoon) one last mournful glance before I cross the living room to pull paper grocery bags out of Tanya's arms.

She slumps back against the open front door with relief. "Thank you."

"Whatever," I tease, hefting the heavy bags in my hold and wandering down the short hallway that leads to the poky kitchen in our ground floor apartment. I place them on the square island in the middle of the room and start pulling out the groceries.

Milk. OJ. Pasta. A jar of pasta sauce. Cheese.

"Guess I know what's on the menu tonight," I muse aloud.

"Nonna would kill you for this, you know." I hold up the generic brand 'Bolognese' (wherein I believe the name is a loose interpretation of what's inside the glass) sauce as Tanya drops two more bags down onto the surface in front of me with a huff of impatience.

"I mean, that ship sailed when she caught you kissing Billy Simmons in Junior year. Jars of sauce are, like, a lesser sin in comparison. And seeing as we're already going to hell…"

I laugh, shaking my head. "Okay, that's a fair point."

"I've been known to make them occasionally." She shrugs a thin shoulder and smirks. "I mean, I *did* steal all the intelligence genes in the womb."

"And the height, too," I growl.

It doesn't matter how many times we have this conversation, being reminded that my wombmate seemingly won the genetic lottery always makes me a little grumpy. I mean, for fuck's sake, I'm the one with the Y chromosome: I'm supposed to be taller. That's, like, a law or something, isn't it? But instead, Tanya (the bitch) is a tall, willowy 5'11" and I…am nowhere near that, having maxed out at 5'8" when I was fourteen and just stayed there. If I believed in a greater power, I'd say they had a pretty shitty sense of humor.

"Awww, come on, Napoleon, chin up: at least when you meet the Daddy of your dreams, you'll fit right into his big, strong embrace, huh?"

I shove the milk into the side shelf of the refrigerator with a bit more force than necessary, my cheeks burning. "Stop it. I only read that stuff. I don't *do* it."

Ever since she discovered my penchant for kinky novels, my darling sister has *not* let me live it down.

She flicks her long, straight hair —dyed bright orange at

the moment, though it tends to change on a whim— over her shoulder and shrugs. "Only 'cos you haven't got the balls to admit that you *want* to do it."

I can feel my cheeks burning, the blush probably deepening as it stretches down my neck and over my ears. "Shut up."

"Hey, at least that's more believable than that series you listened to about the guys getting pregnant." She holds up a hand, forestalling the argument she knows is coming, "And, before you correct me, I'm not talking about trans men and you know it. I'm talking about those wolfy shifter men."

I'm pretty sure my entire body is red at this point. My heart hammers in my chest as the embarrassment sets in and I cover my face with my hands. "Oh, God, *stay out* of my Audible account."

She snorts. "We *share* the account, numb-nuts."

Hang on. What?

"Since when?" I frown. "Have you been logging into my account instead of paying for your own?" How did I not notice that? I make a note to have a proper scroll through my library.

She shrugs. "As long as I listen to the stuff that's included in your membership, I don't see what the problem is."

"The problem is that you're totally invading my privacy."

"Chill, baby bro," Tanya waves me off dismissively, "it's not like I don't know all your deepest, darkest secrets anyway. Twin, remember?"

I roll my eyes. "Last I checked, twins can't actually read each other's minds. I mean, we're close, but we're not *that* close. I still have secrets." I feel a little like a petulant teenager and not a fully grown man in his late twenties when I fold my arms after my final declaration.

She reaches across the small kitchen island and pats my

cheek with a liberal dose of condescension. "You keep telling yourself that."

I'll let her believe that she knows everything. It's far less humiliating than having her know the things I've never said out loud to anyone, things I've never written down or typed or even dared to think about in the presence of other people. My deepest secret is one I have kept tightly hidden, one that seems to simmer at the back of my brain and taunt me more with every passing year since I hit twenty.

I mean, I'm a twenty-eight-year-old virgin.

Mortification tightens my chest at just the thought. It's not like I haven't *tried* over the years. Just like in that Steve Carrell movie – it just never happened. And now I'm nearing thirty and I'm spending my days (when I'm not working my soul-crushing job at one of our local diners) reading and listening to as many gay romance novels as I can get my hands on.

What a life.

At this rate, I'm going to die a virgin.

To be honest, I'd rather that than have my sister —or anyone else— find out, anyway.

We put away the last of the groceries together, our conversation shifting into much more comfortable territory. For all of my complaints, I can't imagine living with anyone other than Tanya. We are probably the very stereotype of twins, even if we don't look alike. We're ridiculously close, have very few boundaries, and have been through all the same life experiences together. Except for when it comes to sex, anyway, which is probably a good thing because even if I read a lot of kinky shit, I'm not into incest. Oh, and then there's the fact that I'm gay.

"You working tonight?" Tanya asks me, trailing me back out

into the tiny living room. She flops down on *my* armchair with a smirk that says she's deliberately trying to push my buttons.

I don't take the bait. I just drop into the other chair, wiggling around until I'm comfortable. "Yeah," I answer on a sigh. "I'm covering for Jamie. They called in sick again."

Tanya frowns. "Again? Do you think it's serious?"

I love that she doesn't automatically assume the worst of people. Or maybe she trusts my judgment about my colleagues. I bite my lip and shrug. "I hope not. Jamie's not exactly in the best place financially. Medical bills would destroy them."

It's not like Tanya and I are flush with cash, either, mind you. But from the bits and pieces I've cobbled together from conversations with Jamie, I know we're far more stable.

"Well, let them know that if they need anything, we're here, okay?"

My sister and her big, bleeding heart. Tears prick the back of my eyes. She can be crude and off-putting, but she has the biggest heart of anyone I know. It's the same heart that had her moving out of home when our Nonna kicked me out as soon as we graduated high school. She had insisted we pool our savings and move in together and never once looked back on the life she was leaving behind. The free room and board, the free meals, the love of our Nonna. None of it mattered to her when she knew I'd be suffering on my own. A decade later, she's never once expressed regrets.

"I will," I reply softly, full of gratitude I don't bother to hide.

The look on Tanya's face tells me that she understands everything I haven't said out loud.

Maybe there is something to that twin mind-meld shit after all.

Chapter Two — Tony

* * *

"You're bussing tables tonight," my boss, Gerald, tells me when I let myself in through the back door of the diner and into the kitchen, having parked the car I share with my sister in the tiny gravel lot out the back. When I make a face, he rolls his eyes before turning back to the burgers he's got sizzling on the grill in front of him. "Jamie's not the only one to call in tonight. We're short-staffed and stupidly busy: that freak club must be havin' one of their open nights again."

'That freak club' is The Grove, a BDSM club located a couple of miles down the road, just inside the industrial part of town. We're the closest eatery by far and, because we're open 24/7, we get a lot of business from the kink community.

I do my best not to scowl at Gerald for his attitude about our clientele. Honestly, the people from the club are always polite, courteous, and friendly, not to mention generous tippers. The same can't be said of the truckers and out-of-towners and road-trippers who make up the rest of our business. Besides, with the amount of kinky romance I've been listening to and reading lately, I think the whole lifestyle has been given a bad rap by people like Gerald.

Narrow-minded dick, I think to myself as I reach for my apron and pull it on. My thoughts drift mournfully to the Bluetooth earbuds in my hip pocket. If I'd been allowed to man the grill, I would have been able to finish off the last of my most recent find on Audible. My favorite narrator had a new release recently, and I've been loving every second of it. But, sadly, it's not meant to be. I'll have to finish listening to it tomorrow, then.

Also, I prefer cooking to dealing with people face-to-face.

Slapping food on a griddle, smelling the delicious scents, watching as I create something out of next to nothing…that's *satisfying*. Forcing myself to try to talk to strangers? Less so. A *lot* less so.

In the front pouch of my apron, I toss in my pen and one of the notepads we scrawl our orders on, then tell Gerald I'm heading out front.

A wall of noise assaults me as soon as I push the double doors separating the kitchen from the service counter open. It's the sound of a packed restaurant of diners talking, of cutlery scraping plates and the jukebox near the front door blasting an old Elvis classic. It doesn't matter how long I've worked here, it still takes me a moment to get my bearings in the din.

I absolutely hate the sensory overload, but I would hate being homeless even more, so I grit my teeth and tell myself it's only six hours. Six hours, and then I can pop my earbuds back in and listen to Spencer Rhodes read me a steamy gay love story.

Another colleague, Betsy, bustles past me to type an order into the far-too-dated old register set up at the center of the long service counter, while Jenny, one of our greener waitresses, pours coffees to a line of patrons perched on stools just down to my left.

"Table twelve only just sat down," Betsy tells me as she passes me by again, heading into the kitchen to pin the order she's just printed up onto the line of fluttering slips of matching paper above Gerald's head, "I haven't taken 'em their menus yet."

"On it," I declare, glancing over to the table in question and grabbing two vinyl-covered menus on my way.

When I get to the table, I greet the men seated there with my standard 'customer service' smile. It feels plastic and doesn't reach my eyes, but my voice is genuine as I say hello and hand over the menus. "Can I get you anything to drink?" I ask, "Or are you okay to wait until I come back for your orders?"

They order a pitcher of Coke and I scrawl it messily onto my notepad, flash them another grin and assure them I'll be back in a moment.

And that pretty much sets the tone for my whole shift. The waves of people coming and going never really slow. Not until it's nearly ten o'clock. Then it seems to abruptly fade away until we're left with an empty diner, save for one or two truckers drinking their coffees and keeping to themselves.

"Holy hell," Jenny slumps against the counter, huffing out a breath to clear a few loose strands of pale blonde hair from her eyes, "that was crazy."

"Theme nights at The Grove'll do that," I tell her, patting her shoulder consolingly. Then I grin. "But the tips make it worthwhile."

She brightens at that and pats her pocket, shooting me a wink. "I did notice that."

We chat idly as we wander the space, refilling salt and pepper shakers and napkin dispensers, wiping down tables and vinyl seats and sweeping the floors. Betsy handles the few customers that trickle in as we work, then declares she's taking her break.

"My feet are killing me," she laments. "I'm breaking in a new pair of shoes."

"Ouch," Jenny commiserates.

I just nod and wave her off. "Go on, we've got this covered."

Maybe ten minutes later, Jenny starts getting agitated. "Sorry," she says, "I've gotta go real bad."

I laugh and shoo her off, too. We've got one old guy perched at the service counter but are otherwise empty. "I'll be fine for the few minutes it takes you to take care of business," I assure her, chuckling at how quickly she scoots away.

Naturally, my luck turns almost the second the door swings shut behind her.

A huge group enters through the front doors, raucous and taking up three booths at once as they sprawl out. I can only assume they've come from the club, seeing as a couple wear kitten and puppy ears (one even has a collar) and…does that woman have a pacifier attached to her shirt with some kind of ribbon?

I give myself a shake and remind myself not to judge, gathering up a whole stack of menus and greeting the newcomers with my usual warmth. I take their drink orders and scurry back and forth between the counter and the tables as I ferry trayfuls of glasses to them. Then I take their orders and hurry to get them entered, printed, and pinned up on Gerald's line.

When the bell over the doors chimes again, I want to groan in frustration.

Where the hell is Jenny?

At least the most recent customers arrive as a single pair. It's two men, both handsome enough. One is quite tall and lean, with a mop of dark hair and warm gray-blue eyes, and the other is shorter and more rounded with softer features, rusty reddish-brown hair, and matching scruff on his cheeks. They both nod and raise their hands in recognition of the other group, but head in the opposite direction in the diner, taking a booth down the other side.

Pulling out two menus, I hustle over to them and begin my usual spiel.

Gingerbread grins and doesn't even bother to open his menu.

"I'll have a Coke and your double bacon cheeseburger with curly fries, please."

His friend scoffs, but the sound is affectionate. "So, a heart attack on a plate, then?" There's something familiar about this other man's voice, but I've never seen him before in my life. He, too, leaves the menu shut and offers me a smile that showcases twin dimples on either side of his mouth. The effect is instantly disarming. "Decaf coffee, black, and a serve of your cherry pie a la mode, please."

"What the hell kinda' order is that?" Scruffy McGinger asks in disgust while I'm scribbling on my notepad.

"The kind where I already ate dinner before we headed out."

"Leftover Chinese food shared with Bob—"

"Frank."

"Whatever the hell you named that evil-ass furball, I don't care. Leftover takeout eaten alone with your cat isn't dinner."

Tall, Dark and Mop-like rolls his eyes and casts me an apologetic grimace. "Sorry about him. He's…an acquired taste."

I'm thoroughly amused by their antics, I have to admit it. But not being able to pick *why* this guy sounds so familiar is driving me crazy. His voice is deeper than he appears it should be, but pleasant. He speaks as though he's weighing his words, the pace and pattern of his speech almost melodic in how measured and smooth it is. I really like it. It sends pleasant tingles up my spine, alongside that curious familiarity.

"I don't know," I try to flirt a little, not knowing what is compelling me to do so. It's not the sort of thing I've ever been interested in doing before. Certainly never with a customer. I feel awkward, but I still wink as I add, "I can't help but agree that our burgers are *way* better than sharing old takeout with a cat."

The taller man gasps with faux indignation, clutching imaginary pearls. "Well I never," he says in an impressive, scandalized southern drawl, and it's like lightning strikes my brain. "That's hurtful, that is."

"S-sorry." I stammer, unable to compute the fact that the man I'm talking to sounds *just like* the voice in my audiobook. Just like the narrator whose works I've been chewing through like a rottweiler in a tennis ball factory.

"Damn, Spence, you broke our server," Ginger-features laughs, leaning across the laminate tabletop to smack at his friend. "Apologize, man. I want my burger."

Spence, my brain echoes helpfully. Because the voice alone could be put down to lucky coincidence, but the fact that my favorite narrator's name is also Spencer probably can't. Can it?

"N-no," I manage to blurt out, feeling the heat of embarrassment crawl over my cheeks, "I just…uh…sorry, are you… I mean, this is going to sound *ridiculous*, but, um, are you Spencer Rhodes?"

His eyes go wide and his jaw slackens. "You got that out of three sentences?"

Holy shit.

Holy fucking shit.

He is.

He *is* Spencer Rhodes.

My heart hammers in my chest and I'm pretty sure my blush covers my entire body at this point. "I'm a fan," I mumble, casting my gaze to the floor.

"No shit," Ginger Spice chuckles, "like that wasn't obvious by the fact you picked his voice so quickly."

"Chance," Spencer's rebuke to his friend is soft but firm, "don't tease the poor kid." He turns those gray-tinted, soulful eyes back on me. "You've got a damn good ear."

"I'm almost thirty," the bizarre defense spills from my lips before anything else can and I cringe. "I mean, uh, thanks."

Smooth, Tones. Real smooth. Just when you'd managed to act normal until now.

Feeling strained silence descending, I hold up my notepad and throw a thumb over my shoulder. "I should get your order in." Then I scurry away before I can further humiliate myself.

It's not until I'm pegging the paper up on the line that it hits me: by acknowledging that I'm a fan of Spencer Rhodes, I've essentially just let those two complete strangers in on my super secret interests. Because Rhodes' narration is niche. Like, he only narrates gay romance, and mostly kinky or taboo stuff at that. And, while I'm sure he doesn't have a problem with it, it might only be a paycheck to him…whereas here I am, listening so much that I can pick his voice out of a freaking lineup after only five seconds.

God, he must think I'm a nerdy, horny little loser.

…But would he be wrong?

"Jenny quit," Gerald tells me just as I'm turning to head back into the diner proper. It startles me out of my thoughts immediately.

"Wait…*what?*"

"Jenny quit," he repeats.

Frowning, I ask, "When?"

He shrugs, slinging burgers onto the grill while he plates up a stack of pancakes for one of the large group's orders. For all my complaints against my greasy bigot of a boss, I have to admit that his multi-tasking skills are second to none. "When she came back from her extended bathroom break."

I can feel my heart sinking into my stomach. "So…she's gone?" My eyes dart to the hook next to the door where, sure enough, there's an apron hanging on the empty hook I'd left behind when I started my shift. "God damn it."

Gerald grunts his agreement.

I glance at the clock above the swinging doors that lead to the front of house and start calculating how long it will be before Betsy's back from her break.

"These are good to go out," Gerald says, gesturing to four plates under the heat lamp. "I'll have the next round ready in two minutes."

Stifling a sigh, I nod and gather the plates in the practiced balancing act I've perfected over the years, using my forearm to help me carry the whole lot. I back out of the kitchen, opening the doors with my butt and turn to move out of their way before they swing shut. Then I hurry the first round of meals over to their respective diners and return to the service window before Gerald can ding the bell.

I make a game of getting back to him for each round until all the diners in the first group have their meals, and Betsy returns just as Gerald is dishing up the burger and pie for Spencer's table.

Spencer.

My heart starts doing a tap-dance in my chest again. In all the rush of the last fifteen minutes, I'd been able to forget my soul searing embarrassment. But it hits me with full force again now.

"Hey, Bets, can you take these plates to table nine?" I ask her, already handing the orders off before she can actually agree. "I've just gotta…" I gesture with my head towards the back of

20

house, implying an imaginary need for the facilities.

"Sure thing," she agrees sweetly, as I knew she would, then turns to do exactly that while I hustle towards the bathroom out back. I hide in a stall and sink down on the closed lid of the toilet, bracing my elbows on my thighs as I cradle my head and focus on calming my breathing.

I tell myself that Spencer Rhodes has probably forgotten all about me and my fanboy moment, and I do my best to believe that.

After leaving the stall, I wash my hands and face at the sink and dab my skin dry with a paper towel, take one last fortifying breath and open the door to leave the men's room…only to find the very object of my obsessive thoughts standing on the other side.

He's leaning against the wall of the narrow hallway across from the door and I swallow reflexively as I take a proper look at him. He's tall and lean, wearing dark jeans that hug his legs and a loose black polo shirt. His face is, as I observed earlier, handsome. Long and angular, but his features are open and inviting. His lips are plump and rosy, and I have a fleeting desire to rise up on my toes and taste them.

That sort of impulse is new for me. Normally, I need to mentally brace myself for that sort of contact, work myself up into feeling comfortable enough to kiss someone I don't know well. But not Spencer. Maybe it's that I almost feel like I do know him? Even if from a distance, just as a fan. He doesn't feel like a stranger, even though he is.

But then it clicks that he's not waiting for a stall. We have three, and the other two are not currently occupied. So, if he's not waiting for a stall, and there's nobody else in there, he's waiting…for me?

"Uh…" Is the incredibly coherent thought I manage to get out past my suddenly dry mouth.

He smiles at me, bringing out those dimples again. "Sorry to startle you," he says, inclining his head. "I'm not the type to stalk guys to the bathroom, but I…well, I got the impression you'd prefer the privacy while I asked for your number."

"Uh…" I understand the words he's saying, of course, but I can't quite process them. Ask for my number? Why would he ask for my number?

"Oh, shit, I didn't get it all wrong, did I? I just thought…" He rubs the back of his neck and his expression turns sheepish. "I mean, you listen to…See, Rhodes is the name I perform under for…um…very specific kinds of novels. Obviously, if you'd said my mainstream name—"

"Oh, no, I'm definitely into in men. I mean, gay. I am gay," I assure him, the words tumbling forth just as awkwardly as everything else I've said to him tonight.

But now Spencer seems to match me with his own blurted, "Oh, good. Me too. Into men, I mean. And women." He pauses to wince and drag his hand over his face, his cheeks turning a bit pink. "I'm bi. But…yeah." Clearing his throat, he sounds hopeful when he asks, "And are you, uh, available?"

I blink at him, struggling to comprehend exactly why he'd be asking that. "Are…are you asking me out?" My voice goes a little shrill with my disbelief. "*Me*? Dear God, *why*? I'm…" I gesture lamely at myself, "nothing special."

Instantly, his expression shifts to something far more serious. "Whoever's led you to believe that is an idiot. Or a series of idiots. There's plenty special about you. In a good way." He rushes to add the last bit, lest I choose to misinterpret him. Not that I could. Not with how earnest he sounds.

Wow. Tonight has taken a seriously bizarre turn.

I don't bother telling him that there has not been a series of idiots. Outside of a few kisses and some dud Grindr experiences which did *not* result in hooking up as planned, there hasn't ever been anyone. Most people find me too odd for friendship, let alone sex. Hence my sad little secret.

And *that* is why I'm convinced I'm nothing special.

Still, I'm not stupid enough to tell him any of it. Especially not while we're loitering outside the bathrooms in the diner where I work, where anyone could overhear me.

"So…" he prompts when I continue to just gawk at him (yet another example of why I'm a painfully single virgin, I'm sure), "can I get your number?"

It's a no brainer, really.

I smile, shyness warring with the bubbling excitement in my belly. "Sure."

Chapter Three – Spencer

"I can't believe you chased him for his number," Chance teases me long after we've settled our bill, leaving hefty tips for both the serving staff tonight, and have started slowly walking down the road to our parked cars. "Was it because he's *a fan?*"

The way my best friend says those last words is more to embarrass me than it is to slight the cute server whose number is now safely saved in my phone under the name 'Tony' with a winky faced emoji beside it. Still, I feel myself prickling in Tony's defense anyway.

"Chance," I say with warning, in a tone I usually reserve for Daddy play, "don't."

Beneath his ginger facial scruff, his lips quirk, knowing that he's hit a nerve. "It *was* cute the way he got all stammer-y and starstruck."

"Chance..."

"And he does seem kinda' perfect for you. He's got that whole 'wide-eyed and innocent' vibe. He practically screams

Boy, doesn't he?"

It's a little frustrating that he's right. I don't give him the satisfaction of knowing that, though, or he'll lord it over me the way only a best friend can.

"I've never seen him at The Grove," I shrug lightly.

"He listens to your kinky books," my buddy counters.

"That doesn't mean *he's* kinky. Besides," I offer with a sigh, stopping in my tracks to face him, "I narrate a lot of stuff under that stage name. From paranormal romance, to Daddy kink, to darker themed BDSM stuff, to MMMMM, to mpreg, to almost anything and everything in between. Even if he *is* kinky," which I doubt, considering how much he'd blushed delightfully at the barest touch of my fingers against his when I'd handed him my phone to type in his digits, "who's to say our kinks align?"

You know what Chance gets out of all that?

"What the actual fuck is *mpreg*?"

Arching an eyebrow at him, I ask, "What does it sound like?"

He crinkles his nose. "Dude. No."

I shake my head at him, my wild mane of hair flying into my face with the action. Brushing it back and tucking it behind my ears with both hands, I say, "You know better than to judge others for their kinks, man. And some of those books are a hell of a lot of fun to narrate. Especially the shifter ones."

"*Shift*—no. You know what? I'm not asking."

Good, I think to myself with amusement as we start walking again, *because explaining knotting might just push him over the edge.*

The silence between us is short-lived.

"So, do you think he might be a Boy?" Honestly, as much as I love my friends, they're all like dogs with bones, never letting a subject go. Chance, being the guy I'm closest to, is the worst of the lot. Or, at least he is with me. He can be a bit more reserved in group settings, and positively shy in large groups of strangers, but with the people he's close to, he has zero reservations.

I stifle a groan. "Does it matter?"

This time he's the one who stops walking, staring at me slack-jawed when I crane my neck around to question what the hell he's doing.

"What?" I ask him.

"Does it matter?" he repeats incredulously, as though he can't believe I even asked the question. "Spence, you're a Daddy. Are you honestly trying to tell me that you'd be down for a vanilla relationship? 'Cos I don't give a flying fuck how cute a guy is; if I can't share my kinks with him, I'm not interested."

"That's you, man, and that's totally your prerogative. But—"

"Seriously?" He doesn't even let me finish, guessing (albeit correctly) that I was about to tell him I didn't *have* to find a Little in order to be happy. He jogs forward on the pavement suddenly, staring me down with intensity. "Spencer. Just because you can manage being single for fuck knows how long it's been since Emma, it doesn't mean that you're not going to want to indulge your Daddy instincts when you *are* back in a relationship again."

"Because looking for a Little has worked out so well for me these last couple of years." The bitter, sarcasm-laced words escape me before I can stop them. I cringe and try to reel back my frustration.

This is an issue I have any time my ex-girlfriend is brought up: I get snappish.

Chance is the only one of the guys who knows the full

story behind my breakup. I almost let it slip a few weeks ago, back when Ted's whole tragic past came to light, but I managed to bite my tongue. Everyone was, understandably, too busy supporting Ted (while simultaneously pretending that we weren't, because he's one of those ridiculous men who 'doesn't need sympathy' and thinks he needs to suffer in silence) and then...well, I guess I didn't want to accidentally trigger Ted myself, I guess.

I mean, how do you tell a guy who lost a child that the reason your girlfriend left you is because, as much as you enjoy playing the role of Daddy in a kinky lifestyle, you categorically refuse to have actual children?

Emma had known it from the start, by the way. It's one of those huge, important topics that everyone should cover when casual dating starts turning into 'are we seeing if there's a future here?' or whatever. And she'd agreed! 'Why would I want a baby when I prefer to pretend to be one myself?' she'd even asked me.

Then, over time, I guess her feelings changed.

Mine, on the other hand, did not.

We had a huge blowout fight over it, the both of us crying and yelling about promises and people changing, and then she'd packed her bags and left. Last I heard, she'd moved across the country to be closer to her family again.

I can admit now that losing her hurt. A lot. But, at the time, I was too angry to admit it.

So now, whenever she's mentioned, it's like someone poking at a scab. There's still pain there. Healing, but not yet gone. And it itches something in my psyche, making me defensive and irritable. Chance knows this, of course, but it doesn't stop him from bringing her up.

Hell, maybe the easy rise he's guaranteed to get out of me is exactly why he does it.

Chance raises both his eyebrows and folds his arms expectantly. Silence, broken only by the distant sounds of traffic on the nearby highway, falls between us. After a long moment, he licks his lips and surprises me with how serious his next words are. "I think you've been punishing yourself, Spencer. And it needs to stop."

"I…" I blink. "What?"

I watch as he rubs a hand down his face, smoothing his scruffy beard while he carefully considers how to explain what he just said. "You didn't want to be a dad, but you love being a Daddy. And whatever the fuck Emma said to you when she left…well, I think it's made you feel guilty about that. So you're depriving yourself—"

"Now, hang on…"

"You're depriving yourself," he continues as though I didn't interrupt him, "of the enjoyment of being a Daddy because…" Chance throws his hands in the air and looks around, as though the words he's searching for might spontaneously appear. "Shit, I don't know. Because some twisted part of you feels like it's wrong now? Except we both know that being a Daddy to a Little is *completely* different to wanting to be a dad, even if some of the fundamental behaviors and instincts are the same. But that girl of yours got in your head and you haven't been the same since."

I'm too stunned to speak. Chance isn't usually the psychoanalyzing type. Of our social group, that's more Ted's forte, or even Charlie's. Maybe even Zephyr's, too. The fact that Chance might have stumbled onto a kernel of truth in all of his ranting is even more surprising.

I *did* spend weeks (months, even) thinking over everything Emma cried at me the night we broke up.

How was it possible that I so enjoyed taking care of her as a Little, but had zero interest in taking care of a real child? Was I really so selfish that I couldn't see the similarities? Would it really be such a bad thing to put those same instincts to love and nurture to use in a more traditional, socially acceptable way?

But, as I had told her, being Daddy to an adult Little and role-playing is something I indulge in to complement my romantic and sexual relationships. There's nothing wrong with enjoying that while simultaneously not wanting children.

Real parenting goes beyond the fun of being a Daddy. You can't safe word out of parenting. You can't step away and take a break or relax into adult time with a real toddler running around. I've seen my siblings' kids in action. I have also seen the way my brothers' relationships with their wives have changed in unappealing ways, and I'm content being a (mostly distant these days) uncle. I don't need to spend more time than is absolutely necessary with children.

The scenes I explore with my Littles are to enhance intimacy and trust between two consenting adults. Looking after real kids is obviously a different kettle of fish: it involves thankless years of commitment to a person whose welfare and upbringing you are responsible for. It involves sacrificing your own needs and desires to put theirs first. It involves sleep deprivation in completely unsexy ways. It's…well, it's just not for me.

That might make me selfish, but at least I'm not going to doom some kid to a life with a father who resents them and doesn't treat them with the unconditional love they deserve.

So, I've spent a long time analyzing why I enjoy being an age play daddy. I've heard people refer to the Daddy/Little relationship as 'pseudo-pedophilia' or 'pedophilia lite', and that hurts deeply. For me, being in a Daddy/Little relationship has nothing to do with sex. Yes, it is considered a kink and, yes, it is a part of the BDSM lifestyle for that reason, but I'm not getting off on the thought of being with a child. I'm with other consenting adults.

It's the intimacy that the roleplay fosters which gets my engines going. There's deep trust exchanged in any of the scenes we partake in. To know that the person I'm with is laying themselves bare, with all their vulnerabilities on display, and is trusting me wholeheartedly to support them and join them as they let go of the stresses of their adult lives gives me a high that nothing else can rival.

I like feeling as though I am my lover's safe space. I am the person they can just let go and be themselves with zero judgment. I'm the person they trust to take care of their needs, whatever they might be. And, in return, I find reward in their love and confidence in me.

I've spoken about this with the guys in my social circle, of course, and they've all said they feel much the same way as I do, which is hardly a surprise. We all came together through The Grove and bonded over being like-minded Daddies.

Over the years, that morphed into a genuine friendship group. We have supported each other through breakups and new relationships, through shootings (Charlie) and a new marriage (also Charlie), through revelations of personal hardships (Matt and Ted) and everything else in between. The group has been slowly expanding as the others find their 'Forever Littles', or Daddies in Matt's case, and Charlie has taken the foundations of our little group and has applied them to the creation of his and Asher's kink-specific social haven: The Little Community Center.

But even though I know they get it, and that I could try and parse out my lingering twisted up feelings over my breakup with Emma with them, I haven't been able to do it.

"Did I hit a nerve?" Chance prompts me, and I realize I've been quiet for too long.

We're still standing on the sidewalk in the dark, and I sigh, running a hand through my hair. I wince at the knots and tangles I encounter. "It's not like that," I finally manage to get out, pulling aggressively at a particularly stubborn tangle. "I don't feel guilty or wrong or…or anything like that. I just…" I lick my lips. "I'm just not going to look *specifically* for someone into Little play. I want a lover; a *partner*. Not just someone to indulge my kinks."

This is only a partial truth, but Chance doesn't need to know that. It's possible that I'm attempting to talk myself out of my deepest desires, because it's been so long that finding the right partner to tick all my dream boxes is starting to sound like a pipe dream.

Charlie said something like that once. After his breakup with what's-his-name. The guy before Asher came on the scene. At the time, I didn't give it a whole lot of thought. I was with Emma and things were good for me. Yeah, Emma was little a lot more than she was big, but it worked for us.

Until it didn't.

Now I get what Charlie was trying to express all those years ago. He wanted to find balance.

Unfortunately for me, 'balance' looks different to everyone. What Charlie has with Asher is a completely different dynamic to the one I had with Emma, though at the time I thought it was similar because Ash approaches his Little persona with the same fluidity that Emma did. But Ash as an adult is *far* more independent than Emma ever was. He's Charlie's equal, supporting his husband with the same intensity that Charlie supports him. Emma wasn't like that in return. She cared about me, but only because of how heavily she relied on me…and I *loved* that.

I still want something like that.

Even if my partner isn't a Little, I want to look after them. I want them to depend on me. I want to be their safe space, like I was for Emma.

I've *got* to stop thinking about her.

It's honestly not even her that I miss anymore. It's more the relationship itself. Being wanted and needed and loved. That's what I miss. So, no, I don't need Daddy/Little roleplay in order to feel those things. It helps cement them for me, but it's not a necessity.

My thoughts are going around in circles now.

"Don't get me wrong," I decide to throw Chance a bone, forcing my feet to start moving again, "if I happen to meet a Little who grabs my attention and wants the same things I do? I'd be all over that like a rash. But I'm not going to turn down an opportunity to see what else…*who* else is out there for me, either."

My buddy mulls over this in silence as we near our vehicles. For a few moments, all I can hear in the still night air is the sound of our measured footfalls on the pavement. Then Chance says, "And if you and this waiter boy—"

"Tony," I correct him.

I don't need to look at him to know that he's rolling his eyes.

"If you and *Tony*," the inflection is teasing, "hit it off, you're telling me you're okay with not being a Daddy again if he's not into it?"

"I only just got his number, man," I bypass the question with a laugh and a shake of my head. "You're putting the cart before the horse. I mean, we might go on one date and find we have nothing in common."

He snorts, finally reaching his car and leaning against it. "The kid listens to the shit you narrate and looks at you with stars in his big, brown eyes. I don't think you'll have a problem when it comes to having stuff in common."

I shrug, pulling my own keys from my pocket now that I'm only a few steps away from my car. "All I'm saying is you're worrying about something that's not likely to be an issue for a long while."

"Uh huh," he doesn't sound convinced. His keys jangle as he raises his hand to point at me in illustration of his final points, "I've watched Charlie, Matt, *and* Ted go from single to super committed relationships in the blink of an eye. Mark my words, Spence: I've seen the way that boy looks at you. These issues'll pop up sooner than you think. And you'd better be ready to face 'em."

Chapter Four – Tony

I have a *date*.

I *have* a date.

I have a date.

I have a date?!

I can't wrap my head around the concept. I mean, I can't even remember the last time I went on a real date. It must have been when I was just out of high school. I don't even think that counts as an adult date. Everything else has been failed Grindr hookups and…oh, God, I've never been on a real date.

Shit.

I don't know what the actual fuck I'm doing.

I'm sneaking around behind my sister's back, for one thing.

I didn't tell her about randomly meeting my favorite audiobook narrator whose voice I've had a crush on for a while now. I didn't tell her that he asked for my number. I didn't tell her that we've spent the last four days and nights texting back and forth like giddy teenagers. (Okay, *I* text like a giddy teenager:

I imagine Spencer's just having a normal conversation on his end.) I didn't tell her *any* of it.

And I especially didn't tell her that I've been listening to Spencer reading me the hottest, smuttiest romance stories in every spare second I get.

Is that weird?

It's weird, isn't it?

I mean...I've met him now. I know him now. I'm going on a date with him now. I should *not* be listening to the books he's narrated anymore. I shouldn't.

Not when I can only picture his handsome face as the sexy heroes in the stories. Not when I close my eyes and let the dirty, sexy words get me all hot and bothered, imagining that he's reading them just for me, maybe even planning to re-enact some of them with me.

Ugh. Down, boy, I mentally hiss at my dick which is starting to take interest in the path my thoughts have taken. I will *not* turn up to my first date with this man (or with any man, really) with a hard on.

I check my reflection in the full-length mirror which hangs on the inside of my closet door. I'm looking good, if I do say so myself. In dark denim jeans and a red button-down shirt, I look more confident and put-together than I feel. Glancing at my watch, the shiny silver one with the large, square face that Nonna gave me for my sixteenth birthday, I note with a start that I need to leave in the next five minutes if I don't want to be late.

Like a gentleman, Spencer had offered to pick me up, but I'd refused. Partially because I don't really know him, partially because I didn't want to risk Tanya being...well...Tanya at him, and also partially because I like to pretend that I have some modicum of control over most situations.

Instead of taking the car, though, I've decided to catch the bus and then walk to the restaurant where I'll be meeting Spencer. I'm not a huge fan of driving in the city. I don't like searching for parking, or trying to maneuver through constantly heavy traffic, or getting lost because there are a bunch of ridiculous one-way streets which make zero sense. And, in taking the bus, I can put my earbuds in and listen to my books without losing concentration.

I probably should *not* be listening to Spencer's narration on the way to our date, should I?

But I can't help myself. It's not just the enjoyment of listening to his talented voice acting, either. The plot in the book I'm listening to right now is great. And the author's style is punctuated with humor that Spencer delivers with perfect emphasis and timing. I actually spend a good portion of my bus trip snickering to myself, uncaring of what the few other passengers might think.

I'm still smiling as I make the short walk from the bus stop through the bustling city streets, tucking my earbuds away into my pocket as I turn the final corner and spy my date leaning casually against the brick wall a few feet away from the restaurant's door.

He straightens up as he sees me approach, a smile tugging up those perfect lips of his, bringing out his dimples.

"Tony," Spencer greets me with warmth, walking a few paces in my direction as though he's just as excited to close the distance between us. "Hi!" He bends to kiss my cheek, and I surprise myself by not flinching away when he enters my personal space so unexpectedly. "You look amazing."

My face burns immediately. Whether because of the press

of his lips to my skin or the compliment, I'm not entirely sure. I bite my lip and look him over. "Right back at you."

It's not even lip service. He's wearing dark khaki pants and a blue polo shirt that seems to set off his dark gray-blue eyes. His hair is still a wild mess of waves, but it doesn't look unkempt. He's tall and lean, and even though he's not the big, muscular bear type I've always joked about being interested in, I can see in the toning of his forearms and biceps that he's probably stronger and sturdier than he appears at a glance.

Spencer offers me his arm and I loop mine in his, my heart beating faster at the innocent contact. I don't usually let strangers touch me, but in my head he's not really a stranger. Not with how long I've been listening to him read to me.

"Did your week improve?" he asks conversationally as he leads me towards the restaurant door. During our text exchanges during the week, I'd admitted that, with Jenny quitting and Jamie still being off sick, work has been more hectic than usual.

I don't want to bring the mood down, even though it's been a pretty stressful few days, so I just smile coyly and squeeze his arm, saying, "It has now."

"Corny," he accuses with a laugh, then tugs me against his side with unveiled affection, "I approve."

We reach the maître d' and Spencer says, "Table for two under Highland?"

I blink. "Highland?"

"Ah, that's my actual last name," he throws over his shoulder as we separate to allow the maître d' to lead us through the maze of occupied tables to our own. "I have a couple of, uh, I guess you'd call them stage names? Rhodes is the one I use for the…um…more risqué stuff."

Spencer's hand becomes a distracting presence on the small of my back as we fall into a single file line, with him urging me to follow the maître d' first. I'm glad my date can't see the flush of my face, because I'm back to being embarrassed over fanboying over him. Especially now that I know for sure he's aware of the kind of books I like to listen to.

Once we're seated, I finally take in the space around us. For lack of a better description, the restaurant is quirky kitsch. It's dimly lit; enough to see properly, but with a darkened sort of ambiance. The walls are open brickwork, and there are random decorations hung around the room. I can see a hopefully faux taxidermy fox wearing a plaid waistcoat. A rabbit with antlers and thick, black framed glasses. Edison bulbs and chandeliers and empty Baroque photo frames painted in neon colors.

The tables and chairs are equally eclectic with none of them in matching sets. I see timber and wrought iron in a mishmash of styles from various eras, with watermarks and scuff marks and chipped surfaces. It's almost like a thrift store threw up in here, but every item somehow feels right for the space.

It's very hipster, I guess.

I can feel Spencer's gaze on me and I tear my eyes away from my exploration to look at him.

"What do you think?" he asks, leaning forward across the scuffed timber surface that separates us. "Have you been here before?"

I shake my head. "No, this is a first for me," I admit, then cast my eyes around the room again. "It's different."

"Ouch," Spencer holds a hand to his chest, "Euphemisms already?""

"No, no," I rush to assure him, cursing myself for letting him think that I don't like it, "I don't mean it in a bad way. I…I just don't get out much."

And I've never been good at subtlety or tact. I usually just say what I'm thinking. The only place I've really been able to prevent myself from doing so is at work, and that's because I make myself stick to a formulated script in my head. The only time I've really gone off script has been with Spencer, and now I have no idea what I'm doing.

I close my eyes against the embarrassment of admitting what a loser I am within the first five minutes of our date. I mean, pathetic much? Yes, I am blushing profusely now. Yes, I do wish the ground would open up and swallow me whole.

"Hey," Spencer's voice is soft and his hand touches mine, making me startle. I blink across the table at him and he gives me a reassuring smile, cocking his head almost like a puppy might. "I was just teasing. I don't get out much, either. And this place is…something else." He tilts his head back, exposing the long, pale column of his neck, and laughs. "Is that a wolf wearing a sheepskin hat?"

I look up and, sure enough, suspended from the ceiling —between the chandeliers— is a wolf wearing a woolly bonnet. "Yeah…" I draw the word out, half-amused, half-confused. When I look back at Spencer, he's rubbing the back of his neck with a sheepish expression.

"So, I didn't choose this place," he admits, shaking his head. "Kate and Cherie, uh, friends of mine did."

"Maybe the food is awesome?" I offer, lifting my menu for the first time.

"God, I hope so, or Cherie's got a lot to answer for." There's fondness in his threat, so I don't think he's actually going to give his friends too much shit if the place turns out to be a bust.

As I scan the menu, I have to admit that it sounds good. Gourmet burgers and wings appear to be the main attractions here, and a glance around the room at other diners' plates is even more encouraging.

Because that's another thing: I'm fussy about food. Still, most places usually have something on the menu I'm comfortable ordering (even if a lot of the time it's the kid's menu and I get weird looks from the servers). Thankfully, this place has a lot of options that sound appealing, even to my limited palate, and that sets me at ease a bit more.

"Share platter?" Spencer suggests, pointing at the option that's caught his eye. He shrugs at me and grins. "I can't choose, so sliders, fries and two kinds of wings sounds kind of awesome to me."

I put my laminated piece of paper down and nod. "Perfect."

A server saunters over almost at the exact same moment Spencer drops his menu on the table. She's dressed in a short, red and black plaid skirt, a short-sleeved white button down and a neon green waistcoat. I blink a couple of times at the ensemble and then realize that it seems to fit the vibe of the place. She's friendly as she introduces herself as Mandy, but not flirtatious, which I appreciate. She asks for our drink orders first, then nods when Spencer tells her we're getting the share platter.

"I know I'm s'posed to upsell you on dessert," she says, leaning forward conspiratorially, "but if you're plannin' on savin' room for it, I'd suggest you go to the dessert bar down the street. It just opened up last month, and oh-my-Gawd, their boozy thickshakes are out of this world, and they make a mean brownie sundae, too."

"Good to know," Spencer grins and hands back our menus. When she's gone, he turns to me and says, "We'd better listen to the lady, huh?"

I probably shouldn't get all giddy about the fact that he's suggesting dessert already, but it's a good sign, right? He's planning on dragging the night out, not trying to rush us out the door and back to our respective homes alone.

"Sounds like a plan to me," I agree, willing my heart not to beat so fast.

My date is thankfully oblivious to my nerves, and he leads the conversation with a casual ease I'm actually a little jealous of.

We've texted a lot over the last few days, so he knows the basics about me, and I know the same about him.

He'd already told me that he was bi, but during the week he sent me a message asking if I was okay with that. I was perplexed by the question. I mean, just because he's attracted to women as well as men (and, presumably, intersex or gender fluid people as well), it doesn't make him any more or less predisposed to wandering eyes…or other parts of his anatomy, for that matter. And, when I responded as such, the reply containing a flurry of cat emojis with hearts in their eyes told me that my answer had pleased him somehow.

Other things I've learned from our texting have been less intense. He's thirty-six, so only eight years older than me, and lives on his own with his cat. He grew up here with his two brothers, and chose a career where his work could be completed literally anywhere in the world, as long as he has access to the right equipment.

In turn, I gave him the Cliff's Notes version of my life. I have a single sibling (my twin sister), we were raised by our Nonna and grew up in a tiny town in bumfuck nowhere, I got kicked out of home after graduating high school, and we stayed in the first place I was able to find steady work.

Because we've already covered the big stuff, tonight our conversation turns more trivial, keeping things light and happy, which I am more than happy to do. He tells me all about Frank, his cat, and I lament that we can't have pets in our poky apartment. Then we discuss some of our favorite TV shows, and I grin when he confesses that he is addicted to baking competition shows.

"Tell me you've discovered *Nailed It!*" I beg just as Mandy, our bright and bubbly server, comes back with the fries and first round of wings from our share platter.

Spencer and I turn to thank her at the same time, shooting each other matching smirks before she nods and leaves us to our own devices again.

"*Nailed It!* is the one with Nicole Byer, right?" he asks me, reaching for a sauce slathered wing. "The one where the contestants are set up to fail?"

I laugh, munching on a couple of perfectly cooked fries. They're crisp on the outside and soft on the inside, not too oily and dusted with a tasty blend of herbs and salt. So morish! "Yeah," I answer after I swallow, "but it's all in good fun, and it's hilarious to watch."

Oh, please let this man have a sense of humor.

"I've only watched an episode or two," he confesses, "but I'll admit, it was pretty funny. I'll have to give it another shot."

Whatever reply I was going to make dies as I watch him suck the bone of the chicken wing free of meat and sauce until it is clean as a whistle.

Holy fuck!

I'm pretty sure my brain short circuits at this point.

Oblivious, Spencer drops the bone into the bowl provided, where it clinks against the porcelain, and he reaches for a small bunch of fries. "So, I know you're also into books," he says, bringing up what has to be the worst subject ever now that my mind is already in the gutter. "Who are your favorite authors right now?"

"Uh…" I give myself a shake, trying to focus. Tearing my eyes away from his lips, I force myself to meet his gaze. "Um. That's a hard, uh, *difficult* question."

That wasn't an awkward answer at all, Russo. Good job! Idiot.

My strange verbal stumble seems to grab his attention, because his lips quirk and he eyes me knowingly.

God damn it.

My cheeks burn and I avert my gaze, quickly trying to explain, "I don't *just* read or listen to porn."

"Noted," chirps Mandy from my side as she drops another selection of wings in between me and Spencer. I close my eyes and groan at her timing.

This. This is why I don't date.

I can't seem to do anything without humiliating myself somehow.

I vaguely hear Spencer thanking her, but my mortification is basically eating me alive from the inside now.

"She's gone," he tells me, but he doesn't sound as amused as I thought he would. Instead, he sounds…concerned? "I didn't mean to make you uncomfortable," he adds softly.

That gets my eyes to fly open in surprise and I gape at him. "I did that to myself," I assure him, shrugging. "I'm…ugh," my hands flap about in the air over our food as I try to put words to my dilemma, "I'm not *good* at social…stuff."

Spencer's gaze is soft and understanding. It almost makes me want to cry. And wouldn't that just top off this date? Jesus, there's no way he's going to want anything to do with me after this.

I'm too much work. Too weird. Too childish. That's what most guys tell me. And I've tried to change. I have. But I can't. This is just who I am. And, right now, I think who I am sucks.

"In that case," Spencer says, then waves Mandy back over and requests everything we've ordered to be packed up to go.

My heart plummets into my stomach.

This definitely has to be some sort of record. Officially fucking up a date so badly that we can't even finish the meal.

With a tight throat, I attempt to fight back the sting of rejection and a little heartache (okay, a lot of heartache: I'd really built Spencer up in my head over the course of the week, after all.) I can feel tears prickling in my eyes and I have no idea how I'm going to walk out of here without letting on just how upset I am.

I'm so distracted by keeping my shit together that I don't even notice Spencer has been talking to me.

"...just wait for our meal to get here and then—*shit*, hey, it's okay."

Spencer's chair scrapes as he pushes it back and makes his way around the table to my side, dropping to his haunches to pull me in for a tight hug. "I should have explained," he says, rubbing my back. "This is totally my bad. I thought we could switch to take out and go eat somewhere less crowded."

"R-really?" I ask, my voice coming out all wobbly and meek. "I thought…"

"That I was cutting it short. Yeah, I just realized that." He sighs, then sounds apologetic when he adds, "I can be impulsive. I forget, sometimes, that the people I'm with can't read my mind."

I snort at that, but I don't pull away from his embrace. Considering how much I generally avoid being touched by other people without advanced warning, it feels good to be held. I haven't really experienced this before. And if this is the only opportunity I get to have this with him, I'm damn well going to drag it out as long as I possibly can.

I'm pretty sure he can feel me calming down, but he doesn't pull back, either. His cologne is subtle but spicy, and his chest is warm and firm beneath my cheek.

His voice seems to rumble through his chest when he speaks. "Do you want to take our food somewhere else? Like…a park, or your place, or mine, or—"

My heart rate increases at the thought of inviting him into my home, or, even more exciting, going back to his. "Your place?" I ask quietly, then explain, "My sister's at mine, and she's…well, meddlesome barely scratches the surface, really."

He snickers. "You met Chance, right? He and my other friends have the market on meddlesome cornered. They mean well…"

"They always do," I nod, thinking of Tanya. She frustrates me, but I adore her. And there's nobody else I'd rather have in my corner.

Spencer squeezes me to his side one last time and then slowly releases his hold on me so he can push back to his feet. He rounds the table and resumes his seat, watching me intently. "You okay?"

I feel embarrassment bubbling beneath my skin at the whole interaction, but I muster a smile and quick bob of my head in affirmation. "Sorry," I tell him, proud when my voice doesn't betray how close to tears I still feel. "Like I said, I'm…not great at social stuff."

"This may surprise you," he responds playfully, "but neither am I."

Chapter Five – Spencer

"**A**re you sure you're okay with me being here?" Tony asks, even as he unbuckles his seatbelt in the passenger seat beside me.

We've just pulled into my driveway, having spent the fifteen-minute drive here in slightly strained silence. He's been tense since I accidentally led him to believe that I was ending our date early, as though he's afraid I only offered to do this because I didn't want him causing a scene or something.

God only knows the kind of people he's gone out with before if he's come to expect that sort of thing.

"Sweetheart," I begin, keeping my voice as soothing and reassuring as possible, "I wouldn't have suggested it if I wasn't."

He licks his perfect plump pink lips anxiously, then smiles. "Okay. Thank you."

I try not to frown as I reach over the center console to squeeze his hand. "There's literally no reason to thank me. We're on a date. A date I asked to take you on. I want to make it a good date for you, because when I ask you to go on a second date, I'm hoping you'll say yes."

His big, brown eyes widen comically, and I swear his jaw actually drops. "A second date?" He shakes his head and laughs, but it's a bitter, self-deprecating sound that sets my teeth on edge. "With me?"

'Who hurt you?' I want to ask. *'Who made you so unsure of yourself?'*

I don't do that, though. Instead, I squeeze his warm, soft hand and say, "Yep. Because you are lovely, Tony. And, while we mightn't know each other very well yet, I already like you a lot." Before he can argue with me or ask me why, I let go of his hand and tap the polystyrene box in his lap which contains our meal. "Come on; let's head inside and eat it while it's still warm."

I climb out of the driver's seat and shut the door behind me, waiting in front of the car as Tony follows suit. I lead the way up the front path to my front door and unlock it when he's at my side, carefully nudging Frank out of the way with my foot when he attempts to make a bid for freedom.

"This is Frank. We disagree on whether he's an inside cat or a neighborhood pest," I explain to Tony, shooting Frank a glare for good measure. "He's an inside cat, for the record."

Frank glares back at me and makes a sound of (what I choose to interpret as) disagreement.

"Aww," Tony coos at him, sounding far too sympathetic to my spoilt housecat's plight, "is your daddy being mean to you, buddy?"

I stand in a stupor as the door shuts behind us, trying not to focus too hard on how much I liked the word 'daddy' falling from Tony's lips.

He was talking to the cat, Highland. Keep it together.

48

The box containing our food is thrust into my hands as Tony crouches down to properly greet the cat in question. "Don't be too offended if he won't let you pet him," I say. "He can be a bit skittish until he knows…" As though he's making a point to prove me wrong, the furry shit practically throws himself into my date's arms, purring loudly. "…you." I finish my thought lamely, then glare at my feline companion. "Okay, fuck you, Frank."

Tony laughs and scoops Frank up, cradling him like a baby as he rights himself back into a standing position at my side. Frank only seems to purr louder, the attention whore. "You are so sweet," Tony tells him, bending his head and *giggling* with delight as Frank cranes up to rub their cheeks together. "Such a pretty kitty."

At this point, I don't think Tony is aware of the major Boy vibes he's throwing, but my heart (and other parts of my anatomy) have noticed. I clear my throat and hold up the forgotten food. "Dinner?"

I swear Frank glowers at me as Tony sets him back down with reluctance.

I saw him first, cat.

I lead the way past the stairs that lead upstairs and the door which leads to my recording studio in the converted basement, and into the small kitchen/dining room.

Tony ducks into the powder room across the hall from the kitchen to wash his hands after cuddling the cat, then joins me at my little square timber dining table. It has four seats, but really only fits two people comfortably.

I open the polystyrene box in the middle of the table and nab a few fries. They're only lukewarm now, but still tasty.

"Your home is lovely," Tony says as he takes his seat, and I

49

watch him look around the space the same way he did when we sat at the restaurant. I wonder how he sees it.

"Thanks," I reply, quickly casting my own gaze around.

My house is like a cozy cottage. The only other room downstairs is the tiny lounge room, while upstairs houses two bedrooms and an interconnected bathroom between them. It's small, I'll be honest, but it suits me. The walls are painted a powder blue, the accents and skirting boards all white. The kitchen is all timber, and the bathroom and powder room are both utilitarian and gleaming white.

Frank leaps up onto the kitchen counter and leans as far as he can across the space between it and the dining table, his black nose twitching as he sniffs at our food.

"Down!" I demand.

I'm pretty sure he rolls his eyes.

"*Frank*," I say warningly. "Get down."

The little asshole trills at me and then plonks his dirty cat butt on the counter.

Whatever argument I planned on having with the furry fiend, I'm distracted by the bubbling giggles coming from the man seated across from me. It's the most relaxed I've seen him yet and I drink the scene in.

His big, brown eyes are bright, his rounded cheeks flushed, and his lips stretched wide into a smile as he tries (and fails) to contain his laughter. And the sound, *oh the sound*, is music to my ears. It's near childlike in how delighted he appears; perfectly innocent and pure and carefree.

Boy vibes for days.

I need to keep getting him to make that sound.

I narrow my gaze at him playfully, waggling a limp fry at him for emphasis, "Is something funny, Tony?"

The giggles peal off into a cackle that is even more enjoyable from my perspective. "T-the cat…" he wheezes as he tries to explain what, exactly, has tickled his funny bone. "A-and the conversation y-you had w-with him." There are literal tears of laughter in his eyes now. "S-sorry," he tries valiantly to catch his breath, then bursts into more hysterics when Frank lets out a soft 'meow'.

"What for?" I ask the question gently, cocking my head and letting my own smile tug at my lips while I wait patiently for his answer.

He's absolutely adorable.

It takes a few more moments before he's gotten his laughter under control, but I'm a bit concerned to watch the shame and contrition steal over his face, replacing his mirth. The change in his demeanor almost gives me whiplash.

"Sometimes, when I've been, uh, emotional, I can get a little manic afterwards," he bites his lip, his cheeks flushed out of some combination of the exertion from his laughter and embarrassment. "I'm weird that way."

Once again, the urge to hurt whoever has given this man such a complex about himself raises its ugly head. I smother it down and reach over the table to grab his hand. "You are not weird," I tell him firmly. "Everyone's brains work differently to process emotional upheaval. I don't think getting the giggles is something you should apologize for."

He snorts and shrugs, "Maybe not in this situation, no. But…it's, um, it's gotten me into trouble before. It can be inappropriate. And, like, I smile when I'm nervous, and that doesn't help…" He blinks rapidly, as though surprised by his own admission, and then winces, "And this isn't exactly great first date conversation, huh? I mean, please, let me tell you *all* the things that are wrong with me."

It takes every bit of willpower I possess to not pull him out of his seat and force him into my lap for a proper cuddle.

Chance was right: everything about Tony has my Daddy instincts firing on all cylinders. But I don't think Tony's a Little. Or, rather, I don't think Tony has explored being a Little. I'm almost certain that, if he did, it would appeal to him.

I can't really explain how I know it. He just seems so… innocent, I guess. Yearning for affection, too. His whole disposition practically begs to be held and comforted and protected. And the things he's let slip about his control on his emotions? I'm willing to bet that if he had the outlet of regressing, of being able to cry out his stresses and hand over control of most decisions for a while, he might find it easier to function on a day-to-day basis.

"There is nothing wrong with you," I tell him, keeping my voice gentle, but leaving no room for argument. "But we'll change the subject if that helps."

He averts his gaze and nods. "Yes, please." Then he finally looks back across the table at me and offers me a lopsided grin, "I swear I'm not a complete freak."

Freak.

I hate that word. Loathe it entirely. But, instead of going into a lecture on why, I just shake my head and assure him, "I told you, angel: I like you a lot, and that includes these parts of you that you're apologizing for – which I disagree with, by the way."

Tony works his jaw for a few seconds, then reaches for a slider, taking a comically large bite which forces him to puff out his cheeks like a chipmunk while he chews.

That settles it. If this man isn't a prime candidate for age regression play, I'll eat my hat.

I get up from the table and head over to the fridge, pulling out a couple of cans of Coke. I set one in front of my seat, and then crack Tony's open for him, relishing the hiss it makes as the air releases. He accepts the drink with a small, grateful smile and takes a sip immediately, washing down his too-large bite of food.

I can't stand the awkward silence that's descended between us, so, as I pick up my own little burger, I say, "You never did answer my question earlier." He blinks at me, midway through another (this time smaller) bite. I smile reassuringly, "The books. What are you into?"

He blushes beet red all over again, but I can't bring myself to regret asking the question, even if he does seem embarrassed by it. "Uh," he flounders for an answer.

"Would it help if I told you some of my favorites?" I ask him. "Of the ones I've narrated as Spencer Rhodes, I mean?"

There's immediate relief in his eyes. I hate that he thinks I'll judge him for whatever it is he's into. It's just books, for Christ's sake. What he likes to read doesn't bother anyone else. And he has to know I'm not exactly vanilla, right? I mean, he knows I visit The Grove, for one thing, and he knows I narrate kinky novels.

"Okay," I think back over the catalogue of books I've narrated, smiling as one stands out immediately. The first age play novel I ever narrated, which was my third book under the Spencer Rhodes stage name. I give him the title, watching his eyes widen, and then I decide if I'm in for a penny, I'm in for a pound, or however the saying goes, adding, "I'll be honest, Tony. I'm a Daddy and I'm into age play. So, I liked narrating that one because I could completely relate to the characters and what they were doing on the page. That's my kink."

His Adam's apple bobs as he swallows roughly. "You... *really?*"

I can't read his tone. Is he surprised because I'm admitting I'm actually practicing some of the kinks I narrate? Is he shocked that, of all kinks, that's the one I'm into? Or is he just surprised that I'm telling him this on a first date?

"Really," I nod.

He bites his lip, averting his gaze as those cute cheeks of his turn pink again. "I...I'm re-listening to that one now, actually."

I swear to God, fireworks go off inside my brain. It's like a billion Christmases have hit me at once. Like a hundred old-fashioned slot machines paying out, *ding-ding-ding*-ing in my head.

Jackpot.

Trying to force myself to play it cool, I reach across our pretty much neglected meal and close my palm over his wrist in what I hope he takes as a gesture of support. "Have you tried age play?"

Tony's reaction is immediate. He straightens in his seat, shaking his head vehemently. But he doesn't withdraw his hand from under my grip, even though his gaze remains glued to where I'm holding him. "No," he says. "No, I...I've never..."

"Never experimented with kink at all?" I keep my voice soft and low, trying to lull him into opening up to me.

"*Jesus,*" he breathes, "that's your 'Daddy's being understand-ing' voice from the book." He completes his observation with a nervous little chuckle, then licks his lips and looks away. "No, I've, uh, I've never..." He squirms in his seat.

"Does it interest you?" I push, my enthusiasm making me

interrupt him. I curse myself for that and remind myself to be patient.

The book I'd mentioned, the one he's *re*-listening to, is one I favor because it doesn't really exaggerate the lifestyle. All the age play interactions are believable and accessible. It's a sweet introduction to the kink, but also gives a lot of information about why the characters enjoy role playing the way they do. If he says yes to my question, if he tells me that he's interested in trying the things he's already heard my voice talking about, I know without a doubt that I want to be his experimental Daddy.

"I…I don't know," he almost whines, then looks down at his lap, the hand not held by mine fiddling idly with the rim of his soda can, his index finger plucking at the pull-tab, making a tinny, echoing sort of sound that could almost be described as musical. "I'm a…I mean, I haven't…It's just that…"

"There's no right or wrong answer," I assure him softly, still not letting his wrist go. I'm only holding it loosely, and I stroke his soft skin with my thumb. "You can enjoy the books and not be interested in age regression in reality. I won't judge you either way. And I'll still like you either way, too."

Tony's eyes close and he tilts his head back to the ceiling, muttering, "It's not even that."

"Okay," I finally realize that I might be pushing boundaries far too early, and I give his wrist one last squeeze before I pull back and give him some space, figuratively and literally. "I'm sorry. I just," I rub the back of my neck and offer him a sheepish smile when he opens his pretty dark eyes again, "I got excited at the prospect that you might be into the same stuff I am. But," I rush to add, "there's no expectation of that, okay? None. Zero pressure."

Real smooth, Spence. Says a voice in my head that sounds irritatingly like Chance. *Keep it up. Are you **trying** to make the poor guy run screaming out of your house on the first date?*

"No, no," now it's his turn to attempt to reassure me. A fine pair we make indeed! Tony leans forward and shakes his head, pinning me with a wide-eyed, earnest stare that makes my stomach flip pleasantly. "I know. I got that. I just…ugh. I don't know what I'm into. Like…um…I don't know what I actually enjoy…like, *at all*."

I blink. "Huh?"

"I'm a…" he clears his throat and the blush that had started to fade comes back with a vengeance, "I've never had sex. Like…*never*. So, um, I don't know if I'm only into the Daddy books because I'm lonely and like the idea of being taken care of, or if I'm actually, y'know, *into* them. I mean, obviously, the sex scenes do it for me, especially when *you're* reading them, but…" He pales. "Oh, God, I can't believe I said that out loud! I'm shutting up now."

Now, I am not some caveman type who gets off on the idea of my sexual partners being untouched and pure and only for me. I'm not. Really. I swear it.

Adults have needs. I don't shame anyone for expressing those needs or going after what they want, as long as they're not putting themselves or others in danger when they do.

But something primitive stirs deep down inside me at Tony's hastily rambled confession. I want to be his first. I want to make it good for him. I want…hell, I just *want*.

"There's nothing wrong with being a virgin, sweetheart," I tell him, frowning when he cringes. "No, I'm serious."

"I'm twenty-eight," he argues back, "it's kind of beyond a joke, isn't it? I mean, if I was avoiding sex for a reason, sure, no shame there. But *I've tried* and…well, let's just say my sexual journey has been a comedy of errors and leave it at that."

I want to know everything, naturally. I want to know *what* he's tried and where things went wrong for him. I want to promise him that not everyone's first experiences (or fifth, or tenth, or hundredth) always go as well as people say that they did.

"Anthony, look at me," I'm not above using Daddy voice, even if he's not a Little. He drags his gaze back to mine with great reluctance. "There's nothing wrong with never having had sex. Plenty of people have perfectly functional relationships without sex."

"I know," he says, sounding almost petulant, "but *I want to*." His voice goes tight with emotion and I want to reach out and hug him. But he powers on, "It just…hasn't happened."

"And that's not your fault."

"But—"

"Tony. It's not. Trust me."

He purses his lips, flits his gaze around the room, then snorts in what sounds like self-deprecation. "I should go."

I want to demand that he stays so we can talk this out, but I know I've probably already pushed him too far out of his comfort zone.

I hold up my hands in surrender. "I'm not forcing you to stay," I tell him, ignoring the voice inside me that screams I should try, "but I want to talk about this with you." Lowering my arms, I reach for him again, but he scoots back his chair. "Promise me you won't dodge my calls?"

His lower lip is once again being mauled by his teeth. "I'll try not to."

Chapter Six – Tony

"Stupid, stupid, stupid," I murmur to myself as I stare unseeingly out of the back passenger window of the Lyft I ordered when I all but ran away from the most successful first date I've ever had.

Yes, that is how pathetic I am: *that* dumpster fire was still the best date I've ever been on.

Spencer offered to drive me home, but I refused. I didn't trust myself not to embarrass myself even further.

Who tells their date that they're a twenty-eight-year-old virgin who gets off on listening to said date narrating kinky novels? *Ugh.* I want to crawl into a hole and die.

He asked me not to dodge his calls, but I can't imagine that he's going to want anything more to do with me. Why would he? I absolutely ruined our date, embarrassed myself in multiple ways, and told him all the ways in which I'm abnormal. If I were him, I would have done a happy dance the second my crazy-ass date walked out the door.

I trudge up the front path to my ground floor apartment

and roll my neck, bracing myself for my sister's interrogation. But, when I open the door into the living room, she's not there. I heave a sigh of relief and, not counting my chickens until they're hatched, scurry down the short hallway towards my bedroom.

It's only once I'm safely huddled in my bed, my fingers hovering over the screen of my phone with the Audible app open, that I let the first tear fall.

I liked Spencer.

I liked Spencer a lot.

And I fucked up any chance of getting that second date.

Through blurry vision, I start removing titles from my audiobook library. I tell myself it's for the best. I don't think I could listen to his narration without further upsetting myself, right?

I'm a sobbing, emotional wreck when I'm done. Even though getting those books back is as simple as a few swipes and clicks on my screen, the symbolism of what I've just done is what has shaken me. I'm heartbroken, giving up one of the things that has brought me so much comfort and joy, and also acknowledging that I'm not going to see the handsome man I'm so very interested in again.

In my hand, my phone vibrates and lights up with a text notification. I sniffle and try to blink away tears, squinting to read it.

'I hope you got home safe & sound. Just want you to know you're perfect as you are & I still want to take you on a second date if you're still interested. XOXO Spence.'

I stare at it until my eyes grow heavy and sleep drags me under.

* * *

"Where were you last night?" Tanya teases me the morning after my disastrous date, cornering me in our tiny kitchen while I attempt to pour myself a glass of orange juice.

My hands shake and the juice misses the glass. "Shit!"

"I've got it," she swoops in and wipes it up with the dishcloth from the sink, rinsing it and coming back for another swipe to remove any residue. Then she takes the bottle from my hands and pours the juice for me.

"Thanks," I say, still cursing myself.

I can feel her stare boring into me. "Alright, spill. And I mean more than just the juice."

Her attempt at humor falls flat between us and I sigh, carefully placing the glass on the bench. I lift and drop my shoulders. "I was out, that's all."

"You're being weird, Tones," her voice is soft and cautious, "talk to me."

I think back to last night and my cheeks flame. "I went on a date," I confess, closing my eyes and willing myself not to cry. "It was an unmitigated disaster."

Her eyes narrow. "Did he hurt you?" She casts her gaze up and down my body, as though checking for injuries. "Was he an asshole? Do I need to take my baseball bat to his kneecaps?"

The ludicrous final question forces a watery laugh from me and I shake my head. "No. He was…" Perfect. Spencer was perfect and I fucked it up. I try to swallow down a sob, failing at sounding anything close to normal. "He's a good guy. *I* messed it up."

"I'm sure you didn't—"

"I *did*!" And then it all comes pouring out of me. All of it. My

60

pathetic love life. Knowing that people think I'm weird. My addiction to my books and the daydreams they inspire. My hopeless crush on a voice —*on a fucking voice*— that turned into a more hopeful crush on the owner of that voice after our stupidly improbable meeting. My rapidly developing crush on Spencer. The date. All the things that went wrong on the date.

And, finally, through tears that refuse to stop now that they've started, I drop my biggest secret on her, too, stammering, "A-and then I t-told him I'm still a f-fucking virgin, and I r-r-ran away."

Tanya, to her credit, takes it all in her stride, like she's done for everything else our entire lives. She pulls me in for a hug and lets me cry it out until I don't think I've got any tears left, then asks, "Where's your phone?"

I reach into my hip pocket, then hesitate. "Why?" The word comes out gravelly and hitches in the middle with my still-wobbly breathing.

Without any respect for boundaries, she slides her hand into my pocket alongside mine and snatches my phone out for herself. "Because I want to talk to this guy before I tell you that I think he deserves a chance."

After my emotional upheaval, my brain is slow on the uptake. It's not until she's swiped at the screen, inputting my passcode (because *of course* she knows my passcode), and has raised the device to her ear that I comprehend what she's doing.

"Tanya, no!"

But it's too late.

Chapter Seven — Spencer

When my phone rings the morning after my date with Tony, I can scarcely believe what I'm seeing on my screen. He never replied to my text message, despite the notification under it that says he read it, but he's calling me!

I drop the manuscript I was reading through and scramble to answer. "Tony! Hi, sweetheart. How are you feeling this morning?"

I am most certainly not expecting a decidedly feminine voice to answer with amusement, "Sweetheart, huh?"

Frowning, I pull the phone from my ear to confirm that the contact definitely reads his name, then bring it back up to cautiously ask, "Who's this?"

"Easy, killer," the woman on the other end sounds like she's enjoying herself. "I'm Tanya, Tony's sister."

Something inside me twists unpleasantly, and I brace myself for some sort of 'Leave my innocent brother alone' speech. "Oh. Sorry. Nice to meet you," I answer politely, adding,

"Tony's told me a lot about you."

"I can see that," she says, still sounding like she's toying with me.

I clear my throat. "Is he okay?" My heart sinks as I reprimand myself yet again for letting him leave here upset. For having upset him in the first place.

"He's…" I can hear his voice in the background, demanding his phone back and I smile, relieved. Tanya carries on as though she's not being harangued by her brother, "a little upset this morning, but I think it's embarrassment more than anything."

"Tanya," Tony's voice is loud enough for me to hear clearly now, "you're overstepping so many boundaries right now…"

"Can I talk to him?" I ask, still half anticipating the 'fuck off and don't call here again' talk.

"That depends."

In the background, I hear Tony reprimand her by name again.

Oh, here we go… "On?"

But what she says next takes me completely by surprise. "Will you join us for dinner tonight?"

I don't even need to think about my response. "What can I bring?"

* * *

I am uncharacteristically nervous when I park my car in one of the three available visitor bays outside Tony's apartment complex. I don't exactly know what I'm walking into. Does Tony even want to see me? He didn't argue with his sister when she invited me, but that doesn't mean he's not doing this under duress.

But I dressed to impress anyway, in dark denim jeans and another nice button-down shirt with the sleeves rolled to my elbows, this one black. I *may* have consulted the group chat for advice, and they were unanimous: I look good in black.

They're also all expecting an update after my 'date' ends. (I did not give them the whole story. I'm not a complete idiot.)

Grabbing the bowl of homemade green salad and the bottle of red wine from my passenger seat, I make my way down the path that leads to the apartment building. It's an older building, slightly run down, but the grounds appear to be well maintained. There are two little courtyards on either side of the front pathway, belonging to the two ground floor apartments. I know that the one on the right is Tony and Tanya's place.

With some juggling of the items in my hands, I manage to unlatch the gate to their courtyard and let myself in, rather than going to the building's entrance and buzzing their apartment. As the gate clangs shut behind me and I wince at the sound, a figure appears at the open apartment door.

It's not Tony.

Instead, it's a tall, willowy woman with vibrant orange hair. I blink. "Tanya, I presume?"

She grins at me, and I see the resemblance to her brother once she smiles. It lightens up her whole countenance. "And you're Spencer." She closes the distance between us, jogging down the couple of steps from the tiny front porch to come take the bowl of salad out of my hands. "Thanks for this, it looks great."

"I hope you don't mind that I pre-dressed it. Just a simple vinaigrette."

"Nope," Tanya hooks her free arm into mine and starts leading me towards the house, "it sounds great. And, hey," she stops us just before we reach the door, pinning me with a serious stare. I'm a few inches taller than her, but she's intimidating. "He really likes you, Spencer. And he's…well, I think you know he's not like most guys. He's…sensitive." She casts a quick peek into the apartment and lowers her voice. "I've, um, I've looked into what you talked about with him. The…Daddy thing?"

Huh. He really wasn't kidding when he said that he doesn't keep much from his sister. Considering how easily flustered he is, this surprises me. But then, I'm glad he has someone he's comfortable talking to.

I nod, not reacting other than to prod, "Yeah?"

"Not gonna lie, I thought it was weird, but," she holds up her free hand, forestalling any potential argument or defense I might offer and her voice dips even lower into a whisper, "I think it would suit him. He's…" a tiny huff of laugher escapes her and she shakes her head, offering me a rueful smile. "Well, you can see it, I'm sure."

I frown a little at that, not exactly sure what she's trying to imply, but starting to get some idea of where Tony's gotten so wrapped up in feeling like he's abnormal. The thing is, I can see that his sister has good intentions, but these judgments she's making, the way she's phrasing her observations…yeah, she's made her brother feel as though his quirks are *wrong*.

"Tony's awesome," I tell her, choosing my own words very carefully. "And, yes, I do think that he'd probably get a lot out of age regression play, if that's what you mean by 'the Daddy thing', but not just because he's so sweet and…" I barely stop myself from saying 'pure', suddenly not liking the implications of the word, even though I've used it to describe him in my head at least a dozen times before now, "innocent?" That also doesn't feel like the right word, either, but it's closer to what I'm trying to get across. "A lot of adults find that handing over the reins to a caregiver provides amazing stress relief. We don't realize just how taxing all the little decisions we have to make during any given day actually weigh on us, y'know?"

She cocks an eyebrow. "Have you ever tried it? Being an adult baby?"

"No," I answer honestly, "but I've been a Daddy for over a decade now, and I have a tight circle of friends in the kink community, including a number of people who do enjoy being little."

I think fondly of Ash, Matt, Josh, Katie and Zephyr. Watching them play together is always entertaining, but warms my heart, too. I am lucky to have friends who trust me enough to let me see them with their guards down; to let me interact as Uncle Spence and play my part in their self-exploration and stress relief. It's not quite the same as having a romantic Daddy/Little relationship, but I like to think that it strengthens our bonds and brings us closer together as friends.

I try my best to express these feelings to her as succinctly as possible.

"So…you don't sleep with them?" she asks bluntly.

I blink. Honestly, the question probably shouldn't surprise me because most people associate BDSM and kink with sex, but it does.

"No," I answer slowly, once again measuring my words, "for me and my friends, the age regression isn't directly linked to sex. I mean, some of them might be into some kinky Daddy bedroom behavior, but it's not the dressing like toddlers or whatever that is getting them off. I can't speak for everyone who ever indulges in age play, but in my world it's about connection, support, and escapism first and foremost." I glance towards the still-open doorway, almost amazed that we've been able to talk for so long without Tony discovering us like I suspect she feared he might.

But then I catch sight of him just inside the living room, leaning against a wall, listening intently.

I, at least, have nothing to hide, so I smile at him. "Hi, sweetheart," I greet him, only a little tentative, unsure of the reception I'm likely to get.

"What if I'm not willing to try it?" he asks, forgoing any greeting. "What if I just want to be in a...a...normal," he makes a face at the word as he says it, and I wonder if he's also been doing some research, or if he is, like Tanya said, just that sensitive, "relationship?"

"Then that's totally okay, too," I answer honestly. I step inside properly, refraining from reaching for him, no matter how badly I want to pull him in for a hug. Instead, after unceremoniously palming off the bottle of wine to his sister, I stop in front of him and look him in the eye. "I'd like to date you, Tony. Exclusively and at your pace. You get to decide what —if anything— we do, romantically speaking."

His dark brown eyes flicker between mine and I get the impression he's weighing the truth in my declaration. I wait patiently, and I'm rewarded when his lips twitch into a small, but genuine smile. "Okay."

This time, I give in to the urge to hug him. He practically melts into my arms, smushing his cheek into my chest. Tanya gives us our space, motioning that we'll be able to find her in the kitchen I can spy just down the short hallway.

"I…I *am* curious about the, um, the age play stuff," he murmurs after a while.

"We'll take it slow," I reiterate, pressing a kiss to the top of his soft, dark hair. "I want to sit down talk everything through properly. We have to be on the same page from the start. Will you be more comfortable if your sister's around for that?"

"Oh, God, *no*," Tony's reaction is immediate, and I can feel him physically recoil in my embrace. After a moment, he seems to press his face even harder into my shirt. "It was embarrassing enough telling her…*you know.*"

I don't know.

"About my Daddy kink?"

He shakes his head and his voice is muffled when he extrapolates, "That I'm a virgin."

"She didn't know?"

Heaving a sigh, Tony explains, "I was…upset this morning. I thought…I thought I'd blown my chance with you. And then she asked me what was wrong, and it all just came spilling out."

Whether he knows it or not, he's *such* a Little. I struggle not to smile.

"And then she called you and, well, here you are." He finally pulls back from the hug and shrugs, his cheeks flushed that adorable shade of pink again. "I've sort of avoided her for most of the day. I know she already thought I was strange for not going out or making friends, but…"

"You're not *weird* or *freakish* or *strange* or anything of the sort," I insist. "Not for being shy or introverted or keeping to yourself, and certainly not for never having had sex. Do you understand me?"

I watch his Adam's apple bob and his blush deepen as his

lips part into a tiny 'o' of surprise. "Y—" he clears his throat, "yes. I understand."

I grin at him and cup his cheek. "Good boy."

Chapter Eight – Tony

I might have been understating my interest when I told Spencer I was curious about exploring age play. After Tanya's meddlesome (but ultimately helpful) phone call this morning, I locked myself in my room, re-downloaded my Audible library, and started to properly Google age regression.

I'm not sure that I'm completely sold on diapers and pacifiers, but I have to admit that some of the other stuff I read about sounded fun. Letting Daddy make my decisions for me, cook for me and bathe me, cuddle me and read me stories (something I already know Spencer is a master at!) and treat me like I'm precious to him sounds like a dream, really. Playing with toys and being silly and free sounds like the ultimate goal in relaxation.

And then hearing Spencer's firm Daddy voice in action seals the deal. Being called a good boy is the cherry on top. It's all I can do to try and keep my growing erection my own little secret until Tanya calls us in for dinner.

As we eat, Tanya questions Spencer lightly about easier

topics. His job, his family, his hobbies outside of BDSM… and he handles her gentle interrogation well. I barely notice that he is pouring me extra water or adding extra salad and veggies to my plate, and when I finally do, he is utterly unapologetic about it. I find that I can't be annoyed. In fact, I kind of like that he was subtly taking care of me already. It didn't feel like I was being babied. Not really.

Nearing the end of the meal, Tanya makes some excuse about having plans to meet up with Braeden, her current boyfriend. She ushers us into the living room after tossing the plates into the old but functional dishwasher, shoots me a wink and a thumbs up, and waltzes out of the apartment, leaving me alone with Spencer.

"Well, I assume that means I have her approval?" he teases lightly.

I stare at the door, marginally flabbergasted at her hasty departure. "Uh…I guess?" Then his words penetrate my brain and I give myself a shake, turning back to frown at him. "Not that we need it. I'm almost thirty." Even if my meltdown this morning would suggest otherwise.

Almost as if he's reading my thoughts, Spencer pats the space beside him on my threadbare two-seater couch and says, "We should talk about everything."

I don't really want to rehash it all, but I understand that he wants to make sure we're on the same page. With a little reluctance, I gingerly sit next to him and stare at him pointedly. If he wants to talk, he can lead the conversation.

I startle when he takes my hand in his. His fingers are long and elegant; my Nonna would have called them 'pianist's fingers'. Between them and his large, warm palm, my perfectly normal hand seems small and pudgy in comparison.

"I'm going to put all my cards on the table, sweetheart. You know I'm a Daddy, and I know that you're a bit curious about that. But I'm not sure I'm comfortable pushing you into role play before I know the extent of your actual experience, and what you already know you like and dislike. However," he continues before I can start telling him what he wants to know, "I also know it's a tender subject for you, and I don't think we need to go through everything all at once."

"But…"

"I think," he keeps going again, giving my hand a squeeze in recognition of my attempted interruption, "in your case, we should just go with the flow and discuss things as they pop up. I want you to set the pace and tell me if there's anything you'd like to talk about, or try, or definitely avoid. I also want you to know that you can safe word at any time." He pauses and gives my hand another squeeze. "Do you know how safe words work?"

I nod. "The, um, the book I was listening to…" I clear my throat, knowing that it was discussion of that book that led to me running from his house last night. "They use the traffic light system."

"Yep, and so do I. I mean, it's not without its flaws, but it's simple enough to follow."

I bob my head in agreement. "Everyone understands traffic lights."

"Exactly. So, if you're uncomfortable at any time, you can say 'red light' and we'll stop immediately, no questions asked. And the same goes for me. If I say it, we stop."

I nod again. "Even if we're not, um, Daddy and Little boy, or whatever?"

"At any time, Tony. I take consent seriously across the board."

I don't know why this settles me, but a huge weight seems to lift from my shoulders with this final declaration. There's absolutely nothing in my past that would suggest it should be a trigger, but hearing the gravity in his words still reassures me that I'm safe with him.

"So…can I…" my heart starts beating rapidly, but I force myself to be brave. He said that I was setting the pace, which means that I have to ask for the things I want. "Can I kiss you?"

The thing I really like about Spencer is that he doesn't try to mask his emotions. I watch as elation and eagerness light up his eyes before a spark of arousal seems to simmer in those gray-blue depths.

"I'd like that very much," he answers me, bringing his free hand to my waist.

I scoot closer towards him, licking my lips in anticipation. He leans in, but doesn't close the space between us, standing by his promise to let me lead for now.

I'm not a complete stranger to kissing, even if it's been a little while since I've kissed someone, so I don't hesitate to press my lips to his. His lips are thinner than mine, but warm and yielding. The sweet, gentle touch of them against mine sends a jolt of happiness through me.

Even though it's a chaste meeting of mouths, I savor it. I savor the slightly sweet taste of the wine we'd shared at dinner still lingering on his skin. I savor the scent of his cologne, spicy but subtle, and the way his hands are now both on my waist, holding me in place.

I savor the tiny sound of appreciation he makes when I part my lips and dart my tongue out to lick at the seam of his. I savor the way he opens for me, still letting me control what we're doing, despite tangling our tongues together when I deepen the kiss.

His hands pull me closer against him, like he can't quite get enough of me, and it's a sentiment I echo in the way I clutch at his back and shoulder blades with my own hands.

I just want to melt into him. We could spend eternity just like this, and I would be forever happy. As we move our mouths against one another slowly, the happiness begins to turn into something with more heat and urgency. It's still a very pleasant feeling, but I pull away with reluctance, breathing heavily and trying to will my swelling cock back into submission.

"Wow," Spencer says, his expression glazed over. He blinks a couple of times and then playfully narrows his eyes my way. "You could have warned me that you're damn good at that."

I preen under the praise, but I'm not sure what to say to him.

Thankfully, he seems to realize this and says, "I'd also say any potential concerns about compatibility or chemistry can be dismissed."

I shift uncomfortably, grimacing at the ache between my legs, constricted by the tight denim I'm wearing, "I'll say." Before the moment gets awkward, I blurt, "Can we do that again?"

Spencer chuckles and nods, already reaching for me, pulling me closer. "You don't need to ask permission to kiss me, sweetheart. Consider it always granted."

"Okay," I answer shyly, and then lean forward to fuse our mouths together again.

Unlike before, this kiss starts heated and gets intense much more quickly. I can't seem to stop my hands from roaming over whatever parts of Spencer's body I can reach. His shoulders, his biceps, his back, his pecs…Beneath the cotton of his shirt, he feels firm and warm and solid.

Somewhere in the middle of our impassioned kissing, I

follow my instinct to climb into his lap, straddling him. He groans into my mouth when I unconsciously move my hips, finding an equally hard bulge in his jeans to mine. I gasp when our clothed cocks rub against each other, and Spencer pulls back, panting, "Too much?"

"Not enough," I tell him honestly, grinding against him deliberately. I grin when he moans and his hands knead my ass.

"You sure?"

"Very," I insist. "I…oh, God…" he's started undulating his own hips now, rocking up to meet me thrust for thrust, and it fries my brain for a moment. "I want…Spencer, I *need*…"

"*Tony…*" I open my eyes, idly wondering when I shut them, to find him looking conflicted.

"I'm not asking you to fuck me," I tell him, even though there's a part of me that really, really wants to. "But…I'm not fragile either, Spence. I'm a hornier-than-I've-ever-been man who is asking his boyfriend—" because he said we would be exclusive and I trust that "—to put me out of my misery and help me come." I take a moment to close my eyes again and enjoy the sensation of our denim clad erections still stimulating each other. "I'll safe word if it's too much. Just… please…*oh…*"

"Okay," he breathes out. "Okay. How do you want…*ungh…*"

Hearing and seeing him just as affected as me is as much a turn on as it is a relief. "I…I don't really want to come in my pants but…ah!" I cry out as one of his hands shifts around to the front of my jeans and fumbles with the fly. "Spence… Spence, I'm *close…*"

"Have you…has someone done this for you before?" He asks, having just undone the button above my zipper.

"What? Given me a hand—oh, *fuck, Spencer!*"

He's wriggled his hand into my briefs and has pulled my hard, flushed, leaking dick out from its confines.

"Answer the question, Anthony."

Jesus Christ. How am I supposed to think straight when his hand is wrapped around my cock and he's using that *tone? And my full name?*

"I...Once...I..." My balls are already drawing tight and I don't want this to be it. "In high school. I..." My chest is heaving with the effort of trying not to blow my load so soon. "Sp-Spencer...not...not here. Bed. Please."

I almost sob when he releases me, and my cock throbs angrily as I struggle to climb back off his lap.

"Are you sure about this?" he asks me again, and I can see his own desperate arousal tenting his jeans, but he only seems to care about me and my needs right now. That's a heady realization and it cements my determination.

Yes, this is only our second date (shut up; I'm counting it as a date, unconventional though it might be), but if I've learned anything from the past couple of days, it's that I should definitely not let a good opportunity slip through my fingers.

"I'm sure," I tell him, looking him in the eye as I do. "Please, Daddy?"

Chapter Nine – Spencer

W hatever vestiges of control I still had over myself disappear when Tony makes his needy plea. I swallow roughly, reminding myself that he made a valid point: he's almost thirty and he knows what he wants. It's not my place to judge whether it's too soon for him or not. If he changes his mind, all he has to do is safe word and I will stop.

"Oh, angel," I bend down to kiss his swollen pink lips tenderly, "of course."

I don't even know if he's realized yet what he's done. The honorific seems to have slipped out without meaning, but he doesn't stammer, apologize, or even blush as he takes my hand and leads me down the short hallway towards the farthest of the two poky bedrooms. It's almost like his resolve has turned off his inhibitions. I kind of love it.

His room is tidy and spartan, with a solid-looking queen-sized timber bed frame pressed up against the far wall, a bedside table next to it and a timber wardrobe along the wall to the right of the doorway.

Once I'm fully inside the room, Tony closes and locks the door behind me, then hovers awkwardly in front of the bed, his confidence seemingly receding.

Even though I told him he was setting the pace, it's apparent that I need to take charge here.

"Traffic light?" I prompt as I reach for the waistband of his jeans.

"Green," he answers without hesitation.

"Okay," I nod. "I'm going to undress you, then I want you to lie on the bed while I get undressed, too. Do you have anything?" When he frowns in askance, I jut my chin in the direction of the bedside table with its single drawer. "Lube? I don't think we'll need condoms unless you'd prefer them for easier clean up."

"Oh," he nods, cheeks pinking, "yeah. Lube's in the drawer."

"Good," I say, then help him out of his jeans and briefs first before pulling his shirt up over his head.

Tony looks a lot younger and more vulnerable than his twenty-eight years when he's finally standing naked in front of me. He's on the shorter side, with smooth olive skin, a surprisingly hairy chest accenting an average build, and maybe just a tiny bit of extra softness around his middle and thighs. His cock is short and thick, too, straining proudly for my attention. It looks almost painful, with its deep purple head glistening with precum.

I drop another kiss to his lips, then one to his shoulder, and a final one to the junction where his shoulder meets his neck, telling him, "You're gorgeous, sweetheart." Some of the tension in his shoulders recedes and I swat his backside gently. "Into bed with you." He scrambles to obey. I grin. "Good boy."

He watches me through dark, hooded eyes as I pull my own clothes off. I kick off my shoes and tug off my socks when my jeans and boxer briefs get tangled around my ankles, then unbutton my shirt with patience I didn't know I possessed.

Finally naked, I slide open his bedside drawer and locate the bottle of lube, setting it on the nightstand as I join Tony in bed.

He kisses me as soon as I'm stretched out beside him, and I let him take control again. I'm curious to see what interests him; what his instincts tell him to do.

He practically glues himself to my front again, kissing me as though this is his one and only chance to do so. Some part of me wonders if that's how he feels, and I make a note to discuss my intentions with him again.

Without clothes, every brush of our bodies against one another is heightened. Tony mewls into my mouth when our cocks rub together, and he rolls his hips with wild abandon, our precum and the heat of our bodies making the skin slick and slippery before too long.

"Oh my God," he breathes, distracted from our kissing by the feel of our hard shafts dragging over each other. "Spence...holy fuck, *Spencer*..."

He's starting to tremble, so I carefully ease him onto his side and follow suit so we're facing each other, with my right arm slid beneath his neck and around his back, pulling him flush against me. "W...what's the lube for?" he asks, and I can't help but chuckle, even as we continue to slowly frot against each other, downshifting from the almost frantic movements we shared while he was on top of me.

"Afraid you're missing out?"

His cheeks redden with more than just arousal.

"It's okay to be curious, angel."

"I'm cl-close again," he says after another beat. His hands grapple at the sweat-slicked skin of my back. "Oh my God. I don't wanna come yet. But," he can't seem to stop himself from moving against me, "I never imagined this would feel so good."

After another kiss, this one slower and deeper, I rest my forehead against his and decide to go with my initial idea. If he wants to extend this, I've got him.

"Roll over, sweetheart," I urge quietly, and his eyes widen for a moment. I nuzzle my nose against his. "We're going to try something a little different. If it's not working for you, tell me and we'll go back to this." I give another roll of my hips for emphasis of my point.

"Okay," he agrees softly, then rolls over to face the wall with his back and his perfect, round ass facing me. I can't stop myself from squeezing the smooth left cheek with my free hand. He pushes back into my touch, "Please..."

I pepper kisses along his shoulder and the back of his neck. "Try to keep your legs together for me, okay?"

Without pulling my arm out from under him, I roll onto my back to reach over for the lube with my free hand, pop the cap open with my thumb, then drizzle a generous amount over my cock. After snapping the cap shut again, I drop the bottle back on the nightstand and give myself a couple of cursory strokes, spreading the lube. There's a lot of it, but that's a deliberate choice.

Then I roll back onto my side, shuffle down the bed a tiny bit, and guide my long, aching shaft into the inviting space just beneath the curve of Tony's ass.

He gasps at the contact.

"Is this okay?" I ask him, whispering into the shell of his ear.

"Yes," he exhales and pushes back onto me again, causing my cock to glide between his closed thighs as intended. His head drops back onto my shoulder when I reach around to grip his leaking erection with my still-lubed hand. "*Oh!* Fuck yes. *Spence…*"

It takes me a few thrusts and minor adjustments of the angle of my hips and of his body, but it's no time at all before I'm rocking into him properly, gliding my hand over his cock in the same pace that I'm fucking the tight, warm, slick space between his clenched thighs. Every so often, the head of my cock bumps into his balls and I delight in the muted mewls and whimpers that elicits.

When I tighten my grip on him just a little, he begins to babble a litany of 'Oh my God' and 'don't stop', alternating and said on repeat. It's insanely hot, and the sounds and pleas go straight from my ears to my dick. In turn, I tell him how good he's being, how amazing he feels wrapped around my cock, how perfectly we fit together.

There's no sense of time right now. Just the feeling of skin on skin, the sounds of pleasure and our heavy breathing, the scent of clean sweat and building arousal, and a hint of vanilla and artificial sweetness from the unexpectedly flavored lube.

"Sp-Sp…" he seems to lock his thighs even tighter, the surprising muscle hidden beneath their smooth, soft exterior closing in around my cock, "I'm…I'm gonna…I'm coming…oh, oh!" His body locks up as his cock jerks in my hand, the first spurts spilling over my fist. "Daddy, fuck, fuck…*Daddy…*"

"*Fuck,*" I echo in a long, drawn-out groan of the word, unable to hold back my own release at the plaintive and unexpected whine of 'Daddy' falling from his lips. If I'd thought his orgasm felt powerful as he shot jet after jet of cum over my hand, it's nothing compared to my own as it sweeps through me like a wave of pleasure and endorphins and absolute bliss.

We're both breathing hard as we come down from our mutual highs, and I kiss the nape of his neck, burrowing my face into him. I have no idea what he's thinking or feeling right now, but I'm feeling oddly overwhelmed.

I don't think I've ever been anyone else's first before. There's an additional emotional connection to him now that I wasn't anticipating. Not so soon.

But he called me Daddy. Three times. I don't think it was a conscious decision, just instinct and the excitement of the moment. I can't describe what that does to my heart and my hopes.

Tony shifts and I pull back, giving him room to roll onto his back. He turns his head to face me, scrunching his nose adorably. "Sticky," he complains lightly, then sucks in his bottom lip and regards me from underneath his long, thick lashes. "Hi."

He's too cute for words.

"Hi," I greet him back, smiling as I dip my head in for a quick, sweet kiss. I curl my right hand up from under him to toy with the ends of his hair and then smooth my palm over the back of his head. "How are you feeling?"

"Is there a word better than phenomenal? 'Cos...*wow*."

I smirk, even while my heart squeezes. "You're very good for my ego."

Instead of flirting back with me, he scoots in for a hug, hiding his face under my chin. "Thank you," he says, his voice tight with emotion.

I don't ask him what for, but I do squeeze him close. "No,

angel: thank *you*."

Chapter Ten – Tony

I just had sex.
   I just had sex.
   I *just* had sex.
I just *had* sex.
I just had *sex*.
I just had sex!

It doesn't matter which way I think it, I have been irrevocably changed. I'm floating on a cloud of endorphins, still unable to believe the turn my day has taken. I woke up feeling like I'd ruined my chances with Spencer, the first man I'd been genuinely interested in in a long while, and now I'm lying in my bed beside him with his cum drying between my thighs and on my balls…and I'm not freaking out about it. Not even because the sticky feeling is a bit gross. I feel good. So good.

And, dare I say it, I'm not really a virgin anymore.

I know it's just a word. I know that I was fixating on it. I know that I probably made a bigger deal out of it than I should have. But I'd always sort of thought it meant there was something wrong with me. Proof that nobody wanted me.

But Spencer didn't make me feel like my inexperience was an issue. He didn't make me feel like I was every other man's unwanted cast off. He told me I was gorgeous. He was hard for me. He came with me.

I don't even realize that I'm crying until Spencer startles beneath me and rubs my back. "Hey," he soothes, sounding concerned, "did we go too fast?"

"No. *God* no." I shake my head emphatically, rearing back so I can face him properly. "I'm just happy. Like, insanely, unbelievably happy."

Genuine relief seems to wash over his face, and it hits me that he actually does care. Not that I really thought it was just lip service, but I guess I wasn't sure just how important my feelings actually were to him. I mean, I know that sometimes people say things just to be placating, but without any real meaning to their words.

I feel kind of guilty for not having given him the benefit of the doubt, even though he can't read my thoughts.

Spencer brings his free hand up and brushes my tears away with his thumb with more tenderness than should be possible for how little we honestly know each other. He brings our mouths together for another chaste kiss and rubs his nose against mine when he pulls back.

"Did you want to talk about it?"

I blink. "Huh?"

For once, it's nice to watch his cheeks flush pink, as though he's suddenly awkward and unsure of himself. "We don't have to," he seems to backpedal a bit, "but, if you wanted to talk about how you're feeling…" He offers me a lopsided shrug. "I just know you were putting a lot of pressure on yourself about sex. And, uh," he clears his throat, "you called me Daddy, Tony. You realize that, right?"

Honestly, the whole experience is a haze of intense pleasure and desire and desperation and need and…holy shit, he's right.

What the hell does that mean?

Where did that even come from?

I didn't only say it once, either. No; if my blissful recollection is correct, I said it a few times.

I mean, I admitted I was curious about his Daddy kink, right? So maybe some part of me was just playing into that and trying to make it good for him?

Except not even I believe that.

No; I was into it. I felt so taken care of in those moments, enveloped by his larger frame, looked after and prioritized and worshiped by him, and I'd just blurted the name out in my excitement.

"It doesn't have to mean anything," Spencer says when it takes me too long to respond. "Like, I'm not expecting you to suddenly be ready to dive into age regression experimentation. Or ever, even. I just…" he licks his lips, "it sounded to me like you liked it. Calling me Daddy. Or maybe I'm just being hopeful. And, you know, it *can* just be a title. It doesn't have to go hand-in-hand with age play."

"No, I…I did like it," I confess, trying not to sound bashful as I do. I just had the guy's impressive cock sliding between my thighs, after all. "It felt *right*. And not just because I know you're a Daddy. But you were taking care of me. You know, last night and then again today."

And let's be honest: even *I* can see that I naturally seem kind of childish at times. Being little probably wouldn't be that big a transition for me, especially if I was in the right mood to start with. But I keep these thoughts to myself, not quite ready to share them yet. Spencer said we'd do things at my pace and I'm not ready to explore that side of my interests yet. Jerking off while I listen to stories is one thing. Trying out the kink in reality is something else entirely. At least in theory.

"I don't think I'm ready for the age regression stuff," I tell him after a moment of contemplation, "but…I'd like to still call you Daddy, if that's okay?"

Spencer brightens even more, his eyes shining with delight. "You can't possibly be real, angel. You're too perfect. I'd be honored to be your Daddy, age play or not."

Not wanting to ruin this happy post-orgasm bubble by correcting him about how imperfect I truly am, I just grin and, still feeling brazen, ask, "Want to shower with me?"

* * *

Is it too soon to want Spencer to stay the night? Or is it normal to get this clingy with the man who just gave me my first real taste of carnal delights?

Is it lame to use the phrase 'carnal delights'? Even in my thoughts? I feel like it is.

(It definitely is.)

Oh, God, I'm overthinking things.

We've just shared a very pleasurable shower, where we soaped each other up and took our time exploring one another properly. I was a bit shy when it came to touching Spencer's cock, but he didn't pressure or rush me. If I didn't want to touch it, that was fine.

But I did. Oh, I really, *really* did.

And, okay, I know I have one of my own, but his is a thing of beauty. It's long and straight, not overly thick, but uncut and veiny. And responsive as hell. There's something addictive in making him harden. Knowing that it's me doing that, that I'm the one with the power to get his already impressive length hotter, purpling at the head and pulsing with need is a heady thing indeed.

I just want to keep doing that over and over again, finding out all the secret, special ways to make it happen.

But then there's this part, too. The part where, after we've stepped out of the shower, he takes my towel off the rack and starts drying me off with an expression I can only describe as besotted.

It's funny how I've always thought I was pretty bad at reading people's expressions, but I find reading Spencer's as easy as breathing. He's just so open, I guess.

He scrubs my hair dry first, making me giggle, then carefully mops up every rivulet and drop of water possible on his way down my neck, shoulders, chest and back. My arms, then my belly, my dick and balls, then my ass. Then my left leg all the way to my foot, and finally my right leg.

By the time he's finished, I'm starting to understand that this Daddy thing is ingrained into him. Whether I'm a Little or not, he's going to take care of me any way he can.

And, God help me, I love it.

I should probably worry that I'm getting too invested in Spencer —in this relationship, even— too fast. But how can I worry when he looks at me like I'm the center of his universe? *Nobody* has ever looked at me that way. Never. I'm going to take advantage of it while I can. Especially when it's Spencer Rhodes. Highland. Whatever.

I wasn't exaggerating when I said I was attached to his voice before I ever met him. Yes, I'd imagined someone bigger, bulkier, bear…ier. But now that I've met him, now that he's shown me what a wonderful person he is, I don't want the fantasy. I want the real man. For as long as I can have him.

He wraps me snugly in my towel before he hastily dries himself off, then he confidently takes me by the hand and leads me out of the tiny bathroom with its peeling paint and mold speckled ceiling and back into my bedroom just a few short feet away. He closes and locks the door behind us, then rummages in my closet and drawers, pulling out briefs, my favorite pajama pants, and a well-worn t-shirt that I only ever wear to sleep in.

"May I?" he asks me softly, holding up the bundle of clothes and gesturing to my towel.

"May you…?"

"Dress you." He says simply.

Like it's a perfectly normal request.

I guess for a Daddy it kind of is.

Chewing on my bottom lip, I give it a moment's considera-tion. Is it really any different to letting him undress me? Or wash me in the shower? Or towel me dry afterwards?

I did really like how all those activities made me feel...

Decided, I nod. "Please," I swallow, close my eyes, and tentatively try, "Daddy."

My heart is hammering in my chest while I wait for ridicule, but it doesn't come. Instead, when I crack one eye open, I find Spencer beaming at me. The tension inside me unwinds.

"How'd that feel?" he asks softly, stepping forward to undo the towel at my chest, wiping me over with it once more before tossing it aside.

"Strangely natural," I answer honestly, stepping into the

briefs he selected for me. I frown a little at them, then snort. They're one of the three-pack that Tanya bought me as a joke last Easter. This one has a little blue cartoon bunny printed over the crotch. Subtle, Spencer is not. I appreciate that about him, though, because subtlety can go over my head.

He doesn't push me to elaborate on my answer, instead pulling the briefs up my legs and running his fingers under the waistband to ensure they're sitting right. My cock twitches in interest, his proximity alone enough to inspire my arousal. But Spencer doesn't react as I start to swell, tenting my underwear. He just grabs the soft flannel pajama pants and takes a knee in front of me again.

My cock *really* likes that.

I can feel myself blushing again, and I wonder how I have enough blood to fill both my dick and my face right now.

"I'm sorry," I apologize, looking away and wishing I wasn't guaranteed to ruin every moment ever with my awkwardness.

"For what?" he sounds genuinely puzzled as he taps one foot and then the other to step into their respective pants' legs.

"Uh…" I quickly jerk my head down my body and look away again.

He makes short work of pulling my pants up my legs and gently takes hold of my chin between his thumb and index finger, turning my head up to look at him.

"That is a totally normal reaction to everything right now." He's keeping his voice quiet, but there's a firm resolve there and his eyes are boring into mine, willing me to hear the truth in what he's saying.

I fight the instinct to look away, uncomfortable with sustained eye contact like this. I trust him, and I know he is trying to make a point.

"For one, everything is new for you. Your body is reacting to that. Secondly, I'm in your personal space, and we find each other attractive, so your brain is sending signals because of that, too. And finally," he licks his lips, "a lot of people get aroused during…uh…this sort of thing." He stops, seems to give himself a shake, then adds, "Little time. I know we're not actually roleplaying, but you're letting me take care of you like I would if you were my little boy, and…well, it's often considered a sexual kink for a reason. It's perfectly normal to get excited while you're little. But," he looks apologetic, "I'm not usually interested in having sex with my partner in Little space. That's something we would have to discuss if it became something you were interested in."

That is a lot to process, but it makes me feel good to hear it all. It doesn't sound like something he's pulling out of his ass, either. It's all factual, but he's also passionate about what he's saying. It soothes me enough for me to be terrifyingly honest with him.

"I like what you've been doing," I admit quietly. "Nothing you've done has felt all that weird. I, um, I thought it would be. Weirder, I mean."

"Well," Spencer pulls me towards my bed, sits down and then tugs me onto his lap. He seems to be choosing his words carefully. "We're not doing anything that strange, are we? Yes, dressing you might be pushing the limits a touch, but it's not that odd for partners to take care of each other, is it?"

"No," I shake my head.

He hugs me close and kisses my cheek, then reaches up to tuck a stray lock of hair back behind my ear. "So, I think as part of exploring your sexuality at your own pace, maybe you should tell me the stuff that are your hard limits: the things you know that you're one hundred percent not interested in. Then, I'd encourage you to research some of the things you're curious about. Read. Google. Talk to me or, if that's too much, I can give you the details for my friends' community center which is geared towards helping members of the kink community."

"Oh, that's a thing? Kink community centers?" I don't know why this surprises me quite as much as it does. "How, uh, how do they even go about advertising that?"

Spencer chuckles. "It's not like they're turning away people who aren't kinky," he says, "but they work in conjunction with The Grove, have a strong online presence in forums and whatever —one of my other friends, Cherie, actually does a lot of the online stuff, but damned if I understand what it is she does— and Charlie also has contacts in the police, too. So…yeah."

"Huh." I mull it over. "I think it would be good to check it out. Send me the details?"

He agrees, then gives me a squeeze. "So. Hard limits?"

Chapter Eleven – Spencer

Tony's hard limits aren't a surprise. He expresses that he's definitely curious about exploring age play now that he's had a taste of what being pampered by a Daddy is like, but that he wants to do a bit more research before he decides on what, exactly, that means. However, he knows for certain that he'll never poop a diaper, and that he doesn't want to be little all the time.

That's a relief because, while it's not entirely a hard limit, I'm really not interested in taking my entire lifestyle (or even just changing) that far. I have tried both things: there was a point where Emma thought we should trial a 24/7 Daddy/Little relationship, however it wasn't for me, and I called it quits after two weeks. I don't know if it was because it felt too close to the lines of actual parenting, or because it impeded our sex life, but I really didn't like it.

Beyond that, Tony can't think of anything else that he's directly opposed to, so I tell him my limits. I will not take part in consensual non-consent, I don't share or indulge in cheating fantasies or cuckolding, and, as he already knows, I'm not really a fan of having sex with my partner when they're in their Little headspace, but being called Daddy and taking control during sex is obviously okay. I explain that I generally prefer to top, but that (as tonight has shown) I'm more than happy to not engage in penetrative sex at all.

"Really?" he asks me with wide, surprised eyes. "Like… never? You wouldn't, I don't know, get bored of me if I didn't want you to…" he trails off and makes a vague gesture. It's kind of cute, but also a sobering reminder that this is all new to him.

I consider my response carefully. "For me, sex is about connecting with my partner emotionally more than just getting off. And I'd rather know that the person I'm with is also having a good time. I'm honestly not going to be happy if you're uncomfortable or in pain, sweetheart."

His cheeks flush and he swallows. "But, I mean, the first couple of times are probably going to hurt, right? I mean, that's what I've read."

Adorable.

I kiss the top of his head and lean my cheek on his silky soft hair. "We're not rushing it, Tony. If that's something you want to explore, we'll start with toys to get you used to stretching and penetration first. That said, you're not wrong: the first time, at least, will probably be uncomfortable and a bit painful, but I'd hope that we'd be able to get past that so the discomfort fades into pleasure."

"Oh, I, um, I have toys. I'm not *completely* untouched, y'know, *down there*. Just…not by another person."

I know he can probably feel me smiling into his hair. It's not like I expected him to say anything else. I mean, the guy's almost thirty. If nothing else, curiosity had to have struck at some point. "Then maybe one day you'll be comfortable showing me your favorites and what you like, but there's no pressure."

Tony's quiet for a moment, then he snuggles into my hold and simply says, "Thank you."

My heart just about explodes with warmth.

I can already hear Chance's voice in my head, berating me for how easily and quickly I tend to get attached, but I brush it away. I know that it's early days with Tony, but something inside me is insisting that I'm onto a good thing with him.

* * *

I am met with Tanya's amused eyebrow raise when I enter the kitchen the next morning, having left Tony sleeping in his bed. He's earned the rest after such an emotional roller-coaster. (Plus, he's far too cute to wake up, with his hair all mussed and his face somehow even younger in repose.)

"Good morning," his sister greets me, grinning smugly.

I grin back. " 'Morning."

"Sleep well?" She asks, then suggestively adds, "Like a *baby*?"

"Tanya," I say in warning. It's not even Daddy voice and there's no hint of playfulness to my tone. I'm just flat out unimpressed. I don't want her making Tony uncomfortable, even under the guise of lighthearted sibling jesting. "Not cool."

Tanya holds her hands up in surrender. "I was just teasing. But," she leans forward in her seat, as if listening out for signs of Tony's approach, then continues, "I want you to know that, if he is into…uh…the Daddy thing? I want to support him. I want this to be a safe space. For him, and for you."

There are two empty mugs sitting in front of the fresh pot of coffee on the counter, and she's already got one on the table in front of her, so I grab the plain blue mug and pour myself a measure of the dark, delicious smelling liquid. Then I turn back to face her and lean my hip on the counter. Regarding her over the rim of my cup, I respond, "I'm really pleased to hear that."

She shrugs. "He's my brother. Not just that, he's my twin. I've been there for literally *everything* he's been through. This isn't any different."

I know there's more to his past than he's glossed over in the short time we've had to get to know each other, and the way she just spoke cements my theories. But I don't push her for information that I'm not entitled to. Instead, I let myself be comforted by the knowledge that he has this strong, feisty, outspoken woman in his corner.

"Good," I tell her, but I don't say anything else on the matter because that would be a violation of Tony's privacy, twin or no twin. Instead I lightly suggest, "Maybe it's worth broadening your horizons anyway? It can't hurt to understand how other people live and love, right?"

Tanya nods, her brightly colored hair swaying with the motion. "Fair point," she acknowledges. "Guess I'm gonna have to do some reading up of my own, huh?" She smirks. "Can you recommend any good books, *Rhodes*?"

I snicker. "I'm not ashamed of my alter-ego or the stuff he narrates, if that's what you're getting at."

"Nah," she waves me off, "I'm just fascinated by the whole stage name thing."

We'd discussed it over dinner, and I'd explained that I keep different stage names for different genres to make things easier for readers/listeners. I don't keep them a secret —anyone who goes looking for my website will find a list of the genres I narrate under each name— but it makes things simpler for people wanting to stick to specific types of book. For example, someone who enjoys my performances of contemporary heterosexual romance might be nonplussed to accidentally listen to some of the kinky gay romances I narrate as Rhodes and vice versa. Some listeners cross over and quite like both, but I like to make things clear, regardless.

We chat about that some more until our mugs are almost drained and Tony stumbles into the kitchen, rubbing his eyes, his dark hair sticking up at odd angles and his pajama bottoms hanging low on his hips. The cuteness is going to be the death of me.

"Sit down, angel," I tell him, ignoring his sister's snort, "and I'll get you a coffee. Cream and sugar?"

"Mmm," he agrees sleepily, tilting his head back for a kiss as I pass by, "thanks, Daddy."

Tanya chortles when he freezes, realizing what he's said, and I pin her with a hard stare, unable to point at her with my hands full of the coffee pot and Tony's mug. "Safe space," I remind her firmly.

"Oh, now *that's* impressive," she says, her eyes widening a little, "do that voice again and you might have us both falling all over you."

"Find your own Daddy," Tony grumbles at her, scowling, "this one's all mine."

I hand him his mug and ruffle his hair, practically floating as I return to the refrigerator in search of the creamer.

* * *

Ash: @Spencer how'd the date go last night?

This is the beginning of the message trail that greets me when I finally take my phone off silent once I'm home again. Frank doesn't come running to greet me, so I head off in search of the little beast while I scroll through the chat.

Ash: Seriously, Uncle @Spencer, I need to know.

Charlie: Leave him alone, baby. Spence'll reply when he's able.

Ash: Oooh, do you think he's still on his date? Did it become a sleepover?

He'd added a gif of Milhouse from *The Simpsons* waggling his eyebrows suggestively.

Chance: I wouldn't be surprised. Diner Boy is his type and then some.

Zephyr: Diner Boy?

Chance: Yeah. Cute kid. Works at the diner near The Grove.

Zephyr: Oh! Short guy? Dark hair and brown eyes? Kinda shy?

Chance: That's the one!

My bestie has topped this off with an assortment of random emojis that I interpret to mean something along the lines of 'jackpot' and 'you win a prize'.

Zephyr: Awww, he IS cute.

Ted: @Zephyr Should I be worried???

He capped his joke off with the emoji sticking its tongue out.

Ted: And, yes, Tony is very much @Spencer's type. I didn't realize he was a Little, though.

Zephyr: @Ted You know his name?! And you're the one who thinks he should be worried???

A gif of an elderly woman with her arms folded and fingers tapping on her exposed elbow follows.

Ted: I've been going to that diner for forever, Zeph. And I happen to pay attention to details like peoples' names.

Zephyr: Uh huh.

I can't help snorting at that.

Josh: @Ted Smart move, Theodore. I suggest chocolate and flowers. Meanwhile... @Spencer, we're gonna need the details, man.

Charlie: @Josh Aren't you supposed to be working?

Josh: Aren't you?

Charlie: I run my company. You're supposed to be out protecting the city.

Ash: Like Batman!

Charlie: NOT like Batman. Jesus.

Josh: Like Jesus?

Charlie: For fuck's sake.

I'm outright laughing now, and I've made my way into the lounge room where I find my lazy lump of a cat sprawled out in front of the glass sliding door that leads to my postage-stamp sized backyard. He's on his back, soaking in the mid-morning sun's rays, and barely cracks an eye open when he hears me approach.

"I bet if I'd been Tony, you would have been excited to see me," I tease, squatting to rub Frank's exposed belly. He wriggles around, enjoying the attention.

"I suppose I should let them know I'm alive at least, huh?" I ask him, and he makes a '*mrrrrow*' sound which I interpret as agreement.

Pushing back to my feet, I head over to the couch where I flop down and start typing. It takes me a few seconds longer than most to get the sentence posted. I've never been the fastest at typing on phones, regardless of the technology improving over the years.

Spencer: Date went well, but I don't kiss and tell.

It doesn't take long before their replies flood in.

Josh: Your poetry's pretty shitty, man. I hope you don't try that crap on him.

Zephyr: @Spencer !!!

The three exclamation marks are followed by a gif of a clip from Grease, with the T-Birds all on the bleachers singing '*Tell Me More*'

Chance: But do you fuck and tell?

Before I can send my reply, he sends another message.

Chance: Nice one @Zephyr. Yeah, Spencer, like the song asks, did ya get very far??

Spencer: @Chance Fuck off.

Chance: That means yes.

Spencer: No, it means fuck off.

Ash: Was the date sweet? What happened? Where did you go? Did you take him somewhere special?

Chance: Yeah, to bed! LOL

Ash: @Chance

The message itself is blank, but a gif of a clearly unimpressed kid with a very flat expression follows.

Spencer: I'm seconding @Ash on this one. Don't be a dick, Chance. I'm not comfortable with you talking about Tony that way.

My phone rings almost immediately.

"Hey," I answer with a smile, letting him know there are no hard feelings.

"So…you only just got home?" Chance is smirking, I can hear it in his voice.

I stretch out along my couch, trying not to grin too widely. "I didn't say that."

Chance whistles, impressed. "He seemed so freaking shy, though. I guess it's always the quiet ones…or is that what they say about serial killers? Oooh, is he a serial killer?"

I think of my sweet, easily embarrassed boyfriend and laugh out loud. "Doubtful."

"Come on, Spence," he whines, changing tact, "I'm your best friend! Don't hold out on me."

"I'm not holding out, I just don't want to cheapen my date by talking about it like it didn't mean anything."

There's a moment of silence and then Chance groans. "You've fallen for him already, haven't you?"

"Okay, I wouldn't go *that* far." Except I like Tony a hell of a lot. More than I expected to after only knowing the guy for barely over a week. And there is something to be said for the connection we're shaping. But I'm not telling Chance about Tony's experience (or lack thereof) or how honored I feel to have been a first for him. Instead, I just say, "But I do think we could have something special between us, given half a chance."

"Huh." My friend sounds marginally surprised. "Well, then, I'm happy for you. But you know what this means, right?"

Now it's my turn to groan. "He's going to have to meet the guys."

I'm just hoping we'll have a bit more time to get comfortable in our relationship first.

* * *

Over the week that follows, I take Tony on a few more dates. We don't discuss age play unless he brings it up and, as promised, I let him set the pace on any further sexual interactions.

He's been getting increasingly more confident with me, though, which has been such a joy to witness.

On our fourth official date, we're cuddled up on a picnic blanket at one of my favorite local parks. There's a gentle slope of neatly trimmed lawn leading down to a pond, and we're perched near the water's edge, watching the ducks and trying to catch glimpses of the small fish that live beneath the surface.

"Why were you single?" Tony blurts seemingly out of nowhere.

I startle. "What?"

"I was just thinking that these last couple of weeks have been so good," his fingers pluck at a loose thread on the grey plaid blanket between our thighs. He fiddles when he's anxious, I've learned that much about him. He keeps explaining his thought process, "And things this good are usually too good to be true. So I don't understand why you were single when we met."

I sigh. He knows I'm bi, that I've been in relationships with both men and women before him, but until now I haven't had to talk about Emma. However, he deserves an honest answer…and, to be fair on him, I really should tell him my stance on children now before we get too invested in each other anyway.

I ignore the little voice in my head that says it's too late. That I'm already too invested. That it will hurt if this conversation goes pear-shaped and it turns out he desperately wants kids.

It's my own fault for leaving it for so long, I know.

"My last relationship ended…badly," I eventually answer him, resolved to do this properly.

Tony tenses and then tentatively squeezes my thigh. "I'm sorry. You don't have to—"

"I do," I interrupt him softly. "It's important that you know."

"Oh," he says, but I can't read his tone.

I guess my words could be interpreted in a number of ways, so I hurry to put the whole story out there. "When Emma and I got together, we agreed neither of us wanted kids. I…I like being a kinky Daddy. I don't want to be a parent."

Tony's tension starts to melt away as he rests against me, and that helps me to relax as well.

"Did she…" he starts to ask and then stops himself.

"Change her mind?" I hazard a guess at his question. He bobs his head, then I do the same. "Yeah. And we fought about it. Nasty things were said, I got all in my head about it…" I shrug. "It took me a while to come to terms with the fact that it's okay to not want kids *and* to want to be in a Daddy/Little relationship."

When Tony tenses again, I realize that I've inadvertently put pressure on him with that confession.

With my arm wrapped around his shoulders, I give him what I hope is a reassuring squeeze. "But I also meant it when I told you that I am happy with the dynamic we have without age play. Emma just…she got in my head, you know? It messed me up for longer than I wanted to admit to even myself."

Tony stays silent as he processes my words. I don't push him. I've learned that he needs time to think things through before he reacts.

While he thinks, I try not to worry that my admission might mean the end for us. I focus instead on the gentle quacking of the few ducks floating on the murky brown water's surface.

"I don't want kids either," Tony eventually tells me. His voice is soft, but the statement is firm and decisive. "I can barely take care of myself, let alone a small human."

Relief washes over me and I'm squeezing him closer to my side again before I know what I'm doing. "You're not just saying that, right?" I'm being uncharacteristically insecure, but once bitten twice shy and all that jazz. "I'm not going to be upset if it's something you really do want. But..." I don't want to say the words.

Winding his fingers into the cotton of my t-shirt and gripping tightly, Tony says them for me. "But it's non-negotiable for you, so we'd probably have to break up."

"Yeah," my throat is tight.

But he doesn't immediately respond to that.

"Is Emma the reason you don't like sex during Little time?"

Tony's question is direct, which I appreciate, and I can follow the logic that led him to it. He deserves an honest answer here, too.

The thing is, it's a complicated question with a complicated answer.

"Kind of?" I offer, knowing that it's not nearly enough. I'm not usually the guy who fumbles for words, so I try to think about what I'm saying before I make a mess of this. "I wasn't really big on it before Emma," I clarify, "and when we were together, we tried it a couple of times and I just couldn't get into it. I felt like I was failing her, you know? But..." taking a deep breath, I admit my real issue, "it wasn't her. Not really. Some part of me gets hung up on the idea that it's skirting a moral line? Even though I know it's not," I rush to add. This is my issue, and mine alone. The one thing where my rational side knows what's up but my emotional one is an idiot. "But I feel it in myself. I hold back. I don't know why, exactly, just that I do. And that's not fair on my partner at the time. So I just generally steer clear of trying anymore."

While he quietly considers my words, I itch to make promises that I don't know I can keep. I want to tell him that I'd try it again for him if he wanted to, but would that just be setting ourselves up for failure?

"I think I understand," he says softly, toying with the fabric of my shirt. "It's hard to try again when you get a mental block about something." There's something far away in his tone now, a wistfulness that makes me wonder what it is he's relating my experience to. I won't push, though. He'll share the information when —*if*— he's comfortable enough. "But that's also why safe words exist, too, right?"

Well, damn.

He's got me there. I can't help smiling. "Yeah, it is."

"Okay." He concludes, effectively closing the subject as abruptly as it started. "I just wanted to know."

"You deserved to know," I assure him. I'm starting to think that it's possible I might not have tried with the right partners, because the concept doesn't feel as awkward when I picture it with Tony. "Maybe one day…"

Tony shakes his head. "Don't push yourself out of your comfort zone, Spence. Not unless you're really ready. It's not something I'm desperate to try right now, and if I ever am, we can talk about it then."

It's funny how the advice that I've given him sounds completely different when it is directed back at me.

"But, Spencer," Tony sits himself up straighter, pushing away from my side so he can look me in the eye. He only really does that with Tanya for any prolonged amount of time, so I take it as yet another sign that he's feeling more comfortable and confident with me. "I really don't want kids." His lips quirk now that he has circled back to the original topic of discussion. "Frank's enough for me."

Those words do things to my insides which I'm definitely

not ready to examine too closely.

"He's enough for me, too," I agree, then we go back to watching the ducks in companionable silence.

Chapter Twelve — Tony

My cheeks burn when, after a couple of weeks of dating (and one night of impulsive online shopping), I carry a large, but otherwise innocuous, brown box into my room. It arrived earlier today and I just collected it from the building's mail room, where all large deliveries are received. Even though there's no way for anyone to tell what's nestled inside the package, I was flustered about being seen with it. But, safe in the confines of my bedroom with the door locked safely behind me, I can breathe again.

I set it gingerly on the bed, then scold myself for being so silly. It's just *things*. There's nothing inside the box that can hurt me.

They could probably embarrass me if the wrong people saw that I had them, but I've kept this purchase tightly under wraps. Not even Daddy knows.

And that's another thing: I don't hesitate even the slightest over calling Spencer 'Daddy' anymore. Not in my head, not out loud, not even around Tanya. I know he loves it, and that makes it even easier for me to do it. And the fact that I've been reading and listening to nothing but Daddy/Little stories in the past couple of weeks hasn't hurt, either.

But that's probably also what inspired me to order the things I did.

I got curious.

Like, super curious.

I was listening to a new book —one sadly not narrated by my amazingly talented boyfriend— and, by three-quarters in, I was deeply invested in what was happening between the characters. I even found myself closing my eyes and imagining myself in place of one of the main characters during a bottle-feeding scene, of all things.

And it felt good. Freeing. *Right.*

At that point, I hadn't wanted to wait: I wanted to try some of those things *immediately.*

Unfortunately, not having access to any of the necessary paraphernalia, I'd resolved myself to two potential resolutions: calling Daddy and asking him to bring some items over for me so I could experiment with age regression, or buying my own and waiting.

The first option *had* been tempting. But I'd chickened out. I know he probably would have driven here breaking all sorts of land speed records, but that was also part of the problem.

I didn't want to get his hopes up.

What if I put on a diaper and hated it? What if I suckled on a bottle and didn't get any of the warm, tingly, excited feelings that listening to the book had inspired?

What if it turned out my fantasy was just that: a fantasy? Then Daddy would be sad, and I didn't want to be the one to do that to him.

So option two, even though it meant delaying my experimentation, was the way I chose to go.

But now the box is here and I'm suddenly shy. In my own room. Alone.

Grow up, Anthony, I tell myself, but then another voice in my head tells me how wrong those words are. The new voice sounds a lot like Daddy. It reminds me that to grow up would be counterproductive to the age regression I want to try out. It also says that I'm allowed to be nervous, and that I'm allowed to freak out and stop at any time. It's comforting, and it provides the impetus for me to reach out a trembling hand and tug at the brown packing tape securing the contents shut.

Peeling back the four panels of cardboard that form the 'lid' of the box, I inhale sharply at the item nestled securely on top.

A package of diapers.

I'd even splurged for ones with cute animal print on them and extra padding. YOLO, right?

The package is sunshine yellow and there's a picture on the front of a young guy built very similarly to me. He's dressed in nothing but a diaper, a blue bonnet, and short, matching blue socks capped with white frill around the ankle. He's beaming up at me, and I find myself unconsciously smiling back.

The plastic packet is kind of squishy to the touch when I lift it out of the box, and I enjoy squeezing it for a moment before carefully setting it aside on my bright orange comforter. It looks strangely at home there, the colors complementing each other perfectly.

Swallowing, I turn my attention back to the box. The next item I reach for is a super soft cotton onesie. It is white with a black kitten printed on the belly, and a bunch of cute, kitty paw prints covering the rest of the fabric. I'd thought of Frank when I saw it and hadn't been able to resist.

I toy with the button snaps for a bit, enjoying the loud *clicks* in the relative silence of my room, before carefully laying the onesie out alongside the package of diapers. A packet of wipes follows along with a container of barrier cream, and I blush at having bought them, because it feels like confirmation of my intention to *use* the diapers.

Beneath these items I find the remaining few things I'd ordered. Two pacifiers, one blue and the other red, some bath toys and bubble bath liquid, and three bottles with different styles of teat.

My heart pounds as I reach for them, and I'm startled to feel my cock swelling at the thought of using them with my Daddy.

It's getting *way* ahead of the program. Besides, Spencer has been clear that he doesn't usually engage in sexual acts when his partner is in Little space. Even though I think he'd try if I said I really wanted to experiment that way, I don't want to push his boundaries like that. Not when there are so many other things I'd like to try first. So, I don't know quite what my dick thinks he's getting out of all this, but he's excited anyway.

I'm alone, so I'm just going to roll with it.

"Okay, let's go wash you so I can try you out," I tell the bottles and pacifiers, gathering them up in my arms and scurrying down the hall and into the kitchen. Tanya's at work and a glance up at the clock reassures me that I have a few hours of precious alone time left, but I'm still paranoid that she'll pop out from behind a corner and see what I've brought into our home.

Not that there's anything to be ashamed of, the voice in my head that sounds just like Daddy says, cool and calm as always.

"There's not," I agree out loud, nodding decisively.

Still, I wash and dry my new items in what has to be record time, selecting a wide, squat bottle with a big, bulbous teat to try first. I fill the bottle with milk, heat it briefly in the microwave, then screw the teat on top. I cover the tiny hole in the silicone nipple with my thumb and give the bottle a shake to even out the temperature. Then I gather up the rest of my items and carry it all back into my room, locking myself back inside.

I've given this a lot of thought since I pressed the 'confirm' button on my purchases. I considered trying things one at a time at first, but ultimately decided that it makes more sense to go all in if I want the best chance at regressing. I figure, the more babylike I can make myself feel physically, the more my brain will get on board.

Well, that's my working theory, anyway.

If it doesn't work and all I achieve is feeling ridiculous, at least I'm in the privacy of my own room and there's nobody else around to witness it happening.

I put the bottle of milk and the blue pacifier on my nightstand and then drop the remaining washed purchases into the box on my bed. Then, taking a deep breath, I start undressing.

* * *

Wearing a diaper is…an interesting experience. It wasn't exactly fun putting it on myself, but when I imagined Daddy doing it, it made the process easier. The padded material is surprisingly comforting, though it's going to take me a while to get used to wearing such bulky underwear. It makes a distinctive papery crinkling sound when I move, forces my stance to widen so I waddle more than walk, and it adds weight and pressure to my dick that normal pairs of underwear do not.

That pressing sensation only increases when I am wearing the onesie with the snaps along the crotch all done up. I can't help but think that it feels good in a kinky sort of way. Probably one of the reasons Littles tend to get hard during Little time.

Stepping in front of the body-length mirror inside the door of my wardrobe, I take in my appearance for the first time. I look *cute*. My already round butt is rounded out further by the excessive padding of my diaper. The onesie itself doesn't quite cover the plastic-treated material of my diaper's exterior, with the cotton brief cut of my onesie exposing the kind of frilly leg cuffs and a bit of the 'cheek' covering too. It actually makes me *feel little* seeing myself this way.

I grab my phone from the bed and snap a photo of my reflection, undecided on whether I'll send it to Spencer or keep it to myself. Either way, I want to commemorate this moment because it honestly feels kind of life changing, like a jigsaw piece snapping into place and creating a clearer picture of who I truly am.

I toss my phone back onto the bed and then move the box of my purchases to the floor, climbing under my soft blankets and reclining onto a pre-prepared nest of pillows with my bottle now in hand. It is lukewarm to the touch now, and I close my eyes as I bring it to my lips.

At first, the mouth feel of the thick, rubbery plastic is foreign and wrong, and it takes me some time to get used to the motion and angle of holding the bottle up and sucking to successfully access the milk. But, once I've got a good rhythm going, I relax into it and let my mind wander.

I imagine I'm lying in Daddy's arms and that he's the one holding the bottle, carding those long, dexterous fingers of his through my hair. He's murmuring sweet words of praise and encouragement, and I'm filled with a warmth that isn't just caused by the milk making its way into my belly.

It's only as I'm sucking at air that I'm surprised to realize that I've drained the bottle and I want more. But, more than that, I want more with Daddy. I want him to be a part of this, to feel what it's like to indulge this whole new side of myself with him.

My head feels kind of floaty at this point, adult concepts and words starting to elude me.

Is this what it's like to regress? Can it really be so easy?

I know I'm not quite there, but I don't think it would take much for me to just let go and *be* little from this point.

As it is, my impulse control is gone enough for me to grab for my phone and send Spencer that photo I took just before.

My phone rings barely a minute later.

"Hello?" I answer him, feeling a bit shy all of a sudden.

"Angel," he sounds bewildered but adoring, *"that picture…"*

I giggle at his near speechlessness. "You like, Daddy?"

There's a sharp intake of breath down the line, and I imagine his pretty eyes widening. "Honey, are…are you *little* right now?"

"Mmmhmm," I wriggle in bed, the pavlovian response of hearing his voice while I'm cocooned in my personal bubble starting to kick in. I slip my free hand beneath my blankie and press down over the top of my crotch to try and stifle it. It only makes me harder. "I was 'sperimenting," I tell him, trying to distract myself. Then I lower my voice into a stage-whisper,

"I like it a lot."

"You're killing me here, Tony," he says, but I can hear the smile in his voice. "You look so cute dressed that way."

I glance down my body and grin. "I bought it for Franky."

Spencer laughs. "Of course you did." His tone goes all soft and sweet when he adds, "I'm glad you like Frank so much. I need my two favorite boys to get along."

"I still like you better than Frank," I tell him, as though it wasn't obvious.

"I'm even more relieved to hear that," he sounds amused. Then he asks, "So, is the onesie and the diaper all you've tried out?"

I shake my head, forgetting that he can't see me. "Nuh-uh. Also got a bottle."

"Oh, I see. And what did you think of that?"

"My belly's full of milk," I answer, some part of me realizing that it wasn't quite an answer. I try to pull my thoughts together, concentrating hard. "I mean, I liked that, too. I want more."

"More milk?"

"Nope. More of…" I gesture vaguely around me, once again having forgotten that he can't see me. "This. Being little. It's… it's really nice."

"Oh, angel, I'm so happy for you."

Those words bring me back to my 'big' headspace some more. He's happy *for* me. Not for himself, despite how much I know he's going to enjoy sharing this with me. No, he's happy *for me*, because I've found something new out about myself. Something good.

"You are?" And yet, I'm still apparently insecure.

"Tony, you're so brave to step out of your comfort zone and

try something new, you know that?"

I swallow, the last of the floaty feeling fading. "All I did was put on a diaper and drink some milk."

He's silent for a moment, before he firmly says, "Listen to me, Anthony; you didn't *just* do anything. You're exploring a kink – that's not something everyone has the balls to do. Especially not a kink that so many people see as taboo. I am so proud of you for having the courage to put yourself first. And I'm honored that you chose to share it with me, by sending me that picture and answering my call. That's even braver, you realize."

He sounds so passionate, and it does funny things to my belly to hear him talking this way about me. *Me!* I'm kind of lame, but he's hyping me up anyway, and it's almost overwhelming that this beautiful man, with his equally beautiful voice and successful career, thinks I'm even the slightest bit special.

It also does very little to distract me from the erection now pushing urgently at the polypropylene inner layer of my diaper. If anything, hearing him specifically saying such lovely things about me while I'm in bed makes me even harder. I bite my lip to stifle a needy whimper.

"Tony? You okay? Is this too much?"

Oh, it's too much all right. But in *such* a good way.

"I…" I squirm and, with my free hand, push down harder on my crotch. That proves to be a mistake. "*Ohh…*" I bite my lip. "Daddy. I'm…I'm big again." I know it's important that he understands that, because I follow it up with, "And I'm *hard.*"

"Oh! Oh, I see." There's a smile in his voice now, but he's sounding sultry all of a sudden. I squeeze myself through the layers, not sure whether I'm trying to prevent things from getting more intense or encourage them further. "Put your earbuds in and get comfy, angel. Daddy's got this."

I guess we're going with encouraging things along, then.

Not at all disappointed with the turn of events, I scramble to do as he asked, retrieving my earbuds from my nightstand, popping them into my ears, and waiting for the sound to transfer over. I'm even more pleased to have shelled out the extra cash for a proper pair that have an inbuilt mic so I can continue the call hands free.

"Done," I tell him, sounding a bit breathless even to my own ears as I settle back against my nest of pillows.

"Good boy," he praises, and my dick jumps for him. "Are you lying in bed, baby?"

"Yeah…I…I have a pile of pillows that I, uh…" I close my eyes, remind myself to be brave, and finish the confession, "that I imagined was you holding me."

"Oh, sweetheart, I wish it was me. But, for now, we're going to keep pretending, okay?"

"Mmm, okay."

Having his smooth, perfect voice in my ears is somehow both so familiar and also brand new. I'm used to listening to him like this through his narration, but to have a direct line to the real thing, to be able to interact with him and be part of the scene is more exciting than I can describe.

"So, lie back on your pillows, close your eyes and imagine I'm there."

I do as I'm told, finding it easier than expected to do just that. Maybe it's having his voice so close, as though he is actually behind me, leaning down to whisper into my ear. With my eyes closed, I can imagine his warm, firm chest at my back and his breath on my neck. "Mmm," I murmur again, already settling deeply into the fantasy.

"Good boy," he says again, his voice turning slightly gravelly. "Now, take your hands and pretend they're mine. Firstly, I trail my hands down over your chest slowly. I pause to tease your nipples through the fabric of your onesie."

I gasp when I do as instructed, my hips lifting from the mattress in search of friction. I get some from the inside of my diaper and I can feel myself begin to throb with need.

"You like that, don't you? I can tell." His breathing is a bit more labored, and I can hear rustling over the phone line. I get even more excited at the thought of him jerking off while he talks me into my orgasm. "I love your nipples, baby. They're so sensitive."

"Uh huh…"

He chuckles. "So then I pinch one."

"*Ohhh…*"

Who knew my nipples were directly connected to my cock? Because hot damn; I'm pretty sure the jolt of pure pleasure I felt just now went straight from one to the other.

"That's it, that's my responsive angel," Spencer pants into my ear. "I enjoyed that so much, I pinch the other one. A bit harder."

"*D-Daddy,*" I mewl as I comply, thrusting my hips up in earnest now. I'm still getting a little stimulation from the diaper, but nowhere near what my body craves.

"Very good…" he groans. "I could play with your gorgeous little nubs forever, Tony." I let out a wordless complaint and his resulting chuckle is equal parts devious and fond. "I won't though. Not tonight. No, tonight I don't have the patience. That's your fault, you know. You look so good dressed up in Little clothes. Does it feel good?"

"So…*so* good," I answer honestly.

Right now, even though I'm in the same outfit as earlier, I don't feel cute or little. Instead, I'm definitely big, and I feel sexier and more powerful and in control of my sexual identity than I've ever felt before. It's an intoxicating feeling, but I'm too horny to manage the words.

"God, that's such a turn on, Tony. I'm so hard for you right now."

That image makes me impossibly harder. "Sp-Spencer, please. I need…"

"I'll get you there. I promise."

I nod and throw my head back. "You always do." Am I talking about the few sexual encounters we've shared together, or the number of times I've jerked off to his narration? I honestly don't know. I don't think I care. He certainly doesn't question me.

"Mmm," he sounds distracted, and I can imagine his long fingers wrapped around his even longer cock, stroking himself while he talks to me. "I do love watching you come undone. Speaking of which: your dick is probably feeling neglected right now, isn't it? You haven't moved your hands without me telling the story, have you?"

My head thrashes from side to side against the pillows. "No. No, I've been good. Please, Daddy. Please…"

"Good boy," this time it's a purr and I'm almost certain I'm leaking precum into the absorbent padding surrounding my cock. "So, as a reward, I drag my hands down your body some more. Can you guess what I find when I reach your crotch?"

"*Ungh!*" After having nothing touching it for so long, the pressure of my hands over the top of my onesie is a blissful relief to my cock.

"Answer me, Anthony."

"M-my erection," I stammer, holding my hands still, but pressing down and doing my best not to buck up, "p-please, Spencer. Daddy. Please. I need to come. Please."

His breathing hitches. "You're still wearing your onesie and your diaper, aren't you?"

I nod.

He can't see me.

I have to force my brain to engage enough to get the words out. "Yes. I…yes."

Spencer's answering groan is deep and I can almost feel it rumbling through me. "Are you going to be a good boy and come in your diaper for Daddy?"

Holy shit.

Is it normal to get as turned on by that concept as I am right now?

Maybe later I'll question both my reaction and how danger-ously close it feels to Spencer crossing his own lines about sex and Little time, but I trust that he knows that I'm in my adult headspace and, if he wasn't comfortable with what he's suggesting, he wouldn't have said it.

My breathing catches and I'm unable to help rocking my hips up towards my hands. My brain almost explodes with the jolt of pleasure I feel at the sensations that causes.

"Tony?" The arousal that's been present in his voice is muted now, replaced by concern. "Was that too much?"

"No!" I cry out, then swallow and will my racing heart to calm down. At a more reasonable volume, I repeat, "No. I… *fuck*, Spencer, I…I'm gonna…"

"*Oh*," I can hear his relief, and then his smile, "you really liked that idea, huh?"

I whine wordlessly.

"Okay, okay," he soothes, then continues, "because you've been such a good boy, Daddy's gonna let you mess your diaper with your cum."

Yeah, we *will* need to talk about this. But not right now. Right now, I'm too lost in the pleasure rocketing through me.

I moan and rock my hips up again, already feeling my balls tightening.

"Imagine I'm there with you, baby. Imagine I'm rubbing your cock through your diaper."

If I'd thought just applying pressure was blissful, it's nothing in comparison to the fireworks in my veins when I start doing just that.

"How does that feel, angel?" his breathing is back to that heavy panting. He sounds strained. "Are you close? Because I sure as fuck am."

"I…I'm…*Spencer*…it feels *so* good!"

"Good, baby. That's…*mmmpph…*so," he pauses to breathe heavily, "*good*…to hear…"

Hearing him unraveling only adds to my bliss. I start thrusting *and* rubbing and then I'm crying out, seeing stars, unloading into my underwear in a way I haven't done since my early teens.

Except it's not underwear. It's a diaper.

I just made a mess in my diaper.

And, okay, I've read enough to know that 'messing' is something entirely different, but I'm never going to do *that*, so I'm just going to redefine the word 'mess' here in my head. Because, as I soften and squirm a little, still pushing down the material, I can't think of a better word for what I've just done.

"Tony? Baby, are you alive over there?" Spencer's voice is soft but still perfectly audible in my earbuds.

"Uh huh," I manage, suddenly feeling sleepy and sated. I silently lament that I missed hearing him come, but I can imagine it well enough, having exchanged a few orgasms together since that first night in this very bed.

"Are you sleepy now, angel? It's been a big evening for you, hasn't it?"

"Mmmhmm," I agree.

He laughs lightly. "All right. I'm going to let you go to bed. I…" He stops himself, then clears his throat. "Thank you for sharing this with me, Tony. Goodnight, sweetheart."

I don't even know if I manage to return the farewell before my heavy eyelids close and dreamland claims me.

* * *

I wake with a start in the middle of the night, my bladder screaming at me for not having visited the bathroom before I went to bed. Having a full bottle of milk beforehand probably didn't help, either.

But, as I grudgingly roll over and attempt to get up, the padding of my diaper, which is substantially less pleasant seeing as I left my cum drying inside as I fell asleep, reminds me of its existence.

In the dark, I blush and wonder if I'm honestly considering going all the way and relieving myself in it.

I mean, you already soiled it with cum. It's not like you weren't going to throw it out anyway...

I'm alone. There's nobody to witness this. If it feels too weird, I never have to do it again and I can just tell Spencer it's a hard limit. No harm no foul. There's no shame in trying, right?

And, seeing as it's just me here and I'm being honest with myself, I bought wipes for this very reason. I was always going to try it when the opportunity presented itself, just to know if it's something I would be willing to try with Daddy.

Jumping in with both feet, remember? None of this step-by-step stuff. Go big or go home.

Yada yada yada.

Just be a big Little boy and pee already.

I lie back, despite my instincts demanding I get my ass out of bed and to the bathroom ASAP, and try to relax and not squirm too much.

It doesn't come immediately. I was potty trained at three-years-old and can't remember the last time I had an accident, but it was most certainly before I reached double digits. Deliberately undermining that training feels inherently wrong, like breaking the rules. I don't like breaking rules.

But eventually my body's valiant attempts to hold my bladder back fail. I whimper as the first squirts into the padding escape me. They're simultaneously mortifying and a release. When the diaper holds, the rest of me finally relaxes and I'm suddenly letting go with a sigh.

It feels really naughty. A bit dirty, but...*unexpectedly satisfying.* It is bizarrely liberating and it does, for the briefest moment, make me feel little, innocent, and helpless, but in a strangely enjoyable way.

The diaper swells under the deluge, the absorbent padding inside doing its job well. There's warmth surrounding me now, and, because I'm on my back, I can feel the liquid trickling over my balls and down my crack, making me squirm with discomfort, scrunching my nose up against the feeling until the padding beneath my ass soaks it up.

Once I'm finished, I bite my lip and reach down, curiously investigating the filled material. It's squishy, warm, and kind of addictive to prod and squeeze.

Let it not be said that I don't have a sensory fixation.

In fact, that's something I wouldn't mind exploring one day…but I'm getting ahead of myself again.

I'm suddenly overcome by the urge to call Spencer and tell him about this whole new discovery, but it's the middle of the night and I have enough impulse control now to know that would be dumb. Besides, exactly how would that call go? 'Hi, Spence, I just deliberately wet myself?' 'Oh, good job, now who's going to clean that up?'

Ugh. I didn't really think *that* part through. I mean, yeah, I bought myself some wipes, but I can't lay myself out on my bed like I did when I put the thing on. What if it leaks, or I drip, or…something? And I'm not attempting it standing up in the middle of my carpeted room for the same reason.

So this means I'm going to have to head into the bathroom after all, and awkwardly take it off and clean myself in there. I shudder at the thought of leaving my nice warm cocoon in exchange for cold tiles and a mildewed ceiling.

Having Daddy lie me down and take care of me sounds *much* more pleasant.

However, I am not calling him over in the middle of the night to change a sodden diaper.

A sodden diaper which, now that it's cooling, is heavy and uncomfortable and damp.

Forcing myself out of bed and cringing at how gross it feels now, I discover walking in it is also an experience. A nowhere near as pleasant experience as wearing it dry. But, curiously, having it wet makes me feel like I'm sinking back into Little space again, compounded by feeling it sag as I attempt to waddle my way across my room.

I fight against that instinct to be little again, knowing that I need to get changed now before the risk of Tanya catching me increases. I don't think I'll be able to keep my new discoveries from her a secret forever, but I'm still not willing to discuss it any time soon.

While I'm wiping myself down, I still can't shake the thought that I enjoyed this whole experience more than I anticipated… and I really want my Daddy.

Chapter Thirteen – Spencer

"So, you've been exploring your little side?" I prompt my cute date.

We're snuggled up on my couch, with Frank draped over Tony's lap like he lives there now, we and are simply enjoying each other's company. We've had a nice, non-eventful dinner and have caught up on each other's past few days, and now feels like the right time to bring this topic up.

"Yeah…" he answers slowly, like he's considering how much he wants to divulge at this point.

I give him a little squeeze around his shoulders. "We're taking this at your pace," I remind him quietly. "If you're not ready to—"

"It turns out Little Me is really good with the diapers." He blurts, cutting me off. "Like, um, *really* comfortable with them."

"Like they excite you, or—"

"Well, yeah, *that*, but…" he clears his throat and shifts around a bit. "The wetting thing is, uh, well it's…*a thing*."

This news does surprise me. He hadn't sounded at all interested in infantilization when we first discussed Daddy/boy play and it's not something I need out of a relationship, so I never pushed. I know he sounded like he was getting off on the idea of coming in his diaper, but actively using them to pee is a big leap from there. Especially for someone so easily embarrassed.

"Yeah?" I ask, gently prodding for more information. "What kind of *thing*? Like…watersports, or—"

"No! God no! I'm not into the pee itself." Tony twists around so that he's looking at me, and Frank makes a sound of protest that we both ignore. With bright red cheeks, Tony explains, "It makes me feel properly little. I don't know why, it just does. And I like that."

Rubbing my hand over his arm in a placating gesture, I do my best to reassure him that it's not an issue. "There aren't any rules on how you enjoy your kink, sweetheart."

"Yeah, but this is something that impacts you. Like," he pitches his voice lower, even though we're the only ones here, "changing me and stuff."

I kind of love that he's got this whole personality contrast going on. He's so confident about exploring this new side of himself, but so awkward and shy when it comes to discussing it.

"And if I had an issue with it, I'd say so. Or I'd safe word," I answer matter-of-factly.

"But…"

"But?" I prompt when he trails off.

He licks his lips and looks down at Frank, gently carding his fingers over the soft, black fur of Frank's side. The cat lets out a little trill of appreciation.

126

"If you're not comfortable—" I start again.

"I was big the first time I...*y'know*."

"Wet?"

He nods.

"Okay…"

"And it felt kinda' satisfying? But it was the after effect that made me feel like I wanted to be little again. So I, um, I thought I should try it while I was little. And I did."

"And you said you liked that."

"Yeah. And I left it, 'cos it made me go deeper and then…" His cheeks look hot to the touch now and he squirms in his seat.

"Then?"

After swallowing roughly, he takes a deep breath and confesses, "I didn't even realize I'd gone *again* until it got really uncomfortable. Like…I had no idea. I was happily playing and then I was, well, y'know."

I won't point out how cute I think it is that he can't bring himself to say 'wetting' or 'peeing'. I want him to be comfortable talking to me about this. But, damn, he's too sweet for words sometimes.

Shifting again, he keeps talking, "And I liked that I had zero control, you know? I felt completely free. There was no stress. No worries. Well, not until…" He stops himself short and bites his lip.

Now I frown, not liking that something about the experience upset him. "What?"

"Not until I realized I had to deal with it on my own." His voice is so small as he makes this confession.

My heart hurts. I cuddle him closer, kissing the top of his head. "You wanted your Daddy. You were little and uncomfortable."

"Yeah. But…uh," he scrunches his nose, "I didn't know it would be like that, so I didn't see anything wrong with trying it out on my own. Just in case I didn't like it, or I was too embarrassed, or whatever. But," he exhales heavily and meets my gaze again, "it was a rough transition back into being big, and without any aftercare, so I won't do it alone again. But I also get if it's something you'd rather not be a part of our relationship as Daddy and Boy when we play together."

Admittedly, Charlie's the Daddy who really gets a kick out of change time. He has a spiel about it. We've all had to hear it. But I don't mind changing diapers, wet or dry, and if it's something that helps my boy properly enjoy his Little time, then it's important to me. So I'm honest and this is exactly what I tell Tony.

"It doesn't gross you out? That I don't even know it's happening? Like, I can't even warn you, I just…" he makes a vague gesture with his fingers, adding a weak hissing sound for emphasis, and it's all I can do to keep a straight face.

Frank looks up at him like he's gone crazy and then meows in protest of his pets having been halted.

"No, it doesn't gross me out," I chuckle, losing the battle against my amusement. "And I *want* to see you lose yourself in how little you get, in whatever way you need to achieve that. To be honest, the fact that you were able to sink that deeply into Little space on your own is impressive. Knowing that it makes you feel good and alleviates your stress makes it even better. It's kind of my job as a Daddy to make your life easier, whether you're little or big. I want to take care of you in every way you'll let me."

His eyes take on a suspiciously moist sheen that reminds

me not many people have ever made the promise to look after him before, and I make a vow to myself to do whatever I can to make this whole experience good for him.

"About that…" he eventually says, biting his lip again and cocking his head. "The other night. When you, um, when we…"

"Had phone sex?"

Tony's cheeks are adorably pink again and he nods, swallowing roughly. "Yeah. That." Clearing his throat, he forges on, surprising me by asking, "Was it too much for you?"

I'm thoroughly confused. "Too much for me?"

"It's just that, uh, I mean, I know you knew I was big, but the stuff you said. *Thecominginmydiaperthing*," he breathes out in a rush, "it wasn't too close to sex in Little space for you?"

"Oh," I pause to really think about it. I'd been caught up in the moment and it was phone sex. It wasn't in person, and I was excited beyond words that he was not only exploring age play, but enjoying it. And he'd been in his adult headspace as I'd spoken to him.

But, yeah, I can see where he's coming from. I appreciate him checking in with me. This give and take is new for me, and I wonder if this is more like what Charlie and Ash share.

Smiling at that thought, I finally answer him, "Not at all. I promise. I enjoyed everything we said and did over the phone, Tony."

He visibly relaxes. "Yeah?"

"Yeah," I press a kiss to his forehead. "But thank you for double checking. It means a lot to me."

And it just makes me even more determined to do everything right by him in return.

* * *

"You are ridiculously smitten, aren't you?"

The question comes from my friend London on our weekly run. Josh is running ahead of us on the sidewalk at a faster pace, his footfalls barely echoing with how much distance is between us.

London is shorter than me, but bulky. His stocky, strong body comes from his years spent as a landscaper, laboring in a physical job day in and day out. Josh's more toned, muscular physique comes from a ridiculously dedicated gym regime. I feel lanky and ridiculous when I run with these men, but I need the exercise and I enjoy the socialization. Sometimes Matt joins us, other times it's Ted or Charlie. Today, though, it's just the three of us.

"Yeah," I pant my response, not even bothering to hide my growing feelings for my boyfriend. My feet slap the pavement as I add, "I can't remember the last time I felt like this. Maybe the early days with Emma?"

Since I've started dating Tony, her name doesn't inspire the same bitterness in me anymore. I don't need a psychology degree to tell me what that means.

London never met Emma, considering she and I were broken up long before he met Matt, but he's heard stories —from me and from the other guys— so the half smile he shoots me is soft with understanding. "That's a good sign, Spence."

"It is," I agree.

We trot side by side in silence for a bit, and I let my thoughts drift to the topic of our conversation.

Tony is kind of perfect for me, even though he doesn't seem

to realize it himself. Our time spent together is always so *easy*. He enjoys me looking after him as much as I enjoy doing it. I've loved him calling me Daddy, even without the age play element, and his bravery to give it a go —to experiment with it even though he wasn't sure to start with— makes me so unbelievably grateful and proud of him.

So proud, in fact, that I blurt, "We're going to trial a couple of scenes this weekend."

Okay, make that proud and excited.

London's pace falters and he swivels his head to face me so quickly I worry that he's given himself whiplash. "Really?" Relatively new to the lifestyle himself, London's the most likely to relate to Tony, despite him being a Daddy where Tony's a Little. "He's okay with that?"

I frown. "I wouldn't ever force him to do anything he wasn't okay with." I resent the implication, and I honestly thought London knew me better than that. None of the Daddies in our group would ever cross those lines.

"No, I know. But from what Chance said about him—"

"*Ugh*. Fucking Chance," I love my best friend, but sometimes I wish he'd keep his nose out of things. He can be a bit melodramatic and make mountains out of mole hills. For a guy who seems shy, he certainly likes to stir the pot.

London rolls his eyes. "He said Tony was already ass over tit when you met." He breathes heavily as we start to make our way up a hill. Ahead of us, Josh is already cresting the top. "So, just be careful that he's not pushing himself out of his comfort zone to keep you happy."

"Fuck" —I breathe heavily— "you. He's...*ugh*...not." This is my least favorite part of our route, and I can barely breathe enough to tell London how wrong he is. My calves burn as we hit the steep incline at the midway point of the hill.

By unspoken agreement, we table the subject until we've reached the top. When we get there, Josh is leaning against a tree in the park to our right. It's the same park where Charlie and Asher got married last year, and further into the area there's a spot overlooking the city. On a clear day, you can see mountains in the distance.

"You two slackers need to pick up the pace," Josh taunts as we slow down to meet him. He shakes his head with a teasing grin. "Letting a Boy like me whoop your asses. Disgraceful."

"I am not ashamed to be outrun by anyone, least of all you," I tell him as I catch my breath. "The fact I can manage to kind of keep up with you at all is a miracle." I turn to face London again and wait as he wipes sweat from his forehead and face. "And I swear, I'm letting Tony set the pace for our scenes. I mean, he's twenty-eight. He knows his own limits. I'm trusting that he will safe word if it's not working for him, and I'll respect that."

With his hands up in surrender, London nods. "Okay, okay, I'm sorry. I didn't mean to imply that you wouldn't. I was just…" he flounders for an explanation.

"Looking out for a Little, I get it." I let him off the hook because I *do* get it. He's a good guy, and if Chance has been filling his head with embellished stories of Tony's *fanboying*, I can't really blame him for his concern.

Josh swings his dark brown gaze between us, arching an eyebrow. "Well," he draws the word out, "sounds like you two have kissed and made up. Are we okay to keep going? I'd like to make it home sometime today."

"Shut up, brat," I laugh, stretching out my legs and giving myself a quick shake. I jump up and down to get the blood flowing, "now let's get going before you earn yourself some corner time."

I take off at a sprint that I know I won't be able to keep up, Josh's laughter at my back.

For the first time in a long time, I'm genuinely invigorated and looking forward to what lies ahead.

* * *

Excitement simmers in my veins today. It's a Sunday, and Tony and I are going to attempt our first real scenes as Daddy and Boy when he finishes work for the afternoon. We've talked through our expectations and rules, gone back over safe words, and have decided on easing into our evening with some matchbox cars, coloring, and, if he gets little enough, stuffies.

But, when I pull up outside the diner and I'm greeted by his red, puffy eyes, my excitement is overridden by concern. I'm out of the driver's seat and wrapping him in a hug on the sidewalk before he can even open the car door.

"What happened?" I ask him, not unaware of how he's clinging to me.

"Just…just a rough shift, that's all." He sounds exhausted and has obviously reached breaking point. It hurts me to see him this way, and all I want to do is storm into that diner and tear into whoever is responsible.

But I don't do that. Instead, I open the car door and gently usher him into the passenger seat, then lean over to clasp his seatbelt for him.

His lips twitch into the ghost of a smile. "Thanks, Daddy."

I let him relax on the drive back to my place and after he

greets Frank, he seems more like his usual self, if somewhat subdued.

"If you'd rather leave our plans for another night…" I start to offer, but he holds up a hand and shakes his head.

"I think I need it more now, to be honest," he says. "But, um, could we…could we do something different than we were going to? Same rules, but…um, never mind."

Stepping into his personal space, I lift his chin gently. "Tell me what you want, sweetheart."

"Can you, um, dress me and then, if it's okay with you, give me a bottle and a binky and just…just cuddle with me? Actually, no, that's boring and stupid, so—"

"*Anthony*," he stops at my tone, big, wet brown eyes blinking up at me. "It's not boring or stupid to want comfort after a shitty day. I'm proud of you for knowing what will help you, and I'm honored that you've asked me."

My poor boy sniffles and nods, and I take him by the hand to lead him upstairs. I take him into what was once a guest room but was converted into a nursery years ago.

It's equipped with an adult sized change table, a sturdy set of dresser drawers, a twin bed with removable side rails, and a toy chest. Tony had been amazed the first time I showed him this room, and I've since decorated it to his tastes and in his favorite colors. I'm glad for having done so now, because it seems to help relax him some more.

"Arms up, angel," I instruct, and then help pull his shirt over his head. Then I help him with his pants and underwear, until he's standing naked in front of me. "Traffic light?" I prompt.

"Green," he says quietly, but without hesitation.

I have him hold my hand as I help him up the painted timber steps at the base of the oversized change table, then guide him to lie back onto its padded surface.

The spongey mat is protected by a waterproof slipcover decorated in tiny black cats, which made Tony giggle when he first saw it. Even now, he turns his head and smiles, running an index finger over the image of a cat licking its paw.

"Kitty," he says, and it's a relief to see him unwinding some more, especially enough to try to get into a Little headspace.

"It is a kitty," I agree warmly, rummaging in one of the drawers beneath the solid, wooden change table and emerging victorious with an adult-sized pacifier, with a bulbous rubber nipple and a bright red shield and ring. I connect it to a pacifier saver clip, the ribbon a bright orange and also decorated in black cats.

Tony's eyes light up when I waggle it in front of him and he reaches towards it with grabby hands. "Please?"

"Good boy," I praise, handing it over and watching in rapt attention as he pops the teat into his mouth and eases into rhythmic sucking. His shoulders relax almost instantaneously.

Good to know.

I fluff out a thick, white diaper and get him to lift off the mat for me, sliding it under him and positioning the seat under his butt *just so*. Knowing that he's likely to actually use the diaper, I slather a healthy amount of barrier cream over his smooth, buttery soft skin, and Tony lets out a tiny little sigh.

I glance up from my task to catch him watching me with drooping eyes. I'm struck dumb for a second by just how precious this moment is, before I bring the front of the diaper up and hold it in place with one hand while deftly bringing the sticky tabs around one of his hips and then the other.

He gives his extra rounded tushy a wiggle, smiling around the pacifier in his mouth, and I'm officially a goner for him.

This beautiful boy is utter perfection.

"Feels good, huh?" I ask him with a smile of my own, reaching for one of the adorable footed onesies we sat and ordered together a few days ago.

"Uh huh," he says, then together we work to get him dressed.

I help him down from the table and pull him in for a cuddle. He feels much more relaxed already, which bodes well for our evening plans.

"Come on, angel," I tell him, taking him by the hand and leading him back down the stairs, "let's go watch cartoons and snuggle, hmm?"

We stop by the kitchen so I can heat him a bottle, and then I get comfy in the corner of the couch with a cushion on top of the armrest to prop my arm up. Happy with that, I tug Tony down, positioning him so his head is supported in the crook of my left elbow and his padded backside is cradled sideways between my thighs. When I move my right leg, it effectively helps me to rock him from side to side like one would a baby or toddler.

Setting the bottle down by my hip, I snag the remote and navigate to Disney+. A few clicks later, I have *The Aristocats* playing and Tony giggles appreciatively.

"Want your bottle?" I ask him, grinning when he blushes and nods.

I hold the bottle to his lips and my grin softens out as he begins to nurse from it.

It's been a while since I've done this. Emma wasn't into bottles or pacifiers, her Little age more akin to a three or four-year-old, but Tony's obviously drawn to being younger. That tracks with everything I've learned about him so far, and I like that he's so different to my last serious relationship. It's like everything is new again.

I'm watching him while he watches the movie. He's boneless in my arms now, eyes drooping as the bottle slowly drains. It's almost an unconscious action on my part when I start bouncing my right leg from side to side, rocking him into oblivion.

I let the movie continue to play while he sleeps. Frank appears and curls up on my other side around the same time Thomas O'Malley launches into his introductory song. He purrs loudly when I reach down to scritch behind his ears and under his chin.

This moment feels utterly domestic and completely perfect. I close my eyes and decide to just soak it in.

I wake from my unplanned nap to the feeling of Tony squirming in my lap.

"Hey," I greet him softly, bringing my hand up to brush his dark bangs out of his eyes, "you okay?"

"Gotta *go*. Gotta go *bad*," he answers, wriggling his hips for emphasis. He doesn't sound *big*, but he's closer to it than he was before he fell asleep.

I smile and shrug. "You're diapered, baby."

He scrunches his nose, a blush creeping up his neck.

"Did you want to go play with your toys?" Maybe taking him off my lap might make it less of a big deal to him? Not that I mind either way. I just want him to be at ease here.

Tony chews his lower lip, then nods slowly, but he gasps and tenses when I go to move him off my lap. His cheeks turn bright red before he burrows his face into the crook of my neck at the same time as a telling warmth blooms over my thigh.

During our negotiations, Tony reminded me that feeling

wet has helped him sink deeper into Little space, so we agreed that I wouldn't immediately offer to change him if it happened. He'll let me know when he's uncomfortable, and I trust him to do that. Still, he feels tense in my arms and I can't have that.

"Are you playing with your toys?" I ask him, as though nothing is different. I glance up at the clock on the archway that leads towards the short hallway. "Daddy has to start making dinner so we don't starve."

Slowly, Tony relaxes and pulls away from where he was hiding. Though his cherubic face is still bright pink, he nods and giggles. "Cars?" he asks, and the single word answer suggests that he's starting to sink back into a deeper headspace again.

I ruffle his hair, delighting in the way it makes it stick up at odd angles. "Whatever you like, angel."

He climbs off my lap and waddles (there really is no better word to describe his wide-legged, toddling walk) over to the brightly colored mat in the corner, upending the bucket of matchbox cars we'd placed there together earlier in the week. He entertains himself, making 'vroom' noises and sending the small vehicles hurtling over the mat at breakneck speeds, and I watch him with fondness for a few minutes before giving myself a shake and heading out of the room to start organizing our meal.

The roast and veggies are just sliding into the oven when he calls out a whiny, "Daddy!"

I close the oven door, take off my oven mitts, and head back into the living room. I find Tony surrounded by tiny cars, a couple of toy trucks, a teddy bear and...I don't even recognize that stuffed dog. He's the eye of a small cyclone of Little exuberance.

"Well," I observe crouching down to zoom a car down the mat myself, "this looks like you had fun."

He nods, then shifts his hips from side to side, scrunching his nose up in that way I'm coming to understand is his 'seriously uncomfortable' face.

"Ahhh, are you wet, baby?"

He picks up the stuffed dog and holds it in front of his reddening face by one floppy gray ear, nodding shyly.

I want to eat him up.

Smothering the urge to pepper him with kisses, I push back up to my feet and reach out both hands. "Let's fix that, hmm?"

He holds out his hands to me, still clutching his new plush toy, and I surprise him by reaching for his underarms and lifting him up that way. After he's stable on his feet, I bend and peck a kiss to the tip of his nose, wink, and then hoist him up again, forcing him to wrap his legs around my waist as I carry him to the foot of the stairs.

"Sadly, sweetheart, I can't carry you up the stairs, so you'll have to hoof it from here," I tell him, and he giggles then complies, his waddle somehow even more pronounced than earlier.

It's insanely adorable.

When we're back in the nursery, I help him up onto the change table again, and smile gently down at him. I can see the nerves swimming in his gaze, even though he's still in a mostly Little headspace. This is a big deal for him, and I want him to know I'm taking it seriously. "If you hate this or you're uncomfortable, I'll stop and you can take over."

He licks his lips, then nods, "I trust you, Daddy."

That is probably the best sentence I have ever heard.

Maybe Charlie's onto something after all.

Chapter Fourteen — Tony

I was right. Daddy changing me makes *all* the difference. He doesn't make a song and dance about it —in fact, he makes short work of helping me out of my onesie and then pulling the soggy, uncomfortable diaper from me, rolling it up and wiping me clean— but there's care and attention and warmth in his actions, and in the way he talks to me.

When I did this for myself, I had to get back into my normal adult headspace to deal with it. But because he's got this, I'm able to stay floating in the relaxing place where the realities of my grown up world don't touch me.

Customers aren't yelling at me because the fry cook got their order wrong, or because it's taking longer to get to them while we're short-staffed. My boss isn't yelling at me for being slow, even though I'm filling in for two other people on my normal shift. I'm not worried about accidentally taking Table 8's coke to Table 3, or dropping and smashing a glass because I tried to clean up a table too hastily.

Sure, all of that did happen tonight (and then some), but

while I'm little, I don't think about it. Instead, I think about how safe Daddy's arms felt as he held me close. How strong he was when he carried me from the living room to the stairs at the front of the house. How fun it was to sit and play with toys, with no expectation to do anything else other than entertain myself.

"Now," Daddy says, breaking me out of my musings, "did you want to stay little for a while longer, or would you like me to get your big boy clothes for you to start thinking about being big again?"

"Hmm…" I hum out loud, completely uncaring that I'm still splayed out on the change mat, my junk on display. The temptation to stay little and hide from my stresses a while longer is strong, but I do also want to spend some grown up time with my Daddy, too. "Big boy clothes," I decide.

Daddy gives me a proud smile (which I think he would have given me either way) and lifts up a pair of brightly colored briefs with a picture of a spaceship on the front. "Training pants," he explains. "Kind of between a pull-up and underwear. Both in case of accidents, but also to help you still feel little for a bit longer."

I feel a bit embarrassed when he says 'accidents', but I do really like the idea of having a middle ground to experiment with. "Spaceship!" I say, clapping my hands.

Daddy chuckles. "That's right, sweetheart. It's a spaceship."

He guides my legs in through the leg holes one at a time, then gets me to raise my hips to tug the underwear up properly. They are quite snug and have a thick crotch. Nothing like a diaper, but definitely thicker than normal cotton briefs. The constriction and sensation against my dick feels good and I rub my palm over the spaceship without thinking. My cock hardens almost instantly.

"Hey," Daddy chides gently, "what's the rule about grown up touching while you're little?"

Biting my lip, I gaze at him sheepishly through lowered lashes. "Is naughty."

The adult part of my brain can tell that he's trying not to laugh. He does a pretty impressive job of schooling his features and nodding seriously. "Exactly. Little boys get excited, but only big boys should be doing anything about it."

I know these rules are Spencer specific. There are a lot of Littles in the online community I've joined recently who have sexy times while they're little, and there's nothing wrong with that. But I kind of like him setting rules like this anyway and, even if we ever do experiment with sex during Little time, I hope these rules don't change. It's fun to feel a bit naughty in this playful way.

"Sorry, Daddy," I tell him, the 'r's coming out as 'w's.

Any remaining sternness in him melts away instantly.

He's such a marshmallow daddy. I love him.

My brain stops.

Did I just...?

Do I...?

I gulp and my heart hammers.

It's only been a few weeks. I can't possibly love him, can I?

I mean, sure, I had a crush on him (or, at least, on an imaginary construction of him) before I even met him. And he has been my first for a lot of experiences, including unlocking this part of me that makes me feel absolutely complete and *right*.

But...*love*? Really? Already?

"Where'd you go, angel?" Daddy asks with quiet amusement,

cupping my jaw with his large hand and smoothing his thumb over my cheek.

"Spaceship," I panic and blurt the first word that comes to me.

Thankfully, Daddy just laughs and shakes his head. "Okay. Well, does that mean you want to wear a spaceship t-shirt?"

I agree quickly and almost sag with relief.

Crisis averted.

* * *

Later on in the night, long after we've eaten dinner (slipping Frank little pieces of roast whenever he begged loudly) and have stacked the dishwasher, Spencer and I are cuddled up in his queen sized bed together.

"Thank you for everything tonight," I tell him, once again 'big' and able to articulate my thoughts properly. "It was just what I needed."

"It was what I needed, too," he says, running his fingers over the back of my scalp in a light head massage that makes me want to purr. After a few more moments, he asks, "Did you want to talk about it? Why you were so upset when I picked you up from work, I mean?"

My lips flatten into a firm line. I'd managed to push most of my disastrous shift out of my mind for the night. "It was just a bad shift," I answer. "Nothing went right, customers were jerks, I broke a couple glasses…" I exhale and shake my head. "I don't deal well with people getting loud and aggressive. I just…broke, I guess."

It had been humiliating bursting into tears when I hung up my apron for the night. I'd hidden in the bathroom, concentrating on my breathing to try and get myself under control before I went out to meet Spencer at the curb. Once again, I can't help thinking that if Gerald would just let me cook instead of deal with customers, I might actually like my job. Sadly, he seems to feel the same way about his and, as the boss, he's decided I should suffer instead. And I have been.

Mustering a smile, I stop to think about everything that happened after my shift ended. "But you made it all better," I tell Spencer.

"I'm happy to hear that," he bends down to press his lips to mine in a sweet, chaste kiss that floods my body with jittery, happy feelings.

I love him.

The words bounce around in my head after he pulls away, smiling dopily down at me.

I love him. I love him. I love him.

I can't get them to stop, but I'm terrified of them all the same. I've *never* felt this way for another man. For anyone. The only person I've ever truly loved is my sister, and this is quite obviously different to that on a number of levels.

It's too soon to be so attached, I reason with myself. Too soon, and there's too much on the line for me to risk blurting the words out and not have them returned. Or, even worse, blurting them out and scaring this beautiful man away.

So, to avoid blurting the words out, I launch up towards him to steal another kiss, which he happily accepts.

Chapter Fifteen – Spencer

There's something different about our kisses now. I can't put my finger on it, but I can feel it deep in my bones. It's like our time together as Daddy and Boy has changed something between us. It's not a bad thing, not even close, but it's different all the same.

Tony seems more comfortable in his own skin. More confident, and more willing to talk things through with me. I can see the way being little has worked his stress away, just like I thought it would, and I need him to know that I'll gladly do this with him every day if it means seeing him glow the way he is right now.

It doesn't take long for our sweet kisses to turn needy, and I throw my head back against my padded, gray linen headboard with a muted *thwump* when Tony starts to suck kisses down my jaw, then my neck, then the V of my partially unbuttoned pajama shirt.

"Jesus Christ, your *mouth*, angel," I praise, unable to prevent myself from thinking about where else I might like to feel that warm, wet perfection.

"Mmm," he murmurs in what I assume is agreement, before he shifts back and toys with the top fastened button of my shirt, nibbling on his bottom lip.

"Can…can I…"

For all my musing that he's becoming more confident, this moment reminds me that he's still so unsure of himself and of his lack of experience.

"What, baby?"

Tony closes his eyes and his cheeks turn that adorable flushed pink as he tries again, "Can I, um, can I suck…" he trails off, and my mind is already filling in the blanks.

Anything, my brain screams, *you can suck anything you want.*

"…your nipples?"

Okay, *not* what I was expecting. I blink back at him, watching as he swallows roughly.

"Like, um, like breastfeeding?" His face is beet red now, his voice pitched up high with his uncertainty. "That's weird, right? You must think I'm…*ugh*. Just…just forget I said anything." He covers his face with his hands and my brain finally kicks back into gear.

Lurching forward, I reach for his wrists and pull his hands away so I can look him in the eye. "It's not weird. *You're* not weird. I just," now it's my turn to blush, and I can feel the heat of it creeping up my neck and over my ears, "thought you were going to ask to suck something else, and I stopped thinking for a minute."

He frowns back at me, cocking his head in mild confusion. "What else would—*oh*." His eyes widen, then glance down to my crotch. A tiny smile tugs at the corner of his lips. "That's, um, next on my list."

Of course he has a list.

Did I mention how freaking adorable he is?

"So," I reach for his hand, squeezing it, "suckling, huh?"

"I…" he clears his throat and nods, "yeah."

"I'll let you in on a secret," I tell him, leaning forward and resting my forehead on his, "I don't think you'll ever suggest anything I haven't already tried or thought about."

"Really?"

"Really."

Some of the scenes in the books I narrate have lit my curiosity over the years. And, having been a member of various BDSM and kink clubs for fifteen years or so has filled in the remaining gaps in my sexual exploration. Yeah, there are things I haven't actually tried, but I honestly don't think he could suggest anything that would catch me off guard.

Instead of saying anything else, Tony brings a shaky hand to my top button and fumbles with it until it releases, then he moves to the next. By the fifth and final button, he seems to have calmed again, his curiosity overriding his insecurities.

I help him along by slipping my shirt off my shoulders and dropping it over the side of my bed. His hands, smaller and stouter than mine, spread over my chest, exploring my pecs almost cautiously.

We've been naked together a handful of times now, but Tony hasn't really stopped to fixate on any one part of me. Until now.

"How do you want to do this, baby?" I ask him softly, still seemingly startling him out of his reverie. "Want me to hold you like I did when I gave you the bottle?"

"Is that okay?" Tony asks in return, almost timidly. "It's not too close to me being little?"

Obviously, we've discussed sex during Little space before, but never like this. Never while we're being intimate, and I'm still warmed that he's concerned about my limits. Nevertheless, I shake my head. "Nope. But you know it's not a trigger for me. I've just struggled to get into it when my partner's Little. I like doing adult things with other adulty adults." I hesitate for only a second before I add, "But if you ever wanted to try it, it wouldn't provoke an anxiety attack or anything. It really is more a soft limit than a hard one. And, baby, you don't have to keep checking in on me…but it's super sweet that you are."

Understanding lights his eyes, then a bit of relief follows. "Okay. That's good to know." He smiles shyly, looking up at me through lowered lashes. "I just want you to be as comfortable as you make me feel."

This beautiful, beautiful man.

Not knowing quite how to respond to such an amazing sentiment, I grab a few of my thankfully lofty pillows and get them positioned under my left arm, then crook my finger, inviting Tony to get comfy.

He lies sideways over my stretched out legs, his own stretched over the mattress to my right on a slight angle towards the foot of the bed. I cradle him with my left arm like I did on the couch and brush his hair out of his face again with my right.

"At your own pace," I remind him gently. "We don't have to — *ohhh!*"

With his beautiful dark eyes closed, he's started showering my left pec with open mouthed kisses, lapping at the skin with tiny kitten licks that send pleasant tingles through my body. Then he latches onto my nipple and the surrounding flesh, suckling with the same practiced, almost lazy rhythm he used on the bottle and his pacifier.

Electricity zips and zaps at my nerve endings. In my pajama pants, my cock becomes rock hard when he starts making small, satisfied sounds. He's got his free hand on my other pec, squeezing and kneading the skin under his palm.

"Oh, Tony, *angel*, that feels amazing," I babble, trying not to thrust up in search of friction. I don't want to ruin this moment for him just because my dick is demanding attention.

"Mmmhmmm," he agrees, then starts moving his own hips.

A glance down confirms that he's just as hard as I am, tenting the front of his own pajama bottoms. I imagine the training pants beneath are catching his precum better than the thin cotton of my boxer briefs, where I can feel a wet spot growing.

"Stroke yourself, Anthony," the urgent instruction surprises both of us, and his eyes open wide to meet my gaze, though he doesn't cease his nursing. I grin. "Show me how you like to be touched."

He groans around my nipple and the sound vibrates through my now sensitive little nub. If that wasn't enough to make my dick ache, watching as he slides his hand off my chest and down to the front of his pants surely is. He shuffles awkwardly as he tugs them down over his hips and ass one-handedly. Then he reluctantly pulls away from my chest with an audible wet *pop* to tug the clothing all the way off.

I gasp when he returns to his activities, bringing his hot mouth back to my nipple, which has been cooling in the night air during the few short seconds he took to take off his pants. He smirks around my pink bud, then closes his eyes again, losing himself in his enjoyment again.

I don't know where to look when his hand travels down his

front —still covered in the soft material of his t-shirt— and then grasps his flushed, leaking cock.

I want to see the pleasure on his face, but I *did* ask him to show me how he likes to be stroked. It would be rude not to pay attention.

Tony grips his shaft and uses his thumb to swipe at the precum dribbling out of his purpled head. He uses it as lube, spreading it over his thick shaft, slowly gliding his fist down and back up the flush-darkened skin. He twists his wrist on every other upstroke, unable to hold back his grunts and groans of pleasure. I feel every sound around my nipple.

"You're so fucking gorgeous," I tell him, clenching my free hand into the bedsheets at my side. I could reach into my pants and jerk myself off, but I don't want to be distracted from the performance he's putting on for me.

He offers me a pleased little moan in response.

Then he takes his hand off his dick and fondles his own balls, teasing them and the skin of his taint with light, tickling motions with his fingers. It's all I can do not to black out, able to imagine those same fingers touching me that way. Imagining the way they would dance over the soft skin of my balls, the featherlight touches warring with the firm suction of his mouth on my nipples or, hopefully one day, cock.

More precum spills over his throbbing erection and he gathers it up with his fingers and spreads his thighs, reaching even lower between them.

"Oh, fuck, Tony."

I can't see his fingers teasing his own hole, but I'm entranced by the movement of his wrist and hand, disappearing between his legs. He writhes, his cock brushing his own forearm while he works himself open.

The nursing at my chest has turned into hard sucking that I'm pretty sure will leave an impressive hickey. I plan on wearing it with pride, because it's going to remind me of this scene for days.

On another deep, reverberating moan, Tony tears his mouth from my skin and begs, "Oh, God, Spencer. *Fuck*. Touch me, Daddy, please. I'm so close. I need...I need..."

"I know what you need, baby," I answer, my voice matching his with tightness and desperation. "Daddy's got you."

He whimpers when I bring up my free hand and wrap it around his weeping cock. His fingers are still buried in his ass, which is no mean feat considering he only used a little bit of precum for lube. He fucks up into my fist and I twist on every other upstroke just like he did, and then he's shouting and coming hard, spurts of his release coating my hand, and landing on his chest and also mine.

With his shirt already soiled, I use it to wipe my hand and drag the hem down to mop over what I can reach of his softening cock and the splashes on my chest.

"That was beautiful, sweetheart," I tell him, honestly. "Thank you for sharing that with me."

His eyelids are heavy, but the blissed-out smile on his face fades and he forces himself to sit up, reaching out and cupping my aching cock through the thin fabric I'm still wearing. The wet spot has spread over the pajama bottoms by now.

"You haven't come yet," he says.

I'm about to assure him that I don't need to when he tugs the material down just enough to release my dick, which practically bounces out once freed from its confines, the head dark and glistening, the length flushed an almost angry red.

"Show me, Spencer," he demands quietly, but confidently. "I

want to see what you like, too."

A burst of laughter bubbles out of me, and I shake my head. "It's going to be a short show," I warn him lightly. "*Someone* just pushed me closer than I've ever been to coming untouched." It's not even an exaggeration: he could probably breathe on it and I'll explode.

Just the mental image of unloading over his face has another stream of precum trickling out and over my length.

"*Daddy*," he whines, giving me big, pleading puppy eyes, "please?"

I groan and take myself in hand, my dick jumping at even that simple contact. It takes three strokes, my fist flexing at the base every time, before I erupt with a shout. I see fucking stars and float for a little while as jet after jet releases over my fist and land God-only-knows where else.

"Mmm," Tony says, sounding equal parts satisfied and contemplative.

I crack my eyes open to catch him scooping a finger through my cum and bringing it to his perfect, unexpectedly sinful mouth.

I can't look away as he sucks the mess from his finger, tasting me for the first time. If I hadn't just had a mind-blowing orgasm, I think I might come again just from that sight alone.

"Next time," he says when he catches me watching, "you're finishing in my mouth."

My brain short circuits.

That's the only excuse I have for what I say next.

"God, I love you."

Chapter Sixteen – Tony

Spencer freezes, clearly not having intended to say those words. The expression on his face is almost comical. I can tell that he genuinely feels the sentiment behind the accidental confession, but there's surprise and a hint of worry in his eyes, and embarrassment in the flush of his cheeks.

Considering I was so afraid of blurting out the same confession, I can't help my giggle. I bring my hand to my mouth and cover it to stifle the sound. Spencer's eyes narrow, and I lose the battle, my delighted laughter bursting out of me while my spirits soar.

Before he can get any more uncomfortable or, worse, try to retract his declaration, I close the gap between us and kiss him, deep and slow. As the kiss comes to an end, I murmur, "I love you, too."

He startles and leans back against the headboard, searching my gaze for any sign of discomfort or perhaps even dishonesty.

Offering him a shy, sheepish smile, I shrug and admit, "It crept up on me when you were changing me earlier. I thought if I said anything, you'd think it was too soon and that I'm a clingy freak."

His eyes go dark and serious. "I hate that word," he says simply, then softens. "But I don't think it's too soon, or that you're clingy, or weird, or anything along those lines. You're perfect, Tony. Okay? You're perfect, and I love you."

My throat is clogged with emotion, my eyes brimming with happy tears. I can only nod and snuggle into him for a hug, heedless of the sticky, drying mess between us.

"But you know what this means, right?" He asks playfully over the top of my head.

I give a little shake in answer.

"You're really going to have to meet the guys now. I've been selfishly putting it off, but we've just done the love exchange. They'll kill me if I leave it any longer."

He's told me a lot about his buddies over the course of the past few weeks. It turns out I'll probably recognize a few of them as customers from the diner, because they're all kinky like Spence himself. Like me, too, I guess. They sound like a really caring group of guys.

"Honestly," he continues talking, his words now tinged with fondness and amusement, "I'm surprised they've respected my request to not stalk you at work. I wouldn't put it past them. Well, some of them."

"Er…" I clear my throat, wondering if I'm about to get some of them in trouble, "well, Chance did swing by with another guy…um, Josh, I think he said his name was?"

Spencer groans and pinches the bridge of his nose. "When?"

"Last week? Must have been Thursday because you had that late recording session."

I feel a bit bad now, because the visit completely slipped my mind by the end of my shift. It wasn't like I'd had much time to stop and chat with the two men at the time, either. We'd been swamped again (it's been happening more often than not nowadays) and outside of a short, awkward exchange, nothing about the encounter had stayed with me.

All of this spills out of me with a sense of urgency, and Spencer is quick to hold me close and assure me that I haven't done anything wrong.

"I don't need reports on who you speak to or when. I didn't mean for you to feel like I was questioning you. I'm just going to strangle Chance when I see him next."

I snort. "To be fair, I just figured they were heading over to The Grove for Littles' Night or something, and we're still the only decent place to grab a bite nearby."

"Hmm," he doesn't sound completely convinced, but I also don't know his friends like he does. After a beat, he exhales and fills me in, "The guys are all worse than stereotypical matchmaking grandmothers. And they're nosy as fuck. I love them, but they can be a bit much."

"That sounds like me and Tanya," I muse with my own fond smile.

"Yeah," he agrees, nodding. "I am closer to them than my bio-brothers, for sure."

I don't know if that's supposed to be reassuring for when I finally meet these people…or intimidating.

* * *

Intimidating is how it ends up feeling when the day to officially meet Spencer's friends arrives. His friend, Ted, has offered to host a get-together at his mansion (Spencer's word, not mine, but I find it's appropriate when we drive up). Apparently with the expansion of their social circle in recent years, it makes more sense to head to the larger space.

Ted's home is stately and takes my breath away on first glance. It's all dappled brickwork on a sprawling two-story house that stretches across a giant block of manicured lawn and gardens, with a cobblestone path leading to the giant double front door.

It's the kind of place that looks like it could eat both my apartment and Spencer's house and not make a dent in its available surface space.

"Ted's place is over the top," Spencer tells me, squeezing my hand as we walk the path to the front door, "but he's totally down to earth, I promise."

I can only bob my head, my heart hammering against my rib cage. I don't belong in a place like this.

As it is, I'm already afraid I'm going to be too weird to fit in. I don't have friends of my own, and social situations terrify me.

But Spencer has not only met Tanya, he's made an effort to include her in our dinners when she's been off work, and I feel like I owe it to him to at least meet the people he sees as found family.

Plus, I remind myself when Spencer rings the doorbell and butterflies take up residence in my belly, I've met Chance and I liked him. Josh seemed perfectly nice for the two minutes I spoke with him, too. And apparently I've met the others as customers.

I just hope none of them were the mean, yelling kind. That could be awkward.

But I don't think Spencer could be friends with anyone like

that, so I'm sure it's okay.

Right?

The door swings open to reveal a gorgeous person wearing a green dress. They are tall and slim, with smooth, dark skin, sparkling brown eyes and a genuinely welcoming smile.

"Spence," they greet warmly, lunging forward to grab my boyfriend in a hug, "you made it on time, I see." They smirk after the lighthearted jibe, then turn to me, yanking me in for a tight hug, too. "Tony! It's so nice to meet you properly. Spencer's been totally cagey about you in the group chat." They step back and sweep their hand over the glossy timber floors. "Come in, come in. Everyone else is out back." They close the door behind us and start ushering us forward. "We're just waiting on Charlie and Ash, and Cherie and Kate. Charlie and Cherie were caught up doing something work related. I wasn't paying much attention."

This person is a whirlwind of exuberance and it's hard not to immediately like them, even if they have just invaded my personal space. It surprises me that their unexpected hug wasn't too unsettling, and that I find myself instantly comfortable around them. They are just likable. Especially when they stop and smack their own forehead with an open palm. "Shit, where are my manners? I'm Zephyr. I'm Ted's—"

"Tiny dancer," an older man approaches, his lips twitching. I'd guess that he's maybe in his late forties, and quite handsome. He looks familiar to me, with his neatly cut brown hair streaked almost artfully with silver at the temples. He's staring at Zephyr with an indulgent expression. "*Language.*" Then he turns to me and offers his hand to shake, which I do quickly before pressing myself back into Spencer's side. "Ted," he introduces himself, seemingly not bothered by my behavior.

His smile is as calming as Zephyr's. "It's good to meet you again."

Zephyr sighs before I can say anything, responding to Ted's earlier light admonishment, "Sorry, Daddy."

Reflexively, I grip Spencer's hand just a bit tighter at the exchange. I'm excited to see other Daddies and Littles interacting so casually, but it still makes me anxious.

"This is a safe space, angel," Spencer says, as if he's reading my thoughts. "You can call me whatever you're comfortable with." He turns to exchange a quick hug with Ted, complete with back thumping, then nods at Zephyr. "Nice dress, Zee."

On closer inspection it *is* a nice dress. It's cut in one of those 50s swing dress styles, tight in the body and flaring out over their insanely narrow hips, the material no longer than their knees. It has teardrop cutouts around the neckline, and it looks like they are even wearing a petticoat underneath it, with the way it swishes when they move.

Zephyr beams at Spencer and curtsies. "Thanks, Uncle Spence. Daddy bought it for me last week."

Ted tucks an errant strand of thick, dark hair behind Zephyr's ear and smiles softly, "Because you were a good boy and you deserved a treat."

The pair share another look that makes my insides squirm with pleasant warmth. It's obvious —even to me— that they adore each other, and it instantly makes me happier to be around them, as though their bright energy is rubbing off on me.

As Ted and Zephyr continue to talk about Ted spoiling his Boy, we follow the two men through the house, past a formal living room and then into a wide, open living-dining-kitchen space. Beyond that, there are large sliding doors which open out to an outdoor entertainment area and a sparkling blue pool. It's too cold right now to consider swimming, but it looks inviting all the same.

The entertainment area is paved beautifully, and the roof extends over it, making it a usable space in most weather. Ted has a couple of big, square timber outdoor tables pressed together with matching seating for sixteen (it takes me a moment to count all the chairs) arranged around them. There's a large outdoor kitchen with an inbuilt grill off to the left, and professional grade patio heaters, too – the umbrella kind you see outside fancy restaurants.

At the table, there are four other men nursing beers and snacking on chips and dips. I recognize two of them as Chance and Josh, the latter being around my age and built like a linebacker with biceps I don't think I could wrap my hands around if I tried.

The other two are new faces and both seem to be as large as Josh. One is older, with a graying beard and shaggy brown hair liberally streaked with silver. His arms are decorated in darkly inked tattoos and, if he didn't have such warm, green eyes, I'd probably be more intimidated by him. He's the more muscular of the pair. The younger guy, also around Josh's and my age if I had to guess, is stockier, with black hair styled into a coif and a squared, clean-shaven jawline.

Spencer's hand finds the small of my back and he gently nudges me closer to the table, making introductions.

"Tony, this is Matt," he gestures to the guy who looks like he'd be right at home in a biker den, then at the younger guy, "and his Daddy, London."

Say what now?

My surprise must show on my face because both men

chuckle at me.

"Yeah," says the older one. *Matt*, I remind myself, determined to remember their names. "We get that reaction a lot." He snuggles into London's side, and I watch as London smooths his hand up and down Matt's thick arm during the sideways hug. It's such a comforting gesture; both to Matt physically and for me to see. "But it works for us."

I press in closer to Spencer's side, offering them a shy smile in return. "Sorry. This is all kinda' new to me. I mean, I read a lot of kinky romance, but never…" I close my eyes and curse myself for babbling.

It's like I have two modes when I'm nervous: shut down or TMI.

The guys don't treat me like the oversharing weirdo I am, though. Instead, they just roll with my random confession.

"Huh," Josh says, leaning forward from his seat on Matt's other side in what seems to be an earnest expression of curiosity, "I never thought about reading age play stuff."

Chance snorts. "You're friends with Spence and you've never thought about books?"

Josh shrugs. "I guess I'm easily distracted."

"That I'll believe," Ted puts in his two cents' worth, handing Spencer a beer and cocking his head at me. "What would you like to drink, Tony?"

"Uh…" I glance around the table. Everyone's got a beer in hand, except Zephyr, who has taken a seat down the end of the table in front of a cocktail glass containing something that looks fruity in nature. "Um, water? Please?"

Ted doesn't comment on my stammering or the unsure way I asked. He just smiles at me and says, "Coming right up." He juts his chin towards the tables. "Take a seat. Eat some snacks before these guys demolish them."

Josh smirks, looks Ted dead in the eye, and takes a large handful of chips with a decidedly challenging air about him. I giggle, then stop abruptly when I realize it's brought everyone's attention back to me.

"Here," Zephyr says, patting the tabletop in front of the seat to his left. "Come sit with me. Josh can be trouble." The words are chiding, but he says them with a smile.

For his part, Josh just laughs. "This coming from you?" He shoots at Zephyr, shaking his head. "Don't think we haven't seen you get bossy with *your* Daddy."

There's something almost secretive about the smile that curls the corner of Zephyr's lip when he casts his gaze towards Ted. "Daddy likes me bossy."

"Damn straight, kitten," Ted agrees, dropping a kiss to the top of Zephyr's head as he places a cold bottle of water in front of me.

I thank him, but he waves me off and takes the seat on Zephyr's other side. Spencer takes the other one next to me.

For the next little while, conversation flows easily around the table. Even though I know Spencer's friends are curious about me, it's a relief when they don't bombard me with questions. Occasionally, one of the guys will stop to ask my thoughts or opinions, but there's no pressure to give detailed answers.

Spencer slings his arm across my shoulders, and I lean into him while Chance teases him about the book series he's just been signed to narrate.

This is a novel experience for me. I haven't had a friendship circle since...well, since grade school. And even then, I only had one or two friends, an outcast from the very start. But watching Spencer and his friends laugh and joke with each other causes tendrils of hope to unfurl in my belly.

Maybe…maybe one day these guys will be my friends, too. I think I might like that.

Chapter Seventeen – Spencer

Tony seems settled in and comfortable by the time Charlie, Ash, Cherie and Kate arrive at Ted's. I know he was anxious about meeting so many people at once, and I would have been happy to take him home if it proved too overwhelming. I'm still selfishly relieved that he pushed through his nerves, and also incredibly proud of him.

Pre-warned of his anxiety, the guys have been on their best behavior. I didn't expect them to be dicks because they are good people, but they can be a boisterous, nosy bunch, especially all together.

Josh does startle Tony when the remaining members of our little gang arrive, though. He shouts his greeting to his brother and brother-in-law, shoving back his chair in his enthusiasm to bound over and hug them. The chair clatters to the ground, and I rub Tony's arm when he jumps at the unexpected noise.

"Sorry, Tones," Josh says, righting the chair. He gestures towards the group who have just entered and performs a quick round of introductions.

Tony gives the newcomers a shy little wave.

"You're a Little, right?" Ash asks as he pulls up a seat across from me: a far cry from the kid who had a panic attack the first time the guys met him.

Chance once told me that Ash could pass as my little brother, and I don't think he's wrong. Sure, his hair is closer to ringlets where mine is wavier, but we both tend to wear our mops wildly around our heads. He's significantly shorter than me, but has a similar body shape, nonetheless.

Ash is a sweet kid, though. Sensitive and appreciative of the found family we've all built together, but also one of the first people to reach out to anyone he thinks might be lonely or hurting. Considering his past, I can understand why he's so determined to welcome everyone with open arms.

It's funny, but I can kind of see parallels between him and Tony, now that I think of it.

Still, ignoring that, it has been good to see Ash come out of his shell over the past few years. He and Charlie are so good for each other, and their relationship is one I can privately admit to being mildly jealous of.

But now that I've been with Tony for a little while, that jealousy seems to have melted away. I suppose there's no reason to be jealous anymore seeing as I appear to have found my own special connection with someone.

"Asher," Charlie warns his husband with a hint of a sigh, "we talked about this. You can't just ask him—"

"It's fine," Tony interjects, though he does lean closer into me while he smiles timidly at the newcomers. His face is turning pink again now that he's noticed that everyone's attention is on him. "I…I *am* a Little. It's very new, but it feels right."

Ash, bless him, bounces excitedly in his seat, then babbles,

"Charlie was my first Daddy, too. I mean, I knew I was into age play before I met him, but I'd never tried with anyone until him. And then it was life changing. Like..." he cranes his neck around to beam at Charlie, "...like having a Daddy was *exactly* what I needed. It completed me." The couple share a quick, sweet kiss before Ash turns back to grin at Tony, holding his left hand up and wiggling his fingers. "And now we're *married*."

Tony's not quite sure what to make of Ash, I can tell. Even though Zephyr's been hovering on the edge of Little space, seeing Ash behaving like a hyperactive child is something else. Ash isn't exactly little right now, but he's closer to that than big. Just as I did with Emma, Charlie has always advocated for Ash to be fluid in his headspaces, and the rest of our group are more than happy to support that and go with the flow. Never knowing which version of Ash we're going to get is highly entertaining.

"That's awesome," Tony replies after only a slight hesitation. "How'd you meet?"

Charlie and Ash exchange glances before Ash nods at his husband and turns back to Tony. His smile is dimmed slightly, and he comes back into an adult headspace as he replies, "My Dad found my stash of Little stuff and kicked me out. Josh found me trying to live on the college campus while I looked for a new place, worked out I was a Little, and brought me to Charlie instead of a shelter."

"I'm so sorry," Tony frowns and pulls away from my side, leaning over the table with a hand outstretched towards Ash, surprising me because he's not usually comfortable touching strangers. "It's not the same thing, but my Nonna told me that once I graduated high school, I had to move out. She didn't approve of me being gay. But I had warning, and time to save up money and make a plan. Plus I had Tanya, my sister," he adds by way of explanation, "so I wasn't alone, but I can only imagine how scary your situation must have been."

Ash takes his hand and they share a moment of silence, acknowledging their mutual trauma. My heart breaks for both of them and a quick glance around the table sees my feelings mirrored on the rest of my friends' faces.

Then Ash seems to notice the quiet that has descended and, because he's no stranger to anxiety, immediately perks back up and distracts Tony by asking, "Would you ever wanna have a play date?"

* * *

"Your boy is ten kinds of adorable," Cherie tells me, jerking her chin towards the stretch of yard beside the pool area, where the Littles are having an impromptu romp around the grass.

The get-together has been a success and, with Ash, Zephyr and Katie all slipping easily into their Little personas, Tony took me by surprise by following suit. He's not as little as he gets when we're in private, but he's currently playing tag with the others, squealing and giggling as though he doesn't have a care in the world.

I can't help grinning goofily, my eyes still following Tony as he races away from Zephyr's outstretched hand. "He is, isn't he?"

"He knows he can come by the Center anytime, right?" She asks. "We've got counsellors on staff now, and I'm sure Ash would be more than happy to sit and answer any questions he has about exploring his Little side."

Nodding, I tear my gaze away from my boy so I can smile

at my friend. "You don't have to do PR here, Cher," I tease. "Charlie's not paying you overtime."

Cherie rolls her eyes and tucks an escaping lock of honey-blonde hair behind her ear. "I know you know what we do, but I also know that you want to keep that sweet, innocent creature all wrapped up in cotton wool and bubble wrap, right?"

Oh, she's got my number, for sure. I can't even deny her assessment.

She laughs and pats my shoulder gently. "You're practically radiating 'helicopter Daddy' vibes, Spence. It's cute, but unnecessary around us. You know that, too, right?"

"Yeah," I answer on a sigh, then turn my attention back out to the roughhousing Littles. "But Tony is…he's…" I struggle to find the words and am reminded immediately of my first meeting with Tanya. Of the way she'd called him 'special' and 'sensitive', as though they were bad qualities. I don't want to focus on his differences, or his anxieties about them, so I finish with, "been through a lot, and I'm protective. Sue me."

"There's nothing wrong with that," Cherie assures me gently. "But we're your friends, Spence. This," she gestures widely around Ted's backyard, "is a safe space. For him *and* for you."

I blink, unexpectedly overwhelmed. "I know that. I love you guys. I'm just…"

"You're still in the early stages of your relationship," Ted cuts in, sidling up to Cherie and me as he hands us each a can of pop, "and he's new to the lifestyle, and to relationships in general."

"Exactly," I agree, then frown at him. "Wait. How'd you know that?"

Neither Tony nor I have said anything about his previous relationships, or lack thereof.

Ted shrugs and takes a sip from his beer. He's not driving, so he's still imbibing. "I'm good at reading people," he says.

"He overheard Tony telling Zee and Ash that you're his first boyfriend," Matt says as he also walks over to join our conversation. He looks out towards the lawn and sighs.

"Why aren't you out there rolling around with the others?" I ask him, ignoring Ted's complaints that Matt spoilt his fun while simultaneously musing over how comfortable Tony must have felt to make such a confession. I know his relative inexperience is something he's still embarrassed about, even though I've tried to convince him there's no reason to feel that way.

The bigger, tattooed man looks down at his feet and admits, "I'm not really so great with the tackling and stuff. Running? Sure, no problem. But getting up from the ground is…an effort."

"It's okay, sweetheart," London's at Matt's side in a heartbeat, rubbing the small of his back. They really do make a striking pair, these tall, burly men. "I'm sure they'll exhaust themselves and will want to play something less physically taxing soon."

"Yeah, Katie's not loving climbing back to her feet either," Cherie adds, gesturing to where her girl is proving our point, complaining loudly as she rolls to her knees and then pushes back to her feet from the grass.

"My fat ass can't take much more of this!" Katie yells at the others once she's up and swatting at grass stains on her curvy jean-covered backside, thighs, and knees.

"Katie," Cherie reprimands from the sidelines we have formed, "*language*. And you know how I feel about *that* 'f' word."

"Sorry, Mommy." Kate wields her big, brown eyes and

rounded cheeks to her advantage and we all chuckle as Cherie melts for her wife.

"Keep playing, babe." Cherie turns back to us, her cheeks flushing pink. "Shut up; I know I'm a pushover."

"We all are," London bumps his shoulder into hers. Then he turns back to me. "So. First boyfriend, huh? Does that mean first—"

"That's not for me to say," I cut him off, shaking my head. "You heard him, though: he had a rough start to adulthood. And he's quite introverted."

A loud squeal from my boy undermines my argument, as does the ensuing battle cry as we turn to watch him tear after Ash, declaring his intent to bring the other Little down.

London laughs. "Yeah," he says with liberal sarcasm, "he seems *real* introverted right now."

I watch, transfixed as Tony continues to play loudly with the others. His inhibitions seem to have vanished and I can't quite describe how it makes me feel. Elated, obviously. He's comfortable with my friends and is finding his footing with people like him. But it also makes me a bit sad, too. Because I've never seen him like this before. Even when we're alone, he's still somewhat shy and reserved.

I want him to feel free to be himself *all* the time.

"Don't stress over it," London instructs quietly, and I don't need to ask how he knows what I'm thinking. Even though he's newer to the lifestyle than the other Daddies in our group, and younger as well, he's mature beyond his age and extremely perceptive. And my face has always been expressive. "The more time he spends experimenting with his Little headspace, the more he'll come out of his shell. Right now," he gestures to where Tony has finally caught his prey and is now spinning on his heel to race in the opposite direction, shrieking with glee, "he's got the buffer of other Littles around him. When it's him on his own, he's probably less sure of how to act."

My eyes follow the pack of Littles and my heart picks up pace at the unadulterated joy on Tony's face. I swallow. "He needs more of this, then. More chance to see that his instincts are normal."

"Which he can come to the Center for," Cherie reiterates playfully, unable to let the opportunity escape her, and I groan.

"Or," Ted laughs, "we get together more often. It doesn't have to be the whole group – I know Zeph would love to have a new playmate visit every now and again."

Zephyr's closer to a Middle than a Little, but I appreciate the offer and tell Ted we'd love to come for a playdate.

Matt clears his throat and says, "I'd like that, too. I mean, Tony seems, uh, *littler* than Zephyr. It might be good for him to see diapers and toddler play normalized, too."

Charlie, Josh, and Chance finally wander over from whatever conversation they'd been having quietly around the corner of Ted's outdoor dining table. They'd waved us off earlier citing 'Center business', but I can't say I'm not curious about the secrecy. I'll wheedle it out of Chance later.

"Ash would be good for that," Charlie acknowledges, catching the tail end of Matt's sentence. He grins at me. "Welcome back to diaper life, Spence."

"You're odd, you know that?" I tease him, but he knows I'm kidding. I understand why it's something he values —the trust and vulnerability Ash shows Charlie being an intense turn on for him— but I'll never turn down an opportunity to playfully taunt my friend.

"We're all odd," he shoots back, still grinning. "All the best people are."

With my gaze drifting back over to the lawn, I find that I couldn't argue with him even if I wanted to.

* * *

Unsurprisingly, Tony is on board with the idea of organized play dates. After that initial meeting with the guys, it's like a switch has flipped and he seems ten times more comfortable in his own skin.

Naturally, we talk about it over the following week, and he admits that seeing other adults confidently slipping into Little headspaces did convince him that it was okay to indulge in this newfound kink.

"There's a part of my brain that still says it's abnormal," he adds as we're snuggled together in my bed. Frank is curled up on Tony's belly, purring loudly, and Tony absentmindedly stokes him while he continues to think out loud, "but playing with your friends felt good. And if they can lead functional adult lives *and* be Little, too, why can't I, y'know?"

I press a kiss to his temple. "Exactly," I respond, unable to keep the smile from my face. "Except there's one thing wrong with what you just said."

He turns his head to peer at me questioningly.

I give him a squeeze with the arm currently wrapped under and around him. "They're not just *my* friends. You've been added to the chat, right?" He nods, biting his lip. "Then it's official: you're one of us now, baby. They're your friends, too."

My heart squeezes painfully as he blinks back tears, his mouth forming an 'o' of surprise.

"I've never really had friends," he confesses quietly.

It's not the first time he's said as much, but we've never really discussed it. I haven't wanted to push him. Even now, I don't quite know what to say.

Clearing his throat, Tony looks back down at Frank and extrapolates, "I've never fit in. Even when I was a kid, I was the *weird kid* that the other kids stayed away from. And I get it: I can be overwhelmed socially and I go off the deep end. I have sensory issues where I either freak out or fixate. I'm fussy about food. It takes me a while to process change. I've never..." he licks his lips. "I mean, I know I'm not *normal*. Because I did okay in school, Nonna never had me tested or anything, but I'm pretty sure I'm *some* kind of neurodivergent. Even I'm not so oblivious that I can't see it. I'm just...not quite the same as most people."

Oh, my heart. I want to strangle anyone who has made him feel like his differences are something to be ashamed of. *"Tony..."*

"It's okay. *I'm* okay," he assures me, turning his head back to offer me the ghost of a smile. "But that's because of you, you know. You haven't treated me any differently, even though I *am* so different. Even Tanya's always..." he trails off and shakes his head. "Not that she meant to. But you haven't ever. And that's made it easier for me to finally accept the fact that being weird doesn't have to mean there's something wrong with me."

"Oh, angel," my voice is tight and gruff with emotion. It hurts to hear him admit that he thought there was something wrong with him. "You're not weird. There's nothing wrong with you. You're perfect."

"Even with my, uh, quirks?"

I shake my head, then rush to explain as his face falls, "It's not an 'I love you *even though'* situation, Anthony. Or an 'in spite of' or 'I can live with' or anything like that. It's an 'I love every single part of you'. Your quirks, as you call them, aren't flaws to be overlooked. They are part of what makes you the man I love." I don't know if I'm explaining myself properly, but I forge on regardless. "And the guys like you for who you are, too. They want to be your friends because they like *all* of you. And, no, it's not just because you're my boyfriend, either. If we broke up tomorrow, they'd still want to be your friends." Feeling the need to lift the mood, I tickle his side lightly, relieved to hear the watery giggles the action elicits. "But we're not breaking up. I refuse."

Tony's quiet after that, and I know him well enough now to understand that he needs time to process everything I've just said.

"Did you want to be little for a while?" I suggest, hopeful that being in a Little headspace will help simplify his feelings and make managing everything easier.

Tony considers this and, after a beat, nods. "Please, Daddy."

I climb out of bed and extend my hand towards him. He takes it without hesitation and I smile. "Let's go get you changed, huh?"

* * *

Even though Little space is beneficial for managing Tony's anxiety, I enjoy spending time with him as equals, too. The more he comes out of his shell, the deeper in love with him I fall. He's clever, witty and amusing. He's sweet and considerate, cheeky and creative. Even while big, he makes it clear that he likes it when I make the decisions for us, when I take charge and take care of him.

Today is one of those days. He's still setting the pace for any sexual interactions, but I've made the decisions relating to our date.

We're going bowling.

Tony's not into sports, and a movie wouldn't give us much chance to talk or interact. But bowling is indoors, we'll get a private lane, and my plan is to order us some hot dogs and fries from the kiosk at the alley. It's casual, low pressure, and fun.

When I park the car outside the alley, Tony grins at me. "Oh, you've made a terrible mistake, Spencer," he says wickedly.

I love this side of him, when he feels free enough to be a bit silly and cheeky. I quirk an eyebrow, "Oh, really?"

"Trust me. You're going down."

I laugh as he says it but, twenty minutes later, he's thoroughly wiping the floor with me. He's not playing a perfect game, but my boy can bowl better than anyone I know. With a handful of strikes, a couple of spares, and a few stray sevens and eights, Tony has definitely lived up to his earlier playful trash talking.

"Where'd you learn to bowl like this?" I ask him as I line up for my third to last turn for this game.

I wriggle my hips, earning myself an amused laugh from behind me, and then take two quick steps, swing the ball at my side and release it down the middle of the lane with force. It hits the polished timber with a crack, then hurtles towards the pins...before wobbling at the end and curving towards the gutter with only a few inches to spare.

Fuck you, gutter ball. I glare at the ten pins that still stand tall and proud, mocking me.

I turn to find Tony trying to hide his amusement behind his

hand. When I raise both eyebrows at him, he snickers, then elects to answer my question, "It was the one sport I actually enjoyed when I was growing up. It's an indoor sport, it's non-contact, it's small teams, and it doesn't involve running or hitting things. So, this is what I played to pass PE. Got pretty good at it."

I look up at the screen displaying our scores and nod. "I'll say."

He turns a little shy. "I can give you some pointers if you like?"

"I'd love that, sweetheart."

I want him to know that our relationship isn't a one way street. I'm only human: I can learn from him, too. Even if it is something as simple as improving my non-existent bowling skills.

My ball has returned, so Tony steps up to the lane with me. He shows me where I've been going wrong, twisting my wrist as the ball releases from my grip. He also suggests that I try a lighter ball to make the swing and release motion easier. After pretending for a few swings, he gets me to try for my spare.

I knock down nine pins.

We cheer and embrace like I've won a championship game, and I lose a little bit more of my heart to this beautiful man.

It's probably the best date I've ever been on.

* * *

"...Daddy?"

Tony's soft question comes as I'm changing him after another post-shift wind-down spent in Little space. Though he hadn't been in tears when I picked him up tonight, it was obvious he was still agitated after another rough day at work. Being Little really does seem to help relax him, though, and I adore these moments together as much as I love our adult dates.

"Hmm?" I ask him, fastening the tabs on his fresh diaper. He asked me earlier to prolong the experience, and I had no reason to deny him. I really am coming to enjoy change time almost as much as Charlie does, not that I'll ever tell my friend how right he is. There's no need to inflate his ego.

Tony sucks on his lower lip before he starts to babble, stuck somewhere between headspaces as he tries to communicate what he needs, "Can…um, can you please read to me tonight? A bedtime story? I don't mind if it's grown up or for Littles, but…um, usually when I'm stressed, I listen to books —listen to *you*— and I just 'membered that I've got the real thing now, not just the nice voice, and it's okay if you don't wanna, 'cos I know you spend all day reading for work, but—"

"Baby, breathe," I chuckle and bend forward to kiss the exposed flesh of his belly, grinning against his golden skin when he giggles. "Of course I'll read to you. I'd love to read a bedtime story to my boy."

In fact, why haven't either of us thought to do this yet? I knew he enjoyed my narration, obviously. And is there anything more comforting than cuddles and bedtime stories?

His big, brown eyes glimmer and his voice cracks as he asks, "Really?"

"Oh, angel," I pull him up into a seated position so I can wrap my arms around him, heedless of the fact that he's only half-dressed. He tucks his face into the crook of my neck and I kiss the side of his head. "I will read to you every single day if you want me to. Twice on Sundays, even. No, *three* times."

My ridiculousness is rewarded by another giggle, even though it's a watery sound. I squeeze him tight. "I'm sorry I haven't done it yet. I know you like my reading voices. And, let me tell you, I do *all* the character voices."

He pulls back and gives me an exaggeratedly solemn nod, his eyes thankfully mirthful again. The tension bleeds back out of him as I watch him slowly settle back into his Little space again. "I didn't 'spect anything less, Daddy."

"Cheeky," I admonish lightly, my heart fluttering at the grin on his face. "Come on," I guide him to lay back down, "We'll get you dressed, and then we're getting a bottle, choosing a book, and going to bed."

And that's what we do. Frank follows us back up the stairs once I've got Tony's warm bottle in hand, and then we choose a book (well, we choose *two* books, because I'm a pushover when it comes to getting the puppy eyes from my boy) and head into my bedroom.

While I'd usually hold him in a nursing position to give him his bottle, that's not going to be conducive to reading, so instead I prop myself up against the headboard and have him snuggle in beside me, holding his own bottle so I can wrap one arm around him and hold our first book with the other. Turning pages will be tricky, but years of being a Daddy have helped me perfect the art.

With only the dim light of the bedside table illuminating the pages, and Frank's fat furry butt squished in the sliver of space between Tony's legs and my own, I start to read.

Tony chose a story about a puppy who gets separated from his Mommy at the grocery store and encounters all sorts of other animal characters on his journey to find her. As promised, I deliver all the voices differently —a deep growly voice for the bear, a high pitched voice for the mouse, a nasal voice for the frog, and so on— and Tony giggles around the teat in his mouth with each one. When the puppy finally finds his Mommy, Tony's finished the bottle and his eyes are drooping as he continues to suck in air.

"Hey now," I pull the bottle away and he whines in complaint, much to my secret amusement, "that'll upset your tummy. Use your binky, baby."

His pacifier is attached to the collar of his onesie via a saver chain, and he grabs for it blindly, sighing once he's popped it past his perfect plump lips. "Next book, Daddy," he demands sleepily around the silicone in his mouth.

I grin, reply, "Yes, sir," and settle in for round two.

He's asleep before we make it past the third page, and I'm struck by the thought that I want this *all the time*. I want it so badly I can almost taste it.

Well. Damn.

That happened a lot sooner than I thought it would.

I guess we'll be talking about living arrangements sooner rather than later, if my heart has anything to say about it. I just hope that he's on the same page.

I know it's fast, but I love Tony more than I can properly express, and I want to experience moments like this one every day for the rest of our lives.

Chapter Eighteen — Tony

Life seems to feel easier after I tell Spencer that I know I'm not neurotypical. It was a fear I'd kept bottled up inside me for so long —for what feels like my whole adult life— and, once I told him, I felt lighter. Even though I don't have an official label for my differences, admitting that I think I might be neurodivergent has been liberating. Almost like coming out of the closet had felt. Like being little feels.

I mean, don't get me wrong. I don't know it for certain, and I don't think I need a diagnosis at this point in my life, but just saying the words out loud helped. Admitting that I've Googled symptoms and signs and have silently ticked a lot of the boxes to myself was a relief. Like there's a reason I'm the way I am, other than just being weird, and that I'm not the only person like this out there.

Beyond that, though, I meant what I told Spencer: he genuinely doesn't treat me any differently even though he knows that I react strangely to certain situations or need extra time to wrap my head around things. Even Tanya gets frustrated with me or expects me to be able to handle change or social situations more easily than I do, but he never seems to.

And he doesn't push me to try to fit in, either. None of his friends do. Not in the group chat, nor in the play dates we have over the weeks that follow that first get-together at Uncle Ted's.

(Yeah, I'm calling him 'Uncle Ted' now. He insisted, and the expression on Spencer's —on *Daddy's*— face made it almost impossible to resist. Plus, that's what Ash calls him, so it caught on pretty quickly.)

I guess I'm feeling much more comfortable with being myself. As an adult out in the world, as someone's boyfriend, and as someone's Boy, too. That's not to say it's all been perfect, though. There are still some things that suck. The biggest of which is my job.

I hate it.

I know I need to work, but the feeling of dread which curdles in my gut before every shift is getting harder and harder to ignore.

I know Daddy can tell. He's been asking me about my options. What would I like to do for work if I had a choice? If I didn't have to worry about making rent every week —if I closed my eyes and just imagined myself doing something I was actually interested in— what would it be?

I brush his gentle questions off, but I know the answer. I've always known.

I want to write.

Even before I graduated high school, I wanted to be a writer. I wanted to go to college and take creative writing classes. I wanted to learn and better my hobby (one I haven't indulged in in years now) in the hopes that maybe one day I could turn it into a career.

It would be perfect for me, really. I could work from home and on my own schedule. I wouldn't have to interact face-to-face with people. I could immerse myself in my fantasies and put them to paper. Escapism and earnings all in one!

But all that went to hell when Nonna told me I'd have to make it on my own. I stopped writing, the words drying up inside me. Even though my hobby was my best method of escapism, I couldn't make my brain cooperate anymore. Nobody would want to read anything I'd created anyway. I was worthless and weird even to my own family. Why would strangers be interested?

So I stuck with reading and with listening to other people's stories for my escape from reality, and that was good enough for me.

But now the itch is building beneath my skin again. The urge to pick up a pen and pretty notebook and scribble away crafting worlds and characters and storylines calls to me again.

It's scary to even admit it to myself, let alone out loud to another person. Even to Daddy.

I know he'd be supportive. I know he'd probably even be excited. He loves books and the creative arts, after all.

But I'm too afraid that I'll try to write and that I'll fail. That the words won't come. That I'll wind up with half-finished narratives and one-dimensional characters. That people won't like it.

That *Daddy* won't like it.

I think I could ignore bad reviews from strangers. I wouldn't have to read them at all if I didn't want to. But I couldn't ignore Daddy's feedback. And if he didn't like my writing, it would probably break me.

Still, I can't help daydreaming about it. About quitting my shitty job and writing for a living. It's a fantasy that gets me through the hardest shifts, when the customers are awful and my boss is being his dickiest. I imagine books with my name on the cover. I imagine the sorts of things I'd write about.

I imagine Daddy wanting to narrate them for me.

But that's a pipe dream. I'd have to work up the courage to tell him I used to enjoy writing, first. Then I'd actually need to write something *and* be okay with letting someone else read it.

I don't think that's ever going to happen. So, I'll just have to suck it up and deal with the fact that my life is almost perfect except for my job. That's the same for a lot of people. In fact, I know I'm better off than a lot of people. I'm definitely better off now than I was even three months ago, that's for sure.

And that takes me right back to where my thoughts started: being with Spencer is the best thing that's ever happened to me.

"Wakey wakey, Tones," Zephyr is smiling knowingly at me, and I blush when I realize I've been zoned out during our play date. Most of the gang has assembled at Asher and Charlie's house today, and I have to admit that I genuinely feel like part of the group now. "We're gonna play with Ash's train set. You wanna join in?"

"Yeah!" I clap my hands together and follow Zephyr over to where Ash and Matty are setting up the train.

I kneel on the carpeted floor of Ash's living room and rest my diapered butt on my bare heels. Today's the first time I've had the balls to wear a diaper and onesie in front of anyone other than Daddy, but nobody has said anything. In fact, both Ash and Matt appear equally padded and more than comfortable with it, too.

"Do you wanna press the button?" Ash asks me when the track is all connected and the train is all ready to go.

I blink at him. "Really? You don't wanna?"

"I can play with it whenever," he shrugs, his curly hair bouncing around his head as he moves. "You should have a turn."

After glancing at the two other boys to be sure they don't mind me getting the all-important job, I lean over and press the button on the console attached to the tracks and feel a jolt of excitement when the train lights up, makes a *choo-choo* sound and then starts clickety-clacking around the large figure eight track.

Ash, Zephyr and Matt cheer, and we all watch as the little locomotive heads over the archway bridge at the center of the eight shape, crossing over the returning track beneath it. I'm looking forward to seeing the train curl around the bend and loop back underneath the bridge. I applaud when it does exactly that.

"If that's not the cutest thing I've ever seen, I'll eat my hat," I hear Daddy say from somewhere behind us, his voice sounding all warm and soft.

"You're not wearing a hat," London's voice jokes, then also adopts the same tone as Daddy's. "But, yeah, it is. I'm starting to believe that there's no limit on the cuteness factor."

"There's not," Charlie's voice agrees. Then he steps into my peripheral vision and bends down to press a kiss on the top of Ash's head. "You haven't been potty in a while," he says, casually as you please, "need to go? Or is today a diaper day?"

I can feel my cheeks burning, but Ash just giggles and

answers, "Potty please, Daddy."

Matty looks at me, then up at his daddy and says, "Me too, Daddy."

Thankfully, Daddy doesn't ask me or get me to join the conversation. I haven't gotten little enough that I've wet without conscious thought, and I don't think I'll ever be comfortable enough for that around these guys. But, then again, a few short months ago, I never would have thought I'd be comfortable enough to even wear a diaper in front of other people, either, nor that I would even want to.

As Charlie and London wander off with Ash and Matt respectively, I let Daddy help me to my feet. He gives me a cuddle and asks me if I've been having fun, and I answer in the affirmative.

"I'm gonna go potty, too," Zephyr declares apropos of nothing, before he flounces out of the room with his dress and petticoat swishing around his thighs. His Little age seems to be older than Ash and Matt's are, so he doesn't seek out his daddy before he disappears down the hallway that leads towards the laundry and downstairs powder room.

Now that I'm alone with Daddy, I squirm. "Daddy," I finally admit in what probably amounts to a stage whisper, "I gotta go, too."

His lips quirk upwards and he kisses my forehead, the picture of doting patience. "Diaper or potty?"

"Potty."

Daddy reaches out and takes my hand, smiling wide. "Good boy," he lauds, then starts leading me through the house.

With his praise warming me from the inside, my thoughts circle back to how happy I am to have found this wonderful man, and how lucky I am to be with him.

And even though I'm not ready to use a diaper in front of our friends, or tell him that I want to be a writer, I'm suddenly aware that there is still something I am ready to share with him.

* * *

"Spence?"

"Hmm?"

We're nestled together on Spencer's couch, *The Great British Bake Off* playing on the TV in front of us. After coming home from the play date at Charlie and Asher's house, Daddy gave me a bath, helped dress me in my adult clothes, then made us a light dinner of grilled cheese sandwiches and tomato soup.

Frank was not impressed by our choice of meal and has been sulking on the end of the couch ever since.

I love that cat.

But I refuse to let myself get distracted by the cute kitty. I'm on a mission tonight. One that hasn't left my thoughts since this afternoon.

"Can we…I mean, would you…" I start and stop, frustrated at myself for not knowing how to ask for what I want.

Spencer lifts the remote and pauses the show, managing to freeze it on Paul Hollywood's intense, steely gaze.

I can't let myself get distracted by that, either.

Focus, Tony.

Taking a deep breathe, I toy with the collar of his shirt and blurt, "Will you fuck me?"

Spencer seems to choke on air. "What?" He twists in his seat, gently pushing me to sit up so he can look me in the eye. "Where'd that come from?"

185

I can't really explain the whole thought process, so I just bite my lip, shrug, and answer, "I've been thinking about it. A lot. And you said I was setting the pace and I just wanted you to know that I'm ready. If…I mean, if it's something you want to do."

It's not like I haven't enjoyed our sex life as it stands. We frot, we mutually masturbate, we suck each other off (and having Spencer in my mouth for the first time was a fucking revelation on its own!) and he fucks me between my legs and teases my ass…but I *do* want to try anal.

I know it's not the be all and end all, that you can have a perfectly fulfilling relationship without penetrative sex, but I want to do it at least once. Plus, I've experimented a bit with toys and I've liked that, so I can't imagine I'll hate having Daddy inside me.

"If it's something I want to do," Spencer repeats with a disbelieving chuckle, shaking his head. He picks up my hand and kisses the back of my knuckles. "Angel, I want to do *everything* with you."

My heart rate picks up, anticipation already bubbling in my belly. "Yeah?" I ask, and I can't keep the excitement from my voice.

"Yeah," Spencer answers, his own voice turning low and husky.

I practically leap into his lap, fusing our mouths together. His hands grip my hips and, while we kiss, we grind against each other in movements that are now incredibly familiar to me. Despite the layers of fabric between us, I can feel his cock swelling against mine. I groan, imagining what it will feel like inside me.

"Let's take this upstairs, hmm?" he suggests when we part

for air, and I nod enthusiastically.

We shed our clothes along the way, and we're both blessedly naked when we fall into his bed together, unable to keep our hands off each other. My cock is steadily leaking precum and it slides against Spencer's skin as we rub our bodies together. It seems crazy to me that I've gone from shy, fumbling virgin to this in only a few months' time.

I whine when Spencer rolls away to rummage through his bedside table drawer, then gasp when he shows me what he grabbed.

"Daddy, what…?"

Spencer smirks at me as he holds the dildo out for my inspection. It's similar to the one I have at home, made of flesh-toned silicon that's supposed to feel like real skin, velvety and sort of spongey. This one looks a bit longer and thicker than the one I own, but still not as big as Spencer's real cock.

"I was thinking we could start with this," he explains, "and go from there?"

We've talked about playing with toys together before but haven't gotten around to it. My dick jumps at the mere suggestion. "I'd like that," I tell him and recline back on the pillows.

"Good boy," he praises and then crawls back over me. I can feel the bottle of lube and the dildo rolling down the dip in the mattress and into my side as we kiss and rub against one another some more, the plastic of each item feeling cool against my heated skin.

When I'm writhing under him, Spencer pulls back and picks the bottle of lube up. "Traffic light?" he asks.

"Green," I answer without needing to think. "Green, green, *green*."

He chuckles and pops the cap, then drizzles a healthy amount onto his fingers. But he waits until after we're kissing again before he brings those slippery digits to my hole. I gasp into his mouth at the almost unexpected sensation of him sliding one and then two inside, pumping and twisting them slowly. His touch feels so new and different to the times I've done this to myself.

I close my eyes and relax against the gentle intrusion, enjoying the feeling of him working me open so carefully. He takes his time and I appreciate it, barely even noticing when two fingers become three.

Spencer's muttered praises help distract me further. "That's it. Good boy. You feel so good around my fingers, angel. So hot and tight."

"Daddy," I whine, undulating my hips, "Daddy, I need *more*. Please."

"Can you show Daddy how you play with yourself at home?"

I almost come from the question alone. "Y-yes," I stammer, trying to form actual words instead of incoherent sounds. "I...yes, Daddy."

He groans appreciatively and steals another deep, delicious, probing kiss. "Good boy, Anthony."

Then he presses the pre-slicked dildo into my hand and guides it down to my ass. I whimper as he removes his fingers, and my hand trembles as I push the bulbous head of the toy past the loosened rim of muscles. With my eyes closed, I can't see Spencer's expression, but I can hear the *snick* of the bottle of lube again, and then his light moans and murmurings as I sink the toy inside me, enjoying the burn of the additional girth.

"Oh, fuck, *Tony*," he says in a strangled voice, and I force myself to open my eyes.

I'm so glad that I do, because he's stroking his cock while he watches me languidly fuck myself with the toy, and it's the hottest thing I've seen yet.

I adjust the angle of the dildo and plant my feet on the mattress so I can arch my back and then: *"Yes, fuck, there!"* I cry out, having managed to stimulate my prostate. I repeat the movement and see stars, my cock dribbling the evidence of how much I'm enjoying this down my shaft and onto my stomach, neglected but still close to the edge.

"D-Daddy," I pant, increasing the speed of the thrusts of the toy, "Sp-Spencer…"

I want to pull the toy out and beg for his cock, but I can't find the words or the willpower to do so. Even though I so badly want him to fuck me, I'm so close as it is. I whine with the indecision.

"It's okay, angel. I've got you." Spencer stills my hand and helps pull the toy from my body, then settles between my spread thighs. "Traffic light?"

"Fucking green, Spencer," I all but cry, missing the feeling of being filled. "Fuck me. Please. Please, Daddy, just…*ohh*…"

He doesn't *look* that much bigger than the dildo, but he definitely feels a lot bigger.

"Breathe and bear down, angel. That's it," he instructs in a low, soothing voice, his lips brushing my ear. "Good boy, good boy…*fuck*, you're so tight."

I can't describe quite what I'm feeling, but the initial pain of being stretched further than I'm used to achieving with only my toys begins to give way to pleasure. I feel stuffed full of Spencer and imagine I can feel the heat of his hot, hard cock pulsing inside me.

I'm so glad that I'd previously told him I wanted to do this bare. The feeling of flesh inside flesh is so damn good. A condom would have felt too…plastic, I guess. And with me being a virgin before being with Spencer, and him testing negative for STIs, we were both happy to go without prophylactics. I don't know how I'll handle the sensory aspect of his cum inside me, but if it turns out I hate it, he can pull out next time or something. (But I haven't hated the feel of his cum anywhere else on my body yet, so I don't think it'll be a problem.)

Spencer bottoms out and stays still, giving me time to adjust even though I can see him quivering with the effort of not moving, his arms braced on either side of my head kind of like he's going to do pushups.

"Are you okay?" he asks quietly, his eyes searching mine for any sign of discomfort.

I lift my head up from the pillow to nuzzle our noses together affectionately. "Better than okay," I assure him, then kiss his lips lightly. "You can move."

He starts off slow, dragging his cock out of me at an even more glacial pace than when he slid in. He pulls almost the entire way out, the head of his cock catching on my rim and making me gasp, before he glides back inside again.

Spencer picks up the pace after a few more movements, shifting his weight on his arms and the angle of his thrusts. He grazes my prostate and I cry out as intense jolts of pleasure spark from inside me, travelling up my spine and through my extremities. Then he repeats the movement. Over and over and over again.

"Sp-Da-*ungh*," I moan incoherently, each deep, forceful thrust of his cock pushing the breath from my lungs, making it difficult for me to form words or think straight. I'm teetering right on the edge of coming, the pleasure inside me having built up to a tension I'm intimately familiar with now, coiled tight and desperate to snap.

"Touch yourself, baby," Spencer demands, his voice deep and breathy all at once. I open my eyes and look up at him, my breath hitching at how dark his eyes have gotten, at how intense his own expression is. He captures my mouth in a deep, rough kiss, then pulls back to say, "I'm close. Need you to come first, honey."

How he can look so debauched and animalistic and then call me 'honey' so sweetly, I'll never know.

I reluctantly pull one of my hands —which had been gripping his hips for dear life— away and wrap it around my aching, leaking dick.

"D-Daddy," I whine without conscious thought, the sound ripped from me as the touch to my cock sends me flying over the precipice of my orgasm, ropes of cum shooting between our sweaty bodies. Some lands on my chest and splatters up near my chin. More shots find their way to Spencer's stomach and chest above me. I close my eyes again and whimper *"Daddy"* with every spurt that leaves my body. *"Daddy, daddy, daddy..."*

"Good boy," he pants above me, and I feel his lips meet the fevered flesh of my forehead, even while his hips continue to rock into me. "You're such a good boy, sweetheart. Fuck, look at you. God, Tony. *Tony.* I'm gonna come."

"Yes," I arch my back for him. "Come. Come inside me, Daddy. Do it. Please. Fill me up." I don't know where the actual fuck that comes from, but it seems to be the right thing to say in the moment, because Spencer shouts and swears and, with one final thrust into me, stills as his cock pulses and jerks

with his release.

He's careful not to squash me as he lowers himself down on top of me, pressing sloppy kisses over my collarbone and neck and mouth. I can taste my cum on his tongue and belatedly realize that he'd been lapping up some of the mess I made only a minute or so ago.

"I love you," he says when we part for air, nuzzling the side of my face with his.

"I love you, too," I sigh.

Yes, I think to myself, following Daddy's instructions to relax while he pulls out and heads towards the bathroom to grab a washcloth, *life's pretty much perfect.*

Now I can only hope that work gets better and then everything *will* be perfect.

* * *

"Sir," I step up to the truck driver who has been berating our newest hire, Steph, loudly for the last minute, "I'm happy to try to resolve this for you, but I'm going to have to ask you to calm down."

He's a beefy older man with an epic beer gut and dirty gray stubble. His plaid overshirt is faded and the white t-shirt beneath it is discolored. I want to recoil from just the sight of him, let alone how loud he's being, but poor Steph is in tears behind me, and fucking Gerald is cowering in the kitchen, letting the 'front of house' deal with it.

"I'm the customer here," he bellows at me, "which means I'm right! Didn't nobody ever teach you that the customer is always right?"

I can't bring myself to look him in the eye, so I fixate on a spot just above his right ear. It's a tactic I rely on a lot in this job.

"I didn't say you weren't, sir," I can feel myself shaking with the escalating confrontation, and I am doing everything I can to keep myself together.

In the back of my head, a little voice has started up, telling me I need my Daddy, and I know I can't give in to it. It would be perfect to escape into my Little headspace, and also disastrous to do it here.

I don't even know what this guy's problem is, but we're a packed house tonight, on account of it being Littles' Night at The Grove again, and I can feel the eyes of all the other patrons in the diner zeroing in on us.

Maybe that's also part of why I'm feeling the compulsion to escape into my Little headspace. There are other Littles here. And Daddies. If they knew I was one of them, maybe they'd help me?

But I can't involve other customers in this. I just need to fix whatever this guy's issue is and then move on with the rest of what promises to be a long, stressful shift.

Not for the first time, I wish I could have taken the night off and gone to The Grove with Spencer. I know Ash and Charlie are going tonight. And Ted and Zephyr, too. Despite my nerves about being little in a more public setting, Zephyr and Ash assured me that The Grove's Playroom is a safe space that I will love. If I can ever get there.

But I had to work. And so did Spencer. So it was not meant to be.

"—you even listening to me, retard?"

It's like the world grinds to a halt at the guy's words, yelled as they are above the general din of a packed house. The whole diner goes silent, and I feel a lump clog in my throat.

"Sir," I try to sound unaffected, but my heart is hammering and my face is burning, and years of childhood taunts are echoing in my brain. I half expect the other diners to get up and start chanting it. "I'll ask you kindly to not use i-inflammatory and d-derogatory language like that, please."

Great. I'm stammering now. I've done so well over the last few months. Everyone's said so. Even though there was nothing wrong with me, even I've felt good about being more confident in social settings. But this is undoing all of that.

"*D-d-derogatory*," the truck driver mocks, laughing cruelly. "Can't you use real words?"

"S-sir," I know that my shaking is visible now, and the wobble in my voice gives away how close I am to breaking. "I'm s-sorry, but I'm g-going to h-have to ask you to l-leave." I turn to Steph for backup, but she's no longer behind me.

In fact, with a sinking feeling, I realize I've been left completely alone out here.

The grin on the big guy's face when he sees me realize this is terrifying.

I try to console myself with the fact that it's a packed house tonight. There are plenty of witnesses. This guy won't get physical. He won't.

"I'm not goin' nowhere," he says.

I can't even remember what his initial complaint was at this point. All I know is I need him gone.

"L-look, sir, your b-bill's comped, okay? J-just…head on out, all right?"

But he doesn't do that. Instead he steps out of his booth and towards me, shaking his head. Then he reaches out and bunches his meaty fists into my shirt, and it's all I can do to not wet myself in fear. "We're not done talking."

"Yes, actually, I think you'll find you are. Now, let him go." Ted's familiar voice is firm as he steps up beside me, forcibly removing the guy's hold on my clothes, and I fight back a sob. I don't know when he got here or how much he's seen, but the relief of having someone on my side —someone I know, someone *safe*— rushes through me and makes my knees go weak.

"It's okay," Charlie also steps up to my other side and wraps an arm around me as though to keep me upright, "I've got you." He pulls me away from where Ted is now arguing with the customer. My customer. My responsibility.

I shake my head, protesting even while I know that the only thing preventing me from collapsing right now is his strength. "I…I can't…I'm at work…I…I have to…"

"You have to go out back and sit down before you have a real panic attack," Ash says, coming to support my other side. If anyone can speak from experience, it's him. We've spoken about our similar traumas a few times now, and I'm still in awe that this confident, attractive guy used to feel a lot like I do. "Come on, Uncle Ted will deal with this guy. He put his hands on you, so he's not getting anywhere near you again."

There's blustering from the angry customer, but Ash and Charlie pull me away. Charlie says something to Ted about calling Josh, and Ash says something about calling Spencer or Tanya, but I'm not paying a lot of attention. I'm too busy trying to hold it together while I'm paraded past tables full of people.

People who have seen me struggle to make eye contact. Who have witnessed me gesture wildly with my hands when I'm flustered. People who saw me stammer and almost cry because some other customer got in my face.

People probably thinking that I'm weak and stupid and pathetic.

These thoughts build and fester as we round the counter and head towards the swinging door.

"What the fuck?" Gerald demands. "You can't be back here."

"If I were you, I'd be more concerned about the fact that you left him alone out there with about a hundred hungry people and one major asshole who *just assaulted him*," Ash snaps back.

"What? So there's nobody out there? Fuck's sake, Russo, get your shit together and man up."

I don't know why, but it's that demand that finally breaks me.

Maybe it's the complete disregard for the fact that a customer reached out and grabbed me with god-only-knows what kind of malicious intent. Maybe the guy just wanted to hold me still while he yelled at me? Maybe he planned on roughing me up a bit? I don't know, and I honestly don't care. An angry man twice my size had his hands on me, and my boss only cares about work? Or maybe it's the raised voice accompanying the instruction to 'man up'. Or some combination of all of it and then some.

Either way, I break, and I break hard.

Through sobs and hyperventilation, the only thing I can think to say —to repeat— is "I want Daddy."

Chapter Nineteen – Spencer

"Y our phone keeps going off out here," Jake, the audio producer I've been working with for the last couple of days tells me as I wrap up a scene. "Like, non-stop for the last five minutes."

I frown and pull off my headphones, already making my way out of the booth. "You couldn't have said something a couple of minutes ago?" I ask him, trying not to sound too frustrated.

He shrugs and rolls his eyes, reminding me why I generally try to avoid working with him. "You were two minutes off finishing the scene. I didn't think two minutes could hurt."

Not wanting to fight with him over the whole concept of emergencies in general, I grab my phone from the desk beside his panel and frown at the number of missed calls. They're from Ted. And Josh.

And Tanya.

My heart plummets into my stomach.

I dial Tanya back immediately.

"What happened?" I ask as soon as she answers, already reaching under Jake's desk for my satchel and rummaging for my keys.

"It's a long story," she tells me, and she sounds exhausted.

"Summarize it." Given how she sounds, I should probably have tried to be a little less gruff. But *obviously* there's something wrong with Tony and I'm worried, damn it.

She launches into a quick recap of what she knows about an altercation at the diner. When she gets to the part where the guy put his hands on my boy, I struggle to maintain my calm. "His new friends —*your* friends— were there," she says while I clench my keys so tightly that I can feel them drawing blood in my palm, "turned up only a few seconds before the guy grabbed him. If they'd been any later…" Tanya sounds pained, and I can empathize. I don't want to think of the possibility of a customer getting violent with Tony. Not now, not ever.

"Is he okay? Where is he?"

Jake's scowling at me, but I'm not really paying attention to him.

Tanya's answer is more important.

"He's…" She begins tentatively, then exhales, and I swear my heart stops for a moment, "I mean, physically he's fine," I release the breath I was holding while she continues, "but he had some kind of anxiety attack and…"

"And?" I prompt.

"He's…" She pauses. "He keeps crying for you. I can't…" She exhales again, frustration bleeding into her tone. "Honestly, Spencer, I don't know what to do here. I've never seen him like this."

"Shit," I mutter, then, apologetically, I offer, "I'll be there soon."

She makes a non-committal sound and I can't help the guilt that creeps up my spine and curls tendrils around my stomach. Tanya has been trying really hard to understand and even participate in Tony's age play, but panic-induced regression sucks for everyone. I imagine seeing her brother like that is jarring, and I know that I'm responsible for bringing out his Little side. For encouraging it. Even if I firmly believe that Tony would have eventually discovered Age Play on his own had we never met, it didn't happen that way and I'm sure that's what Tanya's thinking, too.

From somewhere on Tanya's end of the line, I can hear the rumblings of other people talking, then they get louder as she gets closer to them, or they get closer to her, or whatever. I can recognize the voices, or at least some of them, and it calms me a bit to know that some of the guys are there.

"Is that Charlie?" I ask, "Can I talk to him?"

Tanya doesn't say anything, but I can hear the distinct sounds of the phone being passed to someone else and then Charlie's deep voice is in my ear. "Are you going to be able to make it down here?" he asks me. "Josh is currently taking witness statements, but they need to talk to Tony and he's nowhere near calm enough —or big enough— for that right now. And," he lowers his voice, "man, this boss of his…" Charlie trails off and I can imagine him pinning me with those sharp blue eyes of his. "He can't come back here, you know that, right?"

I'm nodding even though he can't see me. I knew Tony was unhappy with his job, but with Charlie saying the boss is bad news, I'm assuming it's even worse than Tony was willing to let on. "We'll find him something else," I eventually answer. Then I add, "And I am coming. I'll be there in twenty. Oh, and Charlie? Thank you."

"Shut up," he says lightly, "you'd have stepped in for Ash, too."

He's not wrong. Any one of us would step in to help our friends.

Hell, most of us would probably help a stranger in that sort of situation, too.

Jake protests when I hang up and sling my bag over my shoulder, but I glare at him and point at the clock above the window to the booth. "We would have stopped in half an hour anyway. Give me a break. This is an emergency. I'll be back tomorrow. Maybe. I don't know. I'll call."

I don't give him any chance to respond as I turn and race out of the studio and towards the car park.

* * *

The diner is a flurry of activity when I arrive. I bypass the tables of people eating and talking and rubbernecking in the direction of the uniforms. I head directly to the cops, recognizing them both with a relieved sigh.

Josh and Max, Charlie's former partner, both turn to face me as I approach, the latter nodding his blonde head at me before he turns back to the waitress in front of him, his notepad at the ready. I can't help but notice the waitress's red-rimmed eyes. Before I can say anything, Josh steps towards me and puts his big, broad palm on my back, guiding me around the counter and towards the kitchen and back end of the diner.

"The guy's in custody and has been taken in for questioning," Josh tells me quietly as we walk. "From all accounts, he was looking for a fight and Tones stayed calm and professional the whole time. Didn't even break down until he was out back."

I'm not a violent man, but the thought of someone giving my boy a reason to break down at all has my hands clenching into fists at my sides. "What kind of charges can we actually make here?" I ask, some vicious part of me wanting to put the asshole behind bars and throw away the key.

"Well, he didn't get violent, but—"

"He put his hands on my boy, Josh!"

Josh stops us from walking any further, frowning and holding me in place with his hands on my shoulders. It's times like this when I forget that he's a Little himself. He's imposing in his uniform, with arms which almost match Matt's.

"Spence, I get it," Josh speaks calmly, as though he's trying to coax me into being the same, "and I wanna toss him in a cell and throw away the key as much as I'm sure you'd like me to, but we can't just make up our own rules here. And Tones needs you to be supportive and calm right now. No homicidal rage daddies allowed."

I snort at that. "You're right. I know you're right. I'm just—"

"I get it." He cuts me off, and there's a hint of melancholy when he continues, "You're a doting Daddy and a great boyfriend. We should all be so lucky to have that kind of person to rely on." Josh gives himself a little shake, his brown eyes clearing. I want to say that I make a note to follow up on his throwaway comment later, but I'm distracted by his next words. "Anyway, I'm not saying we can't charge him. I *think* we can get him on assault. Harassment at the very least. Dude apparently said some hateful gross things, too."

I nod. "Good. Now, where's Tony?"

* * *

201

Tony is sitting on the stoop outside the back door of the kitchen when Josh leads me to him. He has his knees drawn up to his chest and his face pressed into them, effectively turning himself into a quivering, quietly whimpering ball. Ash is crouched at his side, hugging him and murmuring soothing things into his ear, and he offers me a smile when he notices my approach.

"Hey, look who's here," Ash says cheerily, and I want to applaud the effort. Tony just shakes his head and tries to burrow further into his knees.

My heart breaks even more.

"Oh, angel," I say softly, and *that* gets a reaction. Tony whips his head up to look at me so quickly that I'm worried he's given himself whiplash.

"Daddy," he sobs, launching himself from the ground and into my arms. He presses his face into my chest and cries as I hold him.

When I realize he's *apologizing*, though, I need to put a stop to it. "*Anthony*, you have *nothing* to apologize for, do you understand me?"

"But I did a bad job. I'm not s'posed to cry at work. I'm not s'posed to ask for Daddy."

"You're supposed to be safe from assholes," I mutter, and he gasps.

"Bad word, Daddy."

"You're right. Sorry, baby."

Chuckles sound out around us and I'm reminded that my friends are still here. I look up at them, clustered together a couple of feet away and smile gratefully. "Thanks for looking out for him." I cast my gaze around, then frown. "Where's Tanya?"

202

I know she was here earlier because this is where she had called me from. She'd even handed the phone to Charlie.

"Ted took her for a walk and a chat," Charlie says, and I feel bad for forgetting that Ted had also been here. I shouldn't have, considering Zephyr is loitering with Charlie and Ash.

My brain is scrambled with the stress of the situation, and I need to get my shit together for Tony's sake. Licking my lips, I nod. "Good. That's good." Because if anyone can calmly and smoothly help her understand Tony's escape into his Little headspace, it's Ted.

"Ugh," Tony makes the sound of complaint after a few more minutes pass in contemplative silence. He pulls away suddenly to rub the heels of his palms into his swollen red eyes.

I can't bring myself to release my hold on his hips. I give him a gentle squeeze, whether to reassure him or myself, I'm not quite certain. "You doing better, sweetheart?"

"Uh…" he shakes his head, as if the action is going to clear his thoughts, "yeah. God, I'm so sorry. I…"

"We *just* talked about this," I scold lightly, feeling relief wash over me in a wave now that he's coming back to his Big headspace.

Tony rolls his eyes at me and sighs. "Yeah, well, forgive me for feeling embarrassed for melting down like this. *In public*, at that." His expression morphs into horror and he clutches at me, his cheeks turning as red as his eyes. "Fuck. I totally lost it in front of Charlie and Asher. *And* Gerald."

"After going through something traumatic," Ash informs him. Tony startles and spins around to find that the others are still here with us and I can see him shrinking back into himself.

"It's okay," I soothe him. "Breathe, angel."

Tony brings trembling hands up to cover his face. "I wanna go home."

"Soon, I promise," I hate that I have to break this news to him, knowing that talking about the situation is probably the last thing he wants to do. "But you'll need to make a statement to the police first."

"The police?!"

Folding my arms, I raise an eyebrow at his incredulous tone. "The guy assaulted you. Of course Ted called the police."

Tony shakes his head. "He grabbed my shirt. I…I overreacted."

"Grabbing your shirt and intimidating you *is* assault," Charlie cuts in calmly before I can say anything. That's probably a good thing, because I want to grab Tony by the shoulders and shake some sense into him. Charlie continues, "And the hate speech and yelling was harassment. Not just against you, either."

That last sentence seems to register in Tony's brain and he looks suitably chastened. "Is Steph okay?"

"She's fine," I answer, even though I honestly have no idea. From all accounts, she abandoned him to deal with the guy on his own, so I don't have a huge amount of sympathy for her. If that makes me a dick, so be it.

Tony's quiet for a while, watching his shoes as he scuffs the worn toe of his right foot across the dirty concrete beneath us. "Okay," he eventually agrees. "I'll make a statement."

I run my hand through his hair, finding it sweaty from the exertion of his emotional breakdown, and then cup his jaw. "Good boy. I'm proud of you. And I'll be right by your side."

"Promise?" His eyes are wide and wet and terrified.

"*Always*, Tony."

* * *

"I want to be a writer," Tony declares later in the evening, when we're sitting across from each other at my tiny dining table with a half-eaten pizza in between us and Frank meowing piteously for scraps of meat from the kitchen bench. (I've given up on trying to prevent him from plonking his gross cat butt there, seeing as he does it for every meal now. Tony finds it hilarious, and I'm loathe to stop anything that brings my boy joy. Especially now.)

Tony's words are so quiet that I almost miss them. We've been steadfastly avoiding the topic of work, so it surprises me that he's bringing this up now.

"A writer?" I echo, smiling softly at him. "I didn't know that you write."

My boy looks down and picks off a string of cheese from the slice in front of him, but doesn't eat it. He shrugs. "I used to."

Treading ever so carefully, I ask, "What kind of stuff did you like to write?"

"Romance," he admits, barely above a whisper. He bites his lip. "And fantasy."

"Yeah?"

He nods.

"Tony, that's wonderful."

The snort my words earn me is self-deprecating. "You haven't read anything I've written. It might be ridiculous crap."

I laugh, half tempted to tell him that plenty of people build successful careers writing what others might consider 'ridiculous crap', but I know that's not going to help here. "I doubt anything you write would be either of those things," I insist. "And if you're writing something you'd enjoy reading, chances are there is an audience for it out there."

"I…um," Tony finally looks up at me, "I'm thinking of maybe writing some Daddy/Little romances." He flushes adorably, then goes back to picking at his slice of pizza. "Maybe. I don't know. It's stupid. Forget I said anything."

Nope. Not happening.

"Who better to write about Age Play than someone who has experience with it?" I keep my tone light and gentle. "You can only try."

"But…what if people hate it?"

Now this is something I can answer with certainty. I reach over the pizza and place my hand over his, waiting until he looks up at me again before I speak.

"There will always be people who hate your writing." His face falls and I continue, "But that's the same as any other book. People have different tastes and expectations and you'll never meet them all. Look up the reviews for the classics. Plenty of one stars and DNFs there…and a bunch of five stars, too. I bet there are books you've read and loved that other people have hated, and vice versa."

"What if…" he swallows, those beautiful eyes of his brimming with tears that he does his best to blink away, "what if *you* hate it?"

I can answer this with certainty, too. Even if I've never read his writing before. "Angel," I squeeze his hand, "that's impossible. I love you, and I will love anything you create. And, yes, I am biased: that's the point. I know you. I know your brain."

"My stupid squirrel brain," he mutters.

"*Anthony*," I frown, employing Daddy voice firmly, "you

206

know I hate you talking about yourself like that. Your brain is just like the rest of you: sexy as fuck. And I can't wait to get a glimpse inside it when you're comfortable sharing your writing with me. If you're comfortable. I won't push you."

His Adam's apple bobs as he swallows. Then he sets down his pizza and gets up from his seat, rounding the table to come and drop into my lap and bury his face in the crook of my neck. I rub his back, understanding that he's overwhelmed.

It's a while before he speaks again, and the pizza has gone cold. Frank's still angling for scraps, but he's going to have to wait.

"I can't go back to the diner yet." Tony eventually says, resting his ear over my heart. "I…I think about going back and I feel sick."

"You don't have to go back."

In fact, I'd be much happier if he didn't. I had the distinct displeasure of meeting his boss as we collected his belongings when we left tonight, and I have a new understanding of why Tony's always so distressed after a normal shift.

Between the stresses of having a customer facing job and that awful man as his employer, I'm impressed by Tony's strength and resilience even more than I was to start with: something I didn't think was possible. Still, it's not my place to make that decision for him, no matter how badly I want to.

"But…how will I pay rent?"

"Well…" We've been dating for almost five months now, and he spends most of his time here at my house anyway. "You could move in here. With me."

I'm expecting Tony's reaction to that. He rears back and it's only my hold on him that prevents him from toppling from my lap. "But *Tanya*. She can't afford the apartment on her own. I can't do that to her."

Unbeknownst to him, Tanya's seen this coming. Even before tonight, she's made comments that she has a backup plan lined up for when I 'officially steal Tony away' from her. (Her words, not mine.) Tonight is likely going to escalate them, and she's already texted to let me know that she understands and is glad that her brother has someone who 'cares so fucking much'. (Also her words.)

"Why don't you call her and work out a plan together?" I suggest, and he laughs, the tension leaving his body almost as quickly as it set in.

"You've already talked to her, huh?"

"Uh…" I don't want him to think that we went behind his back, or that we've been making his decisions for him.

He doesn't seem upset, though. If anything, he seems relieved and genuinely happy. He kisses my lips sweetly. "Thank you, Daddy."

Oh, my heart.

Chapter Twenty – Tony

I spend a few days following the incident at the diner just processing the events and Spencer's rescue plan. It's only after the initial stress and panic has faded that I realize I can't just move in and mooch off him.

Yes, I do appreciate that he was being a good Daddy and looking after me, but I'm still a man coming up rapidly on his twenty-ninth birthday, and I can't expect all of my problems to be magically solved for me.

I did that at eighteen, when Nonna kicked me out and Tanya stepped in to make sure I wouldn't have to do all the hard stuff alone. I was there with her, but she did most of the planning. She found our apartment. She organized all the utilities. She even found all the job ads for me to apply for.

It's time for me to start doing things for myself.

It doesn't mean that I don't still need my Daddy to make my smaller life decisions for me. He can still take the stress out of choosing what to eat, or what to wear, or what activities we can do during our free time…but he can't just decide how to resolve my career woes for me.

He just about blows a gasket —as much as I've ever seen Spencer lose his temper— when I tell him that I'm going back to the diner.

"No." Until now, Spencer has been a perfectly doting Daddy. He's never had reason to be genuinely angry at me, but there's fire in his gray-blue eyes now.

"Spencer…" I start and then jump when he smacks a hand down on the dining table's surface, making the cutlery clatter on the porcelain plates.

A few months ago? I would have cowered, or burst into tears, or begged for forgiveness. But now I have the confidence to stare him down, man to man, and tell him he's being unreasonable.

It takes a moment before horror washes over his handsome face. "Shit," he sighs and shakes his head. "You're right. I'm sorry. I just…I hate the idea of you going back there for any reason. Hell, the guys are boycotting eating there on principle."

My phone has been blowing up with messages of support in the group chat: another difference to the Tony of a few months ago. That Tony didn't have the sort of support network that I do now. And that support network is partly why I feel strong enough to go back to work.

"I know," I tell him, reaching for the hand he's left splayed on the table between us, while a metaphorical lightbulb suddenly hovers over my head, "and I love that. I appreciate it. But I need to, Spence. At least until I have another means to support myself."

"But—"

"I can't be financially dependent on you, Daddy," I try to soften my words. "I just…I can't. It's time for me to prove my

Nonna wrong. To prove my school bullies wrong. To prove myself wrong."

The lightbulb is growing brighter as an idea forms. It's not the sort of thing I can actually pull off on my own, but I'm going to do some research before I put voice to it.

Spencer's lips thin. "Why can't you look for a different job, then?"

"I can," I answer, having given this a lot of thought over the past few days. Frank meows from his usual perch on the kitchen counter as though he's backing me up, and I smile. "And I am." Even if I have to fashion one for myself. "But, in the meantime, I have to go back. I've left Betsy and Steph in the lurch long enough."

I give Spencer time to think about what I'm telling him. He's always been a thoughtful man, inclusive and understanding of other people's perspectives. I hope he doesn't let our relationship cloud his fair judgment now.

"You know, even Charlie said you shouldn't go back," he eventually tells me, in what I'm guessing is a last-ditch attempt to get me to change my mind.

I did know that. In a separate, private chat, Asher and Zephyr and I have discussed it at length. Ash explained that his Daddy is the hyper-protective sort, and that Gerald's attitude totally got under his skin. But Charlie's not my Daddy, and even if he was, nobody has the right to make those choices for me unless I give them permission to. Zephyr agreed with me about that, and said that sometimes our Daddies needed a firm hand themselves. They're just people, too. Imperfect like any of us, even if we do put them on a pedestal.

I'm also not unaware that part of Spencer's desire to wrap me in cotton wool and make my decisions for me stems from his last relationship. We've talked about Emma and their dynamic a lot over the past few months. She was needy, and Spencer loved that, so my neediness to this point has filled a void for him. I don't want him to think he's losing that, but at the same time, he has to start differentiating me from Emma. If we've got any chance at making our relationship work permanently, we have to be true to ourselves, not to the ghost of his past relationship.

"Yeah, well," I reply to Spencer, 'I understand why. But I'm still the only person who gets to decide that. Well, me and Gerald, I guess."

Spencer's face twists at the mention of my boss. "He's a jerk."

"You're not getting any arguments from me on that one. But he's a jerk who pays my wages, so, until I do find another job —or he fires me— I'm going back to work for him."

This time after Spencer thinks it over, he exhales heavily and nods. The hint of a smile tugs at his lips. "I'm proud of you for standing up for your rights, Tony. So fucking proud."

That feels better than a thousand 'Good Boy's. We are on the same page, and I can see a bright future ahead.

No more constantly needy Tony. No more ridiculously overly protective Spencer. Balance. Love. Trust. Support flowing both ways. It's perfect.

I beam back at him. "Thanks, Daddy."

After another moment, he asks, "But…will you still move in with me?"

Tanya's moving in with Braeden, but even if she wasn't, I'd still answer the same way: "Hell yeah!"

* * *

Gerald welcomes me back grudgingly. He makes snide comments about me being one of The Grove freaks, which I find irritating but —for the first time ever— not upsetting. Whether it's because his opinion doesn't matter to me, or because I'd expected it, the attitude rolls off my back. I don't pick up as many shifts, just enough to cover my share of the rent for the apartment I share with my sister, and I spend my free time furiously researching my idea.

I still plan to write, of course, but I need an income that's not reliant on Spencer picking up the slack if my books don't sell.

I do up a budget, consider my savings, and I gather the courage to organize a meeting with Charlie and Ted by myself. I know Daddy knows about it, but he refrains from asking to join me. He just gives me a knowing smirk, a peck on the cheek, and a playful swat on my ass when I walk out the door, my research in hand.

After I pitch my proposal to Uncle Ted and Charlie, the two men share a look and then turn to me with matching wide grins.

"This is great, Tony," Ted tells me, holding up the stack of papers I'd handed him as I detailed my idea. "I don't know why it hasn't been thought of before."

"Yeah?" I ask, unsure of myself despite their enthusiastic nods.

"Yeah," Charlie says, running through my proposed budget. "I'd love to get on board as an investor, and I'm happy to arrange talks with The Grove. They'd probably ask for a percentage of the profits—"

"I've already taken that into consideration," I interrupt him, giddiness starting to overtake me. I try not to bounce in my seat. Leaning forward, I point out the line in the expenditures column of my budget. "See?"

Ted gives a low, appreciative whistle. "I'm impressed," he says, then taps his index finger on the sheaf of papers in front of him. "I want in, too. I think it's going to be quite profitable. I can write up the contracts and you can have another lawyer look them over—"

"No," I shake my head. "I trust you. Besides, you wouldn't screw me over. Zephyr wouldn't let you get away with it."

He laughs and sits back in his chair, an indulgent smile on his face at the mention of his boy. "No, he wouldn't. I'd be punished for that." There's something else in his tone that I can't read, but it doesn't sound negative, so I ignore it.

We talk over details some more, and when I leave, we've all shaken hands and I feel the most adult I have ever felt. I'm a businessman now. I'm going into business with two investors at my back.

Charlie has promised that he and Asher will help me learn the ropes on the day-to-day operations, and I know that Spencer will also help me with the set up, too, considering he started his own home business not all that long ago.

When I get back to Spencer's house (I haven't officially moved in yet, and I'm not calling it 'home' until I do) Frank greets me at the door, curling around my ankles and meowing for attention. I drop to my knees to stroke his silky soft black fur, still not over the way he pushes up from the ground to chase more pets.

"Where's Daddy?" I ask him and he trills at me, purring and butting his head against my thigh. I chuckle. "That's not helpful."

It's Frank's turn to complain when I stand back up, intent

on searching Spencer out.

I find him in his basement studio, which is soundproofed and has a red light above the door, indicating that he's recording. I quietly scoot past the recording room door and slip into the closet containing the audio engineering panel — a long desk of buttons, knobs, switches and dials in varying colors and sizes, with tiny etched in white letters beneath each one. There's a thick, soundproof window between the panel and the recording room, and Spencer lights up when he sees me through it. I flick the switch to relay his audio into this space and listen to him as he wraps up his current recording.

It's a shifter romance and I can't wait to hear the finished version, but there's something to be said about getting to experience this moment in person. He's still my favorite narrator, after all, and I feel like the luckiest fanboy ever, getting to watch the magic happen as he records the book.

When he hangs up his headphones, he stops recording from a small panel inside his booth, and then he gestures for me to meet him outside the two rooms, which I am more than happy to do.

I fling myself into his arms, practically vibrating with excitement.

"They're investing!" I tell him with delight. "They're investing in my idea! I'm going to own a food truck, and Charlie's gonna help me work it out with The Grove to have it parked permanently in their car park. Ted will help me take care of the licensing and I'm gonna own my own business!"

It's a rush of information, but Spencer takes it all in his stride, lifting me up and spinning me in a circle. "I'm so proud of you, angel," he tells me as he puts me back on my feet. "You are going to do so great, I just know it!"

"And the best part is I'm still going to be able to write, too."
I'm going to hire staff for the truck so I can pursue my dreams
on the side.

It's all in my business plan, and both Ted and Charlie were
impressed by how detailed my budget was. I tell Spencer all
of this, talking his ear off about my research and the praise
his friends gave me. Instead of being bored —or even insulted
that I didn't talk to him first— Spencer's own excitement only
grows to match mine.

"It doesn't hurt that you're going to be taking business away
from Gerald, either," he mutters darkly, then laughs when I
smack him.

"Daddy, we're not that petty," I tell him.

"You're right, sweetheart." Spencer's words are conciliatory,
but his tone is anything but. I understand, though, so I let it
go.

When I ask, Spencer offers me suggestions and advice on
the practical aspects of applying for permits and starting up
new bank accounts specifically for the business, and tips on
dealing with the trickier paperwork I'll need to lodge when
I register my business, but otherwise he is perfectly content
to leave the control of my idea to me. I appreciate that more
than he can possibly know. It's confirmation that, while he's
my Daddy, he's also my partner and equal when it counts.

The future looks bright with him.

* * *

"That's the last box," Tanya informs us, dusting her palms off
on her jeans once she drops the offending item on the floor in
front of the stairs. "You guys can lug it wherever it needs to

be. I'm done being your pack horse."

I lunge at her, wrapping her in a tight hug. "You're the best," I tell her.

"Excuse you," Zephyr teases me as he descends the stairs with the effortless grace that being a dancer affords him, "but I've just spent the last hour unpacking your clothes and getting them all arranged in the wardrobe and drawers. *You're welcome.*"

"It was twenty minutes, and I helped," Ash adds as he appears behind our mutual friend.

I still can't believe that all the guys have helped me move into Spencer's house. It's a vastly different experience to the last time Tanya and I moved, hiring a U-Haul truck and doing the heavy lifting by ourselves.

"Well, if that's the last of it, I say we get to celebrating," Spencer says, coming up to wrap an arm around my shoulders and press a kiss to my temple.

"Celebrating?" I question.

"House-warming parties are a thing, angel."

I squint at him, confused. "But…you already lived here."

"But *you* didn't. So this is *your* house-warming party." Spencer pulls a blowout party whistle from his pocket —the kind you get from a dollar store— which unrolls and unleashes an unholy bleating sound when he blows it to emphasize his point.

I gasp and blink at him for a moment, then smile widely and make grabby hands, demanding, "Gimme!"

Asher is at my other side almost immediately, doing the same.

Matt and Katie pop their heads out from around the hallway, matching puzzled expressions on their faces until they spy the toy. Then they're bouncing over, too, also begging for a whistle.

Daddy laughs and points back towards the hallway. "The packet's in the lounge room. Go nuts."

We all take off at a run, giggling and shoving at each other to find them, heedless of the voices behind us telling us to be careful.

Any lingering guilt I felt about taking advantage of Daddy melts away as I lose myself in play with my friends.

We blow the whistles at each other and attempt (badly) to bleat out *Mary Had A Little Lamb* with it until Cherie and London break at the same time and tell us it's time to play another game while Daddy fires up the grill in his small courtyard outside.

Ash finds my stuffy collection in the toybox, and soon enough we've handed over our whistles (to our caregivers' obvious relief) and are taking our plush friends on an adventure.

"Mister Bear is an astronaut," Matt says, holding up the soft, floppy brown bear I've dubbed 'Bouncer'. "And this—" he grabs one of the now empty packing boxes "—is the rocket he's gonna take to the moon."

"Well, Lambchop here," Katie waggles my stuffed lion, and I giggle at the name she's given him, "is also an astronaut, and he's going with Mister Bear."

Ash looks at the other toys and reaches for a white bear wearing a beret. "It's a whole crew," he says, "and Fancy Pants is also going to the moon. He's, um, the guy who fixes stuff."

"Mechanical engineer?" Matt offers, sounding amused.

Ash rolls his eyes back at him. "Those words are too big."

We all seem to be hovering at the same sort of Little age, and

I'm a little bit blown away that my friends are doing that for me, matching me where I am comfortable. There hasn't been any discussion about it or anything, but I know that Ash and Matt generally sink into younger headspaces quite naturally. I still only manage that when I'm alone with Daddy.

"I'm academically advanced," Matt teases back, and we all laugh.

"Whatever," Ash sasses lightly, then tosses Fancy Pants the bear into the makeshift rocket. "We're still going to the moon."

I share a look with Zephyr. "You wanna be a Martian with me?" I hold up my chosen stuffy: a toy dog with flopsy ears and big rounded eyes. "This is Marty the Martian pup."

"There's no Martians on the moon," Katie starts, but Zephyr shushes her and grabs for a plush doll with knitted red hair and a gingham dress.

"Mary-Lou *is* a Martian," he insists primly, "and she moved to the moon with Marty because their house on Mars burned down."

"Try saying that ten times fast," Ash laughs. "Mary-Lou and Marty the Martians moved to the moon from Mars."

We all spend a few seconds trying out the impromptu tongue-twister, giggling as we try to speed it up and verbally race each other before Ash shakes the 'rocket' and we return to the game at hand.

The Martians and the astronauts have just made friends when Daddy calls out to tell us that dinner is ready. We scramble up from the lounge room floor, with Ash pausing to offer Matt a hand up, and march towards the powder room to wash up before our meal.

As I come back to my adult self, I can't help but think that this all feels surreal. It wasn't all that long ago that I was a

219

weird, virginal loner in a dead-end job that was making me miserable. Now I have a bunch of friends, and a boyfriend, and I've started to write my first novel.

Oh, and I have a cat. Frank has officially adopted me. Or, at least, that's what Spencer says, and because I adore the black feline who is currently hiding from the influx of visitors, I'm going to say he's right.

The food truck business launched this week with great success, too. I named it *Burgers, Dinonuggets, Shakes & More*, or BDSM for short. We serve a limited selection of quick and easy diner fare with kink-inspired names for each dish. The Grove were enthusiastic about partnering with us, and Charlie is already planning on utilizing the truck for events at The Center as well. I feel accomplished and truly independent for the first time in my life.

On top of that, Spencer also said that he'll teach me the basics of audio engineering and editing to produce audiobooks in his home studio. I'm super excited about that.

I kiss Spencer's cheek and gratefully accept the burger he's put together for me. There's not a lot of sitting room out here, so I just stand beside him as I munch happily and let the conversation around us wash over me.

Yes, it's surreal. But I'm so happy right now, it's not even funny.

Chapter Twenty-one – Spencer

I laugh my ass off the day Chance tells me what he, Josh and Charlie have been so secretive about for the past few months. Just when I thought things were settling into some semblance of 'normal', my best friend is almost guaranteed to turn everything upside down again.

"A Daddy auction?" I echo incredulously after catching my breath and calming down.

"Well, it was Josh's idea, but—"

"Of course it was," I shake my head, my wild hair swaying into my eyes. "I can't believe you're actually going to do it."

Chance has always been kind of shy with people outside our social circle, so volunteering to get up on a stage to be eyed off and bid on is way out of character for him. It's probably also why he's opted to tell me while we're out in public at a café for lunch, knowing that I won't react quite as loudly or as nosily as I would if we were discussing this in private.

To my left, Tony jabs an elbow into my ribs. "Stop it," he frowns, then turns to smile at Chance across the table, "I think it's a great idea. Fundraising for The Center *and* with the possibility of Chance meeting *The One*. Oh," he claps his hands together in delight, "it sounds like a great meet-cute plot for a book!"

"Not gonna happen. This is real life." Chance rolls his eyes back at him before looking at me, "Besides, I'm doing it for Charlie and Ash. You know, *our friends*? Always there supporting us? Ringing any bells for you?"

"You couldn't just donate money?" I ask him in return.

Now it's my best friend's turn to shake his head, and I watch his scruffy red beard barely flutter from the movement. "Not the kind of money they're hoping to bring in from this thing. They're partnering with The Grove and everything."

"Right," I lean back in my seat and contemplate it. "And you just put your hand up and said you'd do it?"

"Nah," he answers, "Charlie, Josh, and —of all people— Katie have been trying to convince me for a while. I've been helping them with logistics and planning, but I finally caved and agreed to be a part of the auction itself just to shut them up."

Tony snorts at that. "You're such a pushover for us Littles, you know that?"

"Unfortunately," Chance agrees with a grin and a quick nod. He eyes me with playful annoyance. "They were gonna ask you, too, but you managed to go and fall in love, so that left me as the last single Daddy in our group. Traitor."

I laugh and pull Tony in against my side, well aware that my boy is poking his tongue out at my friend. "Can't say I'm sorry about that, dude."

Chance's expression turns soft with understanding and a hint of melancholy. "I know. I get it."

"Seriously, though, this is a great opportunity for you," Tony insists, having picked up on the same drop in Chance's mood. I'm so proud of him for noticing, and even more proud that he's attempting to cheer the other man up. "You might have insane chemistry with whoever wins you at the auction and then maybe you *won't* be the only single Daddy in the group anymore...and *then* it's just Josh we have to pair off with someone."

Okay, so nobody said he'd perfected tact yet.

Chance chuckles, still dismissive, "Whatever you say, bud." He throws a couple of fries into his mouth and chews before getting to the crux of why he was finally confessing the big secret to begin with. "So, yeah, that's my contribution to the cause. But the guys are probably gonna hit the two of you up soon, too."

I frown. "They're not auctioning Littles, are they?" I pull Tony just a tiny bit closer against me, feeling a spike of caveman-like possessiveness take over me. I've been a bit this way ever since the incident at the diner a couple of months ago. I don't like the idea of letting him out of my sight for long, even though he's an adult who is more than capable of looking after himself. "And, like you said, we're both taken, so—"

"No, the idea of auctioning Littles or Subs is *bad* with a capital 'B'," Chance agrees, shooting me a knowing smirk. I know he'll give me hell for my behavior later. "But you might want to auction off signed pre-release copies of Tony's book, maybe? Or maybe a personalized audio recording or something? It's not scheduled for a few more months yet, so you'll have time to organize something like that."

Huh. I hadn't thought of that, and they are both fantastic suggestions which won't actually cost Tony and I anything to donate. I share a look with my boy and he nods, seemingly on the same page as me.

I look back at Chance. "Yeah, okay, we'll probably do something like that, then."

Chance grins. "Great. I'll let Ash know."

As conversation shifts to more normal topics —things like work, whether we're going to Littles' Night next week, and placing joke bets on whether Zephyr or Matt will finally snap and propose to their respective Daddies— I let my thoughts drift.

The better part of the last year has been like a dream. I wasn't unhappy before I met Tony, but I can't imagine being happy without him now. I feel needed and wanted in a variety of different ways, and fulfilled as a Daddy to a sweet Little boy who trusts me enough to continue exploring his desires and needs together.

Speaking of...

"So," I interrupt whatever Chance was saying, glancing at my watch and then meaningfully at my boy, "we've actually got plans this afternoon, so we're going to have to get going."

"*Plans*, huh?" Chance asks me suggestively, arching an eyebrow.

Beside me, I know Tony's blushing, but I stare my best friend down. "Yep."

Chance's amusement is almost palpable, but he waves us away, melodramatically declaring, "Fine. Go. Flaunt your perfect relationship and satisfying sex life. I don't care."

I'm still laughing as I drag Tony out of the café by the hand, with plans to do exactly what Chance just accused me of.

* * *

"You can safe word at any time," I remind Tony later in the afternoon. We had to make a few stops for some supplies, and now I feel a bubbling feeling of anticipation building in my gut.

When he had first cautiously asked if I'd try this with him, I'll admit I was nervous. It's not something I've ever actually done, and I want to do it right for him. First and foremost we need to be safe, so we're going to start out tame, but I still worry that he'll get overwhelmed, or overstimulated, or…something. But he wants so badly to try, and I can't deny him anything.

(Being a pushover for our Littles is a trait my entire social circle share, apparently.)

Having shooed Frank from the bedroom, the door is shut and the curtains are drawn, leaving the room dimly lit by the slivers of fading afternoon light that are managing to sneak in through the cracks.

"You can, too, Spencer," Tony replies seriously, no hint of his boyish persona to be seen. I'm glad for that, at least. I love him when he's little but, for what we have planned, I need him as adult as I am.

"I know." I lick my lips, a tiny bit nervous. Then I remind myself that he needs me to be dominant right now, and I swallow back those nerves and try to radiate calmness. We share one last chaste kiss at the foot of the bed and then I raise the blindfold between us, showing it to him. "You ready?

He nods eagerly.

After helping him undress, I tie the blindfold over his eyes and then ask him how many fingers I'm holding up (four), to which he answers, "I can't see a damn thing."

He gets a gentle swat to his backside for the sass and he grins.

"Okay," I help him climb onto the bed and settle him in the middle of the mattress, enjoying the way he looks, spread out for me like he is. "I'm going to tie your hands first, then your ankles, okay?"

He nods.

"I need verbal consent, baby."

"Yes," he answers, then hesitates.

"You can still call me Daddy, Tony," I reassure him softly, moving to his right side to fasten a silky ribbon around his wrist and the discreet hook I've recently installed into the side of the headboard. "I just don't want you sinking into Little space for this."

"Yes, Daddy." Tony sounds cheeky and when I glance down I find him smirking.

Little shit, I muse with affection. Out loud I say, "Good boy."

I move around the bed to tie his left wrist next, and then go for his left ankle.

I've spent a lot of time researching everything about what we're about to do. I've even spoken to Doms at The Grove, doing some practice runs on properly and safely fastening the ties and using the other equipment I've brought into the bedroom with me. I can't betray the trust Tony has put into me by fucking this up.

His cock has swelled and is twitching by the time I'm finished fastening the tie around his right ankle. Still, I pause to quietly ask him, "Color?"

His Adam's apple bobs. "Green."

When I was setting up, he and I discussed the process in depth. He wanted to explore his 'sensory thing' (his words), so all the stimulation for now will be physical only. Neither one of us will speak, except for safe wording and checking in if I feel it necessary. I did offer him sound-blocking headphones, but he refused, concerned that he might freak out at being deprived of both sight and hearing all at once. I am proud of him for expressing his limits, and, if today goes well, we might revisit them in the future.

But for now I keep my movements as quiet as possible. I decide to also undress, so the sound of rustling fabric doesn't forecast my actions. Then I lift the cover from the tray of sensory items I've pre-selected and opt to begin by picking up an ice cube from a bowl full of them.

Tony gasps when I run it over the exposed sole of his foot. He only flinches a tiny bit at first contact, then relaxes into the sensation as I swirl the melting item over the inside of his ankle and then up the inside of his thigh. His cock bobs and his balls tighten with anticipation as I near them, but I skip the area altogether, running the ice down the inside of his other leg instead.

He lets out a breath, whether in relief or disappointment I'm not sure, and his whole body sags again.

Turning back to the tray, I switch out the mostly melted ice cube for a length of the same satiny ribbon attached to his wrists and ankles. I use the very end of it to tickle his abdomen and underarms. Tony squirms a little, but he seems determined not to make any noise if he can help it.

That's not a rule tonight, but it might just be a self-imposed one that I'm not aware of.

Back at the tray, I reach for a shiny new Wartenberg pinwheel. The tines on the little wheel are tiny but sharp. They won't pierce his skin, but with enough pressure they will prickle and scratch a little, and they make tiny imprints in his smooth, golden skin when I roll the gadget down his forearm, then the inside of his bicep, then just shy of his left nipple and then his right. His nipples pucker at the barest hint of attention and I have to bite back a dark chuckle.

I turn back to the tray, returning the wheel. Picking up another ice cube, I hold it in my fist before I close my hand around the base of his cock. His whole body jerks at that, and he whimpers a little as I slowly drag the cube up his straining length. The heat of his flesh here, with the addition of my whole palm, is melting this ice cube faster than the other one, and soon he's left with a little puddle of liquid in his pubic hair and dripping down to his balls.

"Color?" I ask him, noticing his increased squirming, even though he's making a valiant attempt to stay still.

"Green," he whispers, already sounding ragged and wrecked.

Judging by the deep, red flush to his cock, I expect he's close to going over the edge already. The Doms I spoke to at The Grove did tell me not to expect extended sessions to begin with, but I'm still surprised that Tony has reacted so intensely so soon.

I use the remnants of the melted ice cube to tease his hole, working it against the heated pucker until it's nothing but liquid. Tony pants and squirms, his hole clenching as I tease, but he's still quiet.

When I go back to the tray again, my hand hovers between a feather and an artist's paintbrush with thick, soft, smooth bristles.

I choose the brush, and a pot of chocolate body paint, deciding that this will be the grand finale for tonight's gentle experimentation. I spend a little bit of time painting swirls over his skin in spots I know are sensitive for him.

His nipples. The junction where his neck meets his shoulder.

The skin around his belly button. The inside of his thighs. The spot on his neck just beneath his jawline, under his ear. The head of his cock.

Then, after taking a moment to admire the finished project, I suck on an ice cube and start licking up my artwork.

Tony shouts and writhes when my cold tongue meets his left nipple, and I smirk against his skin. The body paint is an explosion of sweetness next to the cold-water taste of the ice and the saltiness of his sweat, and I follow the path I painted myself, listening to Tony breathing heavily and pleading under his breath.

I suck the chocolate from his neck, then head back down to his right nipple, teasing it with the tip of my tongue with tiny kitten licks before nipping with my teeth. Then I head down to his belly button, flattening my tongue and lapping with big, broad strokes.

Tony is quivering with need when I make it to his thighs, and I draw out the delicious torture, sucking the body paint with ridiculous slowness from the inside of one shaking leg and then the other.

All that's left is the splodge of chocolate I'd left on the tip of his cock, which is now mixing with precum and dribbling down his throbbing shaft.

I close my mouth over him and that's all it takes before he explodes, coming hard in thick shooting spurts. I catch most of it and swallow greedily, before licking the remnants from him with satisfaction until he practically sobs, "Too sensitive. Stop, Daddy."

It's not a safe word, but it's damn near close enough and I pull away as requested. When I look up to his face, he's wearing a blissed out grin, so the quick burst of panic in my chest dissipates. I untie his ankles without fanfare, then crawl over him to undo the ties at his wrists.

Finally free, he wrenches the blindfold off and launches himself at me, kissing me deeply.

"That was amazing," he tells me, still breathing heavily. His eyes are heavy lidded, and he pulls me back down into a reclining position on the mattress with him. "Seriously. The best. Like...*wow*."

His words fill me with pride. I wonder if maybe I've got a bit of a praise kink of my own. Brushing a sweaty lock of dark hair from his forehead, I ask, "So we're doing that again, then?"

"God yes," he answers, closing his eyes. "I want to try *everything* with you."

"Good," I say, suddenly feeling a bit choked up, "because I still want everything with you, too."

Tony doesn't answer, except for a light snore, but that's okay. We have time. In fact, we have forever.

Epilogue – Tony

"Did you have fun today?" Spencer asks me as we're picking up the last of the paper plates and plastic cups from yet another get-together at our house, this time an early birthday party Spencer insisted we throw in my honor. Even though it's a smaller space than Ted's, I'm more comfortable exploring my Little side here and nobody else seems to mind spending time in the cramped quarters. Today, our friends (and the phrase still sends a thrill through me) stuck around to help clean up the worst of the debris, so we're just fussing right now. "It wasn't too much? I know crowds still aren't your thing."

Daddy checks in with me like this every single time, and I genuinely appreciate it.

I nod, affection surging through me at his concern. "It was great. Before I met you guys, I'd never really been in a situation like that before. Like…where everyone there was my friend, and there for me. But it makes it less overwhelming. It's safe." I sigh happily. "Still, it's nice to be alone again. Less chaotic.

231

Gives my brain a bit of time to calm down from the over stimulation."

The concern hasn't completely left Spencer's gaze. He takes the trash bag I've been holding from me and asks, "Do you need some Little time? We can cuddle in bed and I can read you a story? The rest of the clean up can wait until tomorrow."

I bite my lip, tempted by the offer, then shake my head. "Could, um, could we go to bed but stay big? I want…"

Even now, after over half a year together, I'm shy about asking for what I want.

But Spencer is patient. He just cocks his head and waits.

So I ramble. "It's just that it's been a while, I guess, and I have the whole oral fixation thing going on and—"

"Angel," Spencer drops the bag on the nearest countertop and reaches for me, cupping my jaw so he can look me in the eye. I can see warmth and amusement in his gaze. "What are you asking for? You jumped ahead a step."

With my cheeks burning, I blurt, "The nipple thing."

"The…" he starts to repeat, then his eyes widen with comprehension. "Oh, you want to suck my nipples again, huh?"

"Only if you're into it. I know it's weird, but I just—"

"*Anthony*. It's not weird. And I love that you're expressing what you want. You know I'm on board. I'm *always* on board with you."

I melt for him all over again. "But…just asking for it like that, when we're not even in bed or anything…"

"Still not weird, baby. I promise."

He takes me by the hand and leads me upstairs, shooing Frank off the bed so we can climb in and scoot together without interruption. Soon enough, we've eased one another out of our clothes and are kissing and exploring each other's bodies like we're not already well and truly intimately acquainted.

When Spencer props his elbow up with pillows and cushions and gestures for me to settle in the crook of his arm in a standard nursing position, I comply and latch my mouth on greedily. Secretly, I still think it's strange that I love doing this —that I get so fucking hard at the feeling of suckling his nipples— but he gets hard, too, so it's okay.

Sometimes I do this just for comfort. When a bottle or pacifier isn't enough for Little me. But right now isn't about that at all.

Besides, the fact that he lets me do this when I'm big and it does turn him on? Well, that's all sorts of awesome, and tonight I'm taking advantage of it.

Spencer's making pleased sounds at the back of his throat as I lavish his nipple with attention. Under my hip, between the V of his spread legs which are cradling my ass in place, I can feel his cock swelling and hardening. His free hand comes down between our bodies to fondle my answering erection and I moan loudly at the first touch.

"That's it, angel," he encourages me when I flick my tongue over the tightened bud in the middle of his pec, "take what you need."

I roll my hips while I suck a little harder, whining when his touch remains light and teasing. I can feel the wet head of his cock beneath me, so I know he's just as aroused as I am. But he's got endless patience where I have none and he chuckles.

"Wanna switch to the other side?"

I moan because, yes, I do, but that means having to release the prize in my mouth and I *don't* love that idea.

Spencer has us located in the middle of his —*our*— large, cushy mattress, so the change in position doesn't involve too much maneuvering. And I realize why he requested the changeover as soon as I'm nursing on his opposite nipple, when his dominant hand wraps itself around my leaking length and strokes me slowly and firmly.

"Oh, *fuck*," I breathe, closing my eyes as the sensation threatens to overwhelm me in the very best way. "D-Daddy…"

"Keep on sucking, angel. I've got you."

This man. This perfect, *perfect* man.

I follow his gentle command without complaint, showing this nipple as much attention as the previous one. Spencer gasps when I graze my teeth gently over it, then groans when I lick it in playful apology.

"You have no idea how fucking hot you look right now," he tells me after a few more seconds where the only sounds are my quiet slurps and sighs and his heavy breaths, "my beautiful boy."

He doesn't usually call me his boy during sex. He's got no problems being called Daddy, as long as I'm big, but this is the first time he's actually crossed those lines, treating me the way he does when I'm little.

I open my eyes and glance up at him, and the stare he's directing my way is intense in so many ways. There's love and affection, and desire and pleasure…but also surprise, like he's just heard himself and isn't quite sure what to make of his own instincts. Even though we've discussed the possibility of it in theory, and we've come *close* to crossing those lines before, this is new, and I don't want him to be uncomfortable.

He always looks after me, now it's my turn to return the favor.

"Color?" I ask him quietly.

The surprise gives way to something softer and warmer.

"Green, sweetheart. Thank you."

I bob my head once, knowing that we'll talk about it properly later, and then take his nipple back into my mouth and he rocks his hips up into me. "I'm close, baby. I'm so close just from this. *Fuck*. How did I get so lucky?"

I'm the lucky one, I want to tell him, but my thoughts are turning disjointed.

I'm not heading towards Little space, not really. But the pleasant fog in my brain feels similar to that.

Maybe it's from the freedom that I feel in this moment, where I'm completely myself and I am certain of his acceptance and his love. Or maybe it's because I can feel my orgasm building. My balls are tightening, and I can feel the tell-tale tingles of pleasure radiating out from somewhere deep in my belly.

Or maybe it's both. I don't know, and I don't care.

I suck harder as the wave of pleasure crests and then, with one final upstroke of Daddy's hand on my cock, the wave of bliss crashes down over me and I paint his abdomen with rope after rope of cum.

"Oh god," he murmurs, "there's nothing better than watching you come for me." His hand leaves my cock and I feel him grasp his own, and I shift in his lap so I can watch him take himself over the edge, too.

When he catches me looking, Spencer pauses his movement, scoops my cum from his skin, then returns his hand to his cock, using the evidence of my orgasm as additional lube. I watch him stroke himself for maybe five seconds before I give in to the urge to take over.

He startles when I remove myself from his lap, but grins wickedly and spreads his legs wider for me when he realizes my intention as I position myself on my belly in front of him. Then I bat his hand away from his cock and lean forward to lick a stripe from his musk scented balls and up his salty shaft. I crinkle my nose at the thought of tasting my own cum and push that from my mind as I suckle at the spongey, leaking head.

I know he's already close to coming, so I don't tease him or draw the experience out like I have in the past. Instead, I lavish the head with attention, giving in to my enjoyment of suckling for a few more moments before I take him in deeper, wrapping my hand around the base of his erection and moving it in tandem with bobs of my head.

Above me, Daddy is babbling praises. "Good boy." "Beautiful boy." "Yes, baby, you feel amazing." "Your mouth is perfection."

The words continue to fall from his lips, lighting me up from the inside and spurring me on. I moan around his dick and it jerks in my hold.

"Tony, honey, I'm close," Daddy warns me, his voice strangled.

"Mmmhmmm," I acknowledge, not wanting to pull away from my prize for even a moment.

"Oh *fuck*," he breathes back, his hips lifting from the mattress as his cock pulses and releases in my mouth and down the back of my throat.

It has taken me a little while to get used to the taste and the texture. It's still not my favorite thing in the world, but I swallow every drop without complaint anyway, and I'm rewarded by a litany of more accolades from Daddy.

"I meant it, you know," he says later, when we're lathering soap all over each other in the shower.

"Meant what?"

Spencer pauses with his hands splayed across my soapy chest, the warm water sluicing over our bodies. "That I consider myself lucky to have found you. To have you in my life." He clears his throat, "And I think I'm coming around on the sex during Little time thing."

I grin at the last bit and nod my head, but I focus on the more important stuff for now. We'll have time later to really explore that revelation.

"I'm the lucky one," I tell him, able to do so now that my mind is clear. "I used to listen to your voice narrating all these awesome love stories and I'd daydream that one day that would be me. That I would get my happy ending with a man who loved me for me. And he'd have a sinful voice and handsome face and understand me when nobody else ever has." Happy tears spring to my eyes as I smile up at him, and I let the gentle shower spray wash them away. "And, against all odds, those daydreams came true."

I don't even have a moment to breathe before Spencer's lips are on mine. He leads me in a slow, sweet kiss, his arms holding me close against his water slicked chest.

"I love you," he says quietly when we part for air, lingering so close that his lips brush mine with every word. I understand why. I don't want to be any further apart from him than is absolutely necessary and I suspect he feels the same way about me.

I press our lips together again, murmuring, "And I love you."

Then I close my eyes and commit this moment to memory, because this really *is* my every daydream come to life, and I have never been happier.

The End

* * *

Thank you so much for reading *Spencer's Satisfaction*. As with my other books, I really do hope that you enjoyed reading it, because I had a hell of a lot of fun writing this one. Who knew I had a secret suckling obsession? Haha.

Anyway, I'd love it if you could leave a review on your retailer of purchase or on Goodreads.

Reviews not only tell the algorithms that our books deserve attention, but honest feedback also encourages and inspires me to keep writing. Even a star rating helps, and I greatly appreciate you making time to do so.

Speaking of my writing: if you're still enjoying the antics of the *Littles & Lace* crew, keep turning the pages for a sneak peek of Book 5 titled *Chance's Choice*.

And, if you'd like a free ebook copy of *Charlie's Contentment* (a 10,000 word zero-angst, high-fluff novella which functions as an extended epilogue for *Asher's Answer,* but can also be read as a super sweet stand-alone) subscribe to my newsletter here:

https://annasparrows.com/newsletter-subscription/

For updates, release dates, competitions and more, follow me on Facebook. The link is in the 'About The Author' page after the sneak peek.

Sneak Peek – Chance's Choice

Chapter One – Chance

"So that's a yes?" My long-time friend Charlie grins at me from across the gleaming countertop of the swanky new bar where we arranged to meet.

Charlie has changed a lot in the last few years. Finding his Forever Boy, ending his career as a cop, and starting a safe haven community center for members of the BDSM/kink community have all played a part in that. He used to be far more serious, less jovial, but now he's quicker to laugh and joke around. Not that he was a stick in the mud before, mind you, but he's more easy going these days. Unless he gets stuck into a new project. A project like the one he has spent months trying to convince me to participate in.

Closing my eyes and giving myself one last opportunity to back out, I sigh. It's a sound of resignation, but I still smile (if somewhat ruefully) at him when I exhale, "Yeah."

Charlie whoops and pumps a fist in the air. "You're the best, man! Thank you!"

"I'm not, like, the only Daddy you've signed up for this thing, right?" *That* thought makes me nervous. This thing I've agreed to? A fundraising auction, where I'm going to be standing up on a stage and (hopefully) having people bid on me. Or, more specifically, a day of Daddy time. With me.

Now, I'll be the first to admit that I love being a Daddy. Like Charlie and the rest of our social circle, I enjoy the emotional connection between a Daddy and a Little. I like being needed. Nurturing and caring for someone else makes me feel valuable. Even if it's just for the odd scene at The Grove, our local premium BDSM club, I feel *good* after taking care of a Little.

But what Charlie (and, by association, some of my other friends) have been bugging me to agree to seems a bit more daunting.

For one, I'm not going to meet the Little who 'buys' my time until after the fact. Sure, Charlie made sure to ask our lawyer friend, Ted, to write contracts that emphasize the importance of consent for both parties, with a clause that if either me or the winner of the auction are uncomfortable once we meet, a different 'prize' will be arranged by The Center commensurate with the value paid for my time…but it still feels like a lot of pressure on me to make it work, regardless.

Secondly, I might be a Daddy, but I don't consider myself an overly outgoing guy. Standing up on a stage, being *judged* and *bid on* terrifies me. I mean, what if there aren't any Littles in the audience who are into a bearded ginger with a dad bod? I can't imagine I'll feel very good if I don't bring in any money at all. But, on the other hand, what happens if I bring in a ton of cash for The Center? Then we go back to my first concern that there'll be additional pressure on me to make the experience worthwhile.

"No," Charlie answers my question with a shake of his head and an earnest smile, his blue eyes shining brightly with his excitement, "a few other Grove members have volunteered, too. But the more people that volunteer, the better. And," he leans forward conspiratorially, even though the din of chatter around us makes this a private conversation anyway, "you're my favorite to bring in the big bucks."

I snort at that. I can't help it.

"Me?" I ask, my voice pitching higher with incredulity. "How slim are the pickings at The Grove these days, anyhow?"

Charlie's jovial expression fades into consternation. "Chance, come on. You're a catch."

"Uh huh. That's why all you hot Daddies have boys and I'm still painfully single." I keep my tone light, even if the words themselves are bitter. I can't help it. My social group is kind of aesthetically intimidating to an average Joe like me. Even limiting my assessment to *just* the Daddies in our group, I know I'm the odd man out.

To start with, there's Charlie. He's tall and broad and muscular, not an ounce of fat on him, with biceps that broadcast the fact that he's spent far too long in the gym. He's got one of those generic Hollywood pretty boy faces: an angular jawline topped with neatly trimmed dark stubble, piercing blue eyes and one of those *The Bachelor* style 'more on top' haircuts to his dark brown head of thick hair.

Then there's Ted. Rich, suave, sophisticated Theodore Masters – a silver fox if ever I've seen one. He might be nearing fifty, but his salt and pepper hair only adds to his charm. He's also handsome and lean, and I'd seen many a twink throw themselves at him before his boy, Zephyr, caught his attention.

Next we have young London, a relative newbie to our group and to the world of Daddy/Little dynamics as a whole. He's stocky, but just as broad as Charlie (if a little bit shorter), with lush black hair he keeps coiffed in a rockabilly style, and a square jaw I'd kill for.

Finally, there's Spencer. My closest friend in the group, and probably the next likely to consider himself 'average', though his height and his voice are superior to mine in every way. The latter isn't really a surprise, considering his chosen career is as a voice actor and audiobook narrator. He's tall and lean and charismatic in ways I can only dream of being.

All in all, I've always felt like I've been riding these guys' coattails. They're the cool kids on the playground and they've been kind enough to let me sit with them, but I know I'm out of place.

"Chance," Charlie repeats my name, sounding a little horrified now. He reaches across the narrow counter that separates us, closing his wrist over mine. His blue eyes feel like they are searching my soul, and he frowns as though he's just read my mind. "Do you really feel that way?"

Of all the guys in the group, Charlie's not the one I thought I'd ever share this sort of deep and meaningful conversation with, but here we are.

I shrug and play dumb. "What way?"

"Like you're not one of the hot Daddies, for one." The phrase 'hot Daddies' sounds ridiculously silly coming from him, especially with that serious frown marring his handsome face, but I don't laugh.

"I know who I am, Charlie," I answer reasonably, "and I'm a realist. You put me in a line up with the rest of you and-"

"And you're just as hot as any of us."

I scoff at that.

"I'm serious," he insists.

"I'm not looking for sympathy or fishing for compliments," I respond calmly as I take a deep drag from my beer and then smack my lips together once I've swallowed. "I'm just saying, I know I'm…average in comparison. Plain. Boring. Whatever. And that's okay. I don't *want* to work for abs like you and Josh do, or go running like Spence does, or…y'know, anything like that. I'm comfortable with who I am. I just know it's not as…uh…cover model-y as the rest of you. And sometimes I get irrationally jealous of that."

Charlie's still looking at me like I've kicked his puppy or something. "I don't like that, man." He scratches the back of his neck, discomfort etched all over his face. "I never realized you thought of yourself like that, and I don't know what to say to fix it."

"There's nothing to fix," I assure him, feeling stupid for having made the confession to begin with. Sometimes, my brain and my mouth don't connect before the latter engages. This is definitely one of those situations. "Like I said: I'm comfortable with who I am. I am. I just have moments sometimes. But don't we all?"

Something darker and more melancholy flickers in his eyes and he nods, takes a fortifying swallow or three of his beer, then admits, "After I got shot, I questioned whether I'd be a good enough Daddy for Ash. I couldn't physically do things the way I wanted, you know?" He sighs and shakes his head. "And even now, even years later, I have moments where I wonder if I'm still good enough for him now that I'm not a cop." That surprises me, but before I can turn the tables to tell Charlie he shouldn't feel that way about himself, he continues, "So, yeah,

I think I get it. I don't like it, but…I get it."

"See," I say instead, understanding that I won't be able to talk him out of his self-deprecation any more than he can talk me out of mine, "we're all fucked up." I lift my glass to him and he laughs as I add, "Cheers!"

Conversation shifts back to the auction once our strange, emotionally charged moment has passed. I ask him about whether it's just sessions with Daddies and Doms being auctioned, and he explains that The Center and The Grove have both received donations from other kink-friendly places in the city and beyond. Day spas, hotels, photographers, costume designers and even a guy who builds custom adult nursery furniture have all donated their time and services as prizes to be bid on. The Grove has come to the party with discounted memberships for anyone signing up or renewing on the night of the auction, too.

"This whole thing is genius," I tell Charlie as he finishes explaining the deal he's made with The Grove to split the funds and, if the whole thing proves to be a success, the plan to make it an annual event.

"Yeah," he agrees, his smile turning proud, "Josh came up with it."

"No way."

Josh is Charlie's Little brother. And, yes, that's Little with a capital 'L'. He's a cop, like Charlie was, and is generally the joker of our entire group. He's also known to be kind of a brat, though the guy has a heart of gold and we all love him, even if we give him shit.

"Gotta hand it to him, then." I say when Charlie just nods at me. "He's much smarter than he pretends to be. Then again, didn't he just ace his Detective exams or whatever? I've gotta learn to give the kid more credit, huh?"

"He did. Mom threw a party and everything," Charlie chuckles, but he's still wearing that proud expression. "I'd say we should all start giving him a bit more credit."

"Except when he says something stupid in the chat." Which is almost always. We're all aware that he does it for the attention, but Charlie is almost always guaranteed to take the bait where his younger brother is concerned,

Now it's Charlie's turn to tilt his glass towards me in acknowledgement. "Except for that," he agrees.

After circling back to the original topic of conversation, we start to wrap up our meeting.

"So," Charlie says as he stands and slides on a black, form fitting jacket, "I'll have Cherie send you the contract and we'll go over what else we need from you as we get closer to the date. We'll probably need a bio, some examples of your favorite kinds of Daddy/boy interactions, that kind of thing. A list of your hard limits, too. Pretty much anything you'd bring up during negotiations."

I nod and climb off my own bar stool, draining the last of my glass of beer before placing the empty glass down on the countertop. "Sounds like a plan."

I just hope it's nothing I'll come to regret.

About the Author

I've been writing* for as long as I can remember. I started with silly short stories as a kid, moved on to fanfiction in my teens (and still write it now), and am also a published MF romance author under a second pen name.

I have been an avid reader of MM romance my whole life. (Ask me about my beginnings with *Buffy* fanfic, haha.) I wrote a sweet and kinky MM romance novel in 2022 and the reader response changed my life. From there, I knew I had found my niche.

And thus Anna Sparrows was born.

*All of my writing is 100% my own. No part of it is generated by Artificial Intelligence (AI) software of any kind. Yes, that means that it's sometimes flawed, but I'm okay with that.

You can connect with me on:

🌐 https://annasparrows.com

📘 https://www.facebook.com/AnnaSparrowsAuthor

🔗 https://www.instagram.com/annasparrows

Subscribe to my newsletter:

✉ https://annasparrows.com/newsletter-subscription

Also by Anna Sparrows

I write ridiculously sweet & steamy MM romance with guaranteed HEAs…and sometimes with a side of kink.

Littles & Lace Series
The Littles & Lace series is an MM Age Play series, following a group of like-minded friends in the BDSM community. You'll find mild ABDL, light Pet Play, Femme Play and more here.

Book 1: Asher's Answer

Book 2: Matteo's Mettle

Book 3: Ted's Temerity

Book 4: Spencer's Satisfaction

Book 5: Chance's Choice

Book 6: Josh's Jackpot

Dads & Adages Series
Visit Australia's sunny Gold Coast where an assortment of single dads find love and even learn a few life lessons along the way.

Book 1: Where There's A Will

Book 2: You Don't Know Jack

Book 3: A Match Made In Evan (release TBA)

Shifters Sanctuary Series
In a world where alphas are thought to be extinct, a number of 'human' men are about to have their worlds rocked.

Book 1: His Alpha Unlocked

Book 2: His Prodigal Alpha (release TBA)